THE BROKEN HOURS

THE BROKEN HOURS

JACQUELINE BAKER

HARPERAVENUE

The Broken Hours
Copyright © 2014 by Jacqueline Baker
All rights reserved.

Published by Harper Avenue, an imprint of HarperCollins Publishers Ltd

First edition

HarperCollins books may be purchased for educational, business,
or sales promotional use through our Special Markets Department.

HarperCollins Publishers Ltd
2 Bloor Street East, 20th Floor
Toronto, Ontario, Canada
M4W 1A8

www.harpercollins.ca

Library and Archives Canada Cataloguing in Publication
information is available upon request
ISBN 978-1-44342-566-7

Printed and bound in the United States of America
RRD 9 8 7 6 5 4 3 2 1

For John

The sleep of reason brings forth monsters.

GOYA

ONE

I

Providence, Rhode Island

{1936}

DESPERATION, SOME SAY, is but a particular form of madness.

Indeed I felt so, toting my valise up College Street like a vagabond in the blowing rain, the address blurred on a scrap of wet paper in my hand, the lights just beginning to come on in the windows of the great houses against the evening gloom. The spring has been late this year, and leonine, on the heels of a bitter winter, and the rain blasted sideways, soaking my trousers and threatening to wrench my battered umbrella like some shining black jellyfish into the watery aether. The air stank of the sea, as it always does here in such weather. So chilled was I, so tired from the long walk I had undertaken to save the few pennies of trolley fare, and so generally unwell my state of mind, I confess I would have given it all up but for the fact—why dissemble?—I had nowhere else to go.

So I pressed on along the steep, cobbled street, past lampposts yet unlit and wrought iron gates and the white marble edifice of the university library, where, briefly, I considered seeking shelter. The light so dim beneath the dripping elms, I could not make out his smeared address and cursed my own carelessness in allowing the paper to become damp.

Engrossed as I was, I scarcely noticed the man and the bicycle there until I stumbled into them, dropping my valise and almost toppling the bicycle, and the man, over.

I do beg your pardon, I said, setting the bicycle to rights again.

The man shot me a mild look of annoyance from beneath his crumpled fedora. He appeared to be of the street himself, as I suppose a good many of us must look, these lean times making vagrants of us all. He was accompanied by a boy in a grey woollen hat, and galoshes, and a coat far too heavy for even such inclement weather, and with a great crimson scarf wound exceedingly tight so that it seemed all that kept his head from tumbling from his little shoulders. He looked up at me, eyes pale and disinterested in their sockets like watery eggs in their cups.

Quite the weather for an outing, I observed.

We were caught in it, the man said, in a voice that smacked of the northern hills. *My own fault. I could see it coming. But boys, you know. Can't keep them shut up all day.*

He seemed understandably anxious to be off.

Do you live here, then? I asked. *In College Hill?*

He wiped the rain from his nose before nodding toward a large yellow house on the back side of the street. *Boarding house across the way.*

I see.

Just for a time, he added quickly, as if I'd suggested otherwise.

I pitied the man his embarrassment. I had felt as much often enough myself in recent months.

Well, I won't keep you, I said. *But, say, do you know where I might find Number Sixty-Six? Behind the John Hay Library, I was told.*

He shot me an odd look. *Sixty-Six?*

That's right.

The rain dripped from his fedora.

You'd be standing smack in front of it, he said. *This place right here.*

I lifted my umbrella and there it was, set back from the street in a small overgrown courtyard at the end of a short lane. A two-storey colonial with a monitor roof, bone-coloured with black shutters framing windows darkened by heavy draperies drawn tight against the coming night and the storm. The man looked at me with a new interest.

Sure it's Sixty-Six you're looking for?

I consulted the paper again. *Quite sure.*

Visiting, are you?

In fact, I'll be living here, temporarily. You see, I've been engaged—

Daddy, the boy said then, *isn't that the house—*

Never mind, James, he said shortly.

The rain pattered around us, filling an uncomfortable pause.

Do you know something of it, then? I asked.

Daddy—

The man cast his son a pointed look before saying, *There was a suite for rent there, the main floor, when we come to the neighbourhood last week. But the wife—*

Mama wouldn't—

James, he said, firmly.

The boy looked chastened.

Well, she wouldn't, he said, mostly to himself. He lifted the end of his wet scarf and put it between his lips.

I looked from son to father.

Wife didn't much care for the place, the man offered.

Oh? Why not?

He glanced across to the boarding house.

Fancies herself, he began, dropping his voice, *a what you call it, "sensitive."*

Sensitive?

Sees things. Or senses them, or what have you. Her and the boy both.

I smiled. *I'm afraid I don't go in for that sort of thing myself.*

Nor me, he said, hastily. He hesitated, then added, *But . . . the other tenants, upstairs. She'd heard talk. Gossip, like. Just women stuff. Nonsense things. But in such close quarters.* He shrugged.

You've met them, then? The upstairs tenants?

The man shifted his boots on the wet cobblestones. The old bicycle creaked.

Can't says we got that far.

What do you mean?

Mama wouldn't go past the landing, James put in. *She said—*

We should be getting on. The man laid a heavy hand on the boy's shoulder. *Suppertime.*

I repressed another smile at their country manners. And their country superstitions, too. I've known their like.

At any rate, I said pleasantly, *I suppose we'll be neighbours.*

I extended my hand, noticing with some surprise my fingertips were stained blue with ink from the wet slip of paper I carried. I checked an impulse to wipe them on my overcoat. The man must have noticed as well for he hesitated before extending his own.

Crandle, I said.

Baxter. This is my boy—

James, I finished, extending my hand to the child.

James reached out a sodden mitt in surprise at his name, as if I'd divined it rather than heard his father speak it.

We had a whole house, the boy said, marvelling himself at the fact, *all to our own selves. And a red barn too before we come here.*

Hard times, the man said.

For us all, I agreed.

Well. The man seemed to hesitate, but then he said only, *Come along, James.*

And with that they were gone, the boy clutching his father's trouser leg and looking up at darkened number Sixty-Six as they wheeled their rusted bicycle to the boarding house lit warmly there beyond, in the gathering dusk.

I PAUSED ON THE STREET a moment, wondering at the kind of house into which I'd been employed. Certainly the man Baxter had been odd about it. Inclined to see darkness everywhere, in spite of his denying it. Sensitives, of all things. I'd been under the impression that had gone out with the Victorians. I recalled the boy's pale, unnerving gaze. And that business about the wife and the landing. The gossip—whatever it was—about the upstairs tenants, surely that referred to my employer.

Still, no matter the house, no matter the situation, the truth was I'd run out of alternatives. There could have been nothing so bad I would have walked away from it then.

So I plucked my valise from where it lay in the puddle, giving it a useless shake. A vicious gust whipped the elms unbeautifully and sent cold rivulets down the back of my neck as I ducked quickly into the narrow, overgrown lane. The sunken path had pooled with rainwater and I skirted the edges where a creeper vine tendrilled out over the cobblestones, emitting a distinctly medicinal childhood aroma of peppermint as I trod upon it. I did not pause when I emerged into the small courtyard but made straight for the front door, unadorned but for two electric lantern lights which, though I was expected, were unlit. Another blast of rain hit me from behind. I hesitated only briefly.

Then I rang the bell.

DID I HAVE A SENSE even then of—not foreboding—but an uneasiness about my new engagement, my new employer? His name meant nothing to me. I'd gathered from the temporary agency where I'd applied only that he was a gentleman writer of some small reputation who, due to personal circumstances, had fallen behind in correspondence and manuscript preparation and therefore required assistance in such matters along with basic domestic chores. As the clerk at the agency had, earlier that afternoon, read out to me doubtfully between bites of a heel of bread: *"congenial lodgement and small remuneration in return for light secretarial and housekeeping services—"*

I'll take it, I'd said.

The clerk reached over and stabbed the desk lamp on with his thumb, blinking at me in the dim green light. Crumbs clung to his lower lip. His office reeked of old meat.

Housekeeping, he said again, pronouncing it oddly: *hiss-keeping*.

He might have said fish-gutter, garbage collector, grave-digger. It mattered not.

I'll take it, I repeated.

He bit again, then brushed his mouth with the back of his hand before taking up a pen and writing painfully, cross-checking each number. Beyond the spattered windows, the storm swelled blackly in from Narragansett Bay. Great, roiling clouds swirled above the courthouse and Westminster Arcade and the distant, dark hunch of Federal Hill. Thunder, I thought, but a second later a metal trolley stacked with files passed the open door, pushed by a young page who looked in at us uncuriously.

The clerk cleared his throat and handed me the number on a slip of sticky paper, not waiting for my thanks but spinning away on his chair to a file cabinet at the back of the room.

I made the call immediately from a telephone in the lobby, worrying at a hole in the musty carpet with the heel of my shoe as I waited for an answer.

At first, I'd thought it was a woman. The voice high, reedy, weak.

Candle, you say?

Tired, but with a strained, sad quality which I put down to the effects of a poor connection. I felt the line vibrate and tremble between us like a live thing.

Crandle, I corrected mildly, neither wanting to give offence nor cause upset to someone who, if the connection were not to blame, sounded so tremulous.

I wonder, Mr. Candle, he repeated, though from poor hearing or willful perversity, I could not have said, *I wonder if you would enlighten me as to the provenance of such an upstanding cognomen.*

He said it without humour, but I was not ignorant to his little joke.

Crandle, I stressed, *is an Irish name, if that's what you mean, sir.*

The line crackled and clicked and hung suddenly silent between us so long I had the disconcerting impression I'd been talking to myself.

Is that the Pawtuxet Crandles, he finally said, the line humming to life again.

Fall River.

A Catholic, then.

I'm afraid so.

I said it lightly. Perhaps I gave a small, apologetic laugh. Among men of my standing, it has ever been thus.

Spoken like a true Catholic, Candle, fear being a great motivator of papists the world over. Forgive me, I mean to give no offence. Their graveyards are unparalleled. They die, it is said, beautiful deaths. But listen, don't mind Old Grandpa. You must take what I say cum grano salis. *It is important only that we become acquainted with one another, our particular idiosyncrasies, you see. I intend no insult.*

None taken, sir.

Though I felt not a little affronted and suspected his idea of getting to know me meant conjuring me—the way men of his class have always done to men of mine—in an already predetermined and hardly flattering image: a paddy; a fish eater; a Fall River yob. I knew his type too, of course, the old Rhode Island guard, the intellectuals, the blue bloods.

I take it, then, Father Candle, that you are not of the venerable Crandle line of northern New England who made their fortune in textiles?

My father made his fortune as a mill worker, sir.

He made a noise, possibly of distaste, though perhaps I only imagined this as well, sensitive as I am to the matter of what some among his class would consider my "low birth."

You have been educated.

Yes, sir.

Your father sent you to university.

Yes—

Not to Brown.

I studied in Boston.

Indeed?

Not without certain sacrifices on behalf of my father, and that of my mother—

She is not a mill worker, I presume, your mother.

No, sir, she is—

Indeed.

I took from his tone of weary courteousness that he was on the brink of dismissing me and I put in quickly, *I am an excellent worker, always punctual.*

Hardly difficult, sleeping where you work.

I pride myself in efficiency.

Nothing worthwhile achieved in haste.

And I think I can claim to be more than usually dependable, and honest—

No man less so than he who claims—

Perhaps among certain classes, sir.

I confess I was a bit sharp.

So, he said, after a short pause, *the flame doth scorch a bit, after all.*

I attempted a stuttered retraction but he said, sadly, *I have often, myself, wished to be of a little more fire and a little less wax.*

I knew not how to reply, so said only, *I assure you I am equal to any task which—*

Might I ask what you studied? At BU?

I hesitated. *Astronomy, sir.*

You don't say? His voice showed new interest.

I laughed, again, apologetically. *I realize it isn't—*

One must follow one's heart, is that right, Candle?

Yes, sir, I believe so.

And your father, did he also believe in following one's heart?

Again, I hesitated. *He might have wished for something more—*

Practical?

Yes.

A solicitor, say? A numerary?

Numerary?

An accountant.

Yes, perhaps.

I cannot say I disagree with him, your father. But when one is young—

I make no claim to that, sir.

Do you not? Well, no matter. Neither do I. But tell me, how did you enjoy it, this study of the stars?

I judged it best to speak frankly.

I found I hadn't the heart for it, after all.

Too much of the abstract?

Too much, I said, *of the infinite.*

The line rattled.

No, he agreed. *No, you are not young.*

An empty pause, as if we'd again lost the connection, a crackling static during which I could not make out what he said, and then he was back.

—you cook?

Cook, sir?

You know, heat up things in cans. Chili, or spaghetti, or what have you. Baked beans. There are an increasing variety of good things that come in cans, I have found.

The mention of food caused an involuntary clenching at my abdomen. I had eaten so little in recent days that I had reached a point beyond hunger. Or perhaps I had only convinced myself it was so. We make a virtue of necessity when we must.

I've done my own cooking, sir.

It wasn't a complete fabrication. I had done some.

Just the basics, I clarified, *but I know how to economize. And housekeeping as well.*

Self-made man, and all that?

I have, I believe, striven for self-sufficiency.

And can you type?

I can type, sir.

This much, at least, was true.

Two, or how many?

I was stumped. *Words per minute?* I ventured.

Fingers.

Why, all of them, sir.

He made a humphing sound which might have been admiration or might have been disbelief.

I cannot say I've taken to it, myself. I like to think it is because I have the hands of a pianist, not—he said, giving the word a distinctive snap—*a stenographer.*

You are a musician, then?

My mother is rather gifted. I am, sadly, not. Snapping that word again, elastically. *But I do feel there is no harm in indulging in a bit of wishful thinking now and again, providing one does not make of it a habit. By such means of self-flattery do we often comfort ourselves for what we lack, isn't it so, Candle?*

Indeed, sir.

You are not one to imbibe in hallucinogenic and incapacitating liquid refreshments, certain, as they used to say, aqua vitae?

I beg your pardon?

You are not a drinker, are you, Father Candle? It does run high among certain of your pontifical denomination. All that Blood of Christ business. Sets up a damned poor precedent, if you see my point.

I told him I did. He did not seem convinced.

It is, he went on, *the greatest unrelieved evil to any delicately cultivated civilization. I am nauseated by even the distant stink of any alcoholic liquor. And not one to use tobacco, either, I hope. I find it worse than nauseous. I can think of no greater horror than a smoking car.*

He coughed.

I am neither a smoker nor a drinker, I assured him.

And neither are you then what is commonly called a family man? Which is not to say I have anything against it. But I assume you are not connubially leashed, lest you would not be applying for such a position, in domus, *as it were.*

Sir?

I assume, apart from your good mother, there is no Mrs. Candle, no Lady Candle, no Candle of Perpetual Sorrows. That would complicate things, of course.

There is no Mrs. Crandle.

I felt a sudden twinge, a black spot spreading on my soul like mould on pale fruit. I saw Jane's face, white-lipped, that December afternoon in Boston, where we had walked along the Charles River, Molly running ahead making figure eights with her little footprints in the snow—in and out among the trees with stilted grace—like the trails of deer. Jane had stopped with a hand on my arm to watch the flakes hit the brown water and disappear. She'd said, *It's a kind of extinction, isn't it. Each one. So permanent.*

How grief collapses time. A year ago, two? Last month? It might have been yesterday, a lifetime. When Jane had turned her face up to kiss me, or rather to be kissed, I had hesitated, the snow seeming all at once cold and soiled and hopeless, fallen angels in the failing light. All was dirty, then, all was rot, the child's black footprints like burned things, the twisted limbs of trees grotesque against a bled sky, the foul, drunken swirling of the river. The stench of it, the unbearable decay. *All*, I thought, *all*.

By lesser means had I often been tipped into despair. It was a failing in me, to be sure.

Jane mistook me, then. It was not uncommon between us, these misreadings. I should have kissed her. But when I looked at her, I saw only blackness, a pit into which I was forever falling; my own inevitable failings.

Mama?

Molly stood all at once still in the snow, staring back at us, as if something unspeakable had just occurred to her.

The flakes settled on her blue felt hat like the loosed feathers of a hunted swan.

She looks flushed, Jane said.

Molly's cheeks flamed in the cold, her black eyes bright, glittering. Jane bent to fuss with the scarf hanging askew around her little throat.

It's the fresh air, I said, and walked on, leaving Jane to follow with Molly. It was well past lunch and I was hungry and underdressed for the cold.

Will you wait, Jane called.

—and bring whatever small, personal items you require, came the voice over the telephone. *The room which will be yours at the very top of the house—splendid views—is comfortably and tastefully furnished in the colonial manner. You will be quite at liberty to make yourself at home.*

It was a moment before I realized what he was saying.

Thank you, sir, I said. My voice trembled embarrassingly.

Are you quite sure of your way? he asked.

I believe so.

Nevertheless, he proceeded to give detailed, colourfully descriptive, one might even say atmospheric, directions to his home behind the Brown University campus. I was given to understand that a sister or mother or some other elderly female relative (not a wife, to be sure) who normally handled such matters was to be away for a time convalescing from *a somewhat prolonged and exceedingly virulent case of the grippe,* as he put it, and that I was to be employed for at least the duration of her absence. This would be some few weeks and perhaps, all going well, a good while afterward, he added, if I were agreeable to such arrangements.

I assured him I was most agreeable. In the meantime there was a more immediate concern.

I beg your pardon, I began then, hesitantly. *We have not discussed . . .*

I had hoped he would take up the hint, but I was met with only silence. It was awkward, to be sure. I would not have brought it up had my situation not been quite so desperate.

. . . the matter of salary.

More muffled humphing or, possibly, coughing. Perspective, I have found, is everything.

I do feel, Candle, that between gentlemen talk of money is a coarse matter.

I only ask . . . my circumstances are what one might call strait-ened. I laughed apologetically. I sensed it was not the first time I had done so. *I do realize this is out of the ordinary, inappropriate even, certainly not something I'm in the habit of—*

You are guttering, Candle.

Might I receive a small portion of my salary in advance? It is rather urgent—

Yes, yes, he said wearily. *I find this talk of such low mat-ters—*a cough here, he seemed to be growing breathless—*degrading to us both. Please, let us speak no more of it.*

He asked then if I needed a review of the directions to his home, and I assured him I could find the place easily and that I would begin making preparations for my move within the hour—another fabrication as there were no preparations to make, only myself and my shoddy valise there in the dank, panelled lobby and outside the lowering skies over the city and the coastal gusts rattling the windowglass, the promise of the storm to come.

That I need not face it, this storm—another night on the cold, wet streets among the other desperate and unwashed, urinating in the park like an animal, waiting in the damp at the back of the line for the soup kitchen only to arrive at the front to find the kettle had just been scraped—was only just beginning to settle. I assured him he could expect me before nightfall. In truth, I could not get there soon enough to suit me, but I did not say as much to him. It did not do, I had found in such situations, to appear too eager.

It is a splendid thing you are not a woman, he said, out of the blue. *I wasn't quite sure how I would manage it. A pleasant surprise, Candle. I expect our time together to be quite—*he wheezed—*illuminating.*

And then he was gone.

I STOOD IN THE RAIN on the doorstep of darkened Number Sixty-Six, waiting for an answer to my ring. When none came, I stepped back into a puddle and looked up at the building.

It rose, modest but elegant, two square storeys plus an attic in the typical Rhode Island colonial style, with small-paned windows and a carved fan above the panelled front door. Still, while handsome, there was something unwelcoming about it, too, tucked away there in the trees behind the university, a kind of squat and sublimated misanthropy. It struck me often, the similarities between buildings and people; not that they resemble us, but that we resemble them. We, too, only hollow frames subject to the slow indignities of decay, the darkening that age brings. I wonder, sometimes, what lives in us. I wonder what comes calling, what we invite inside.

But such thinking always troubled Jane.

The streaked windows of Sixty-Six remained unlit. A sudden movement there and I lifted a hand in greeting before realizing, with some embarrassment, it was only the trees and the storm reflected darkly in the glass. The rain blasted against me. Feeling a flicker of irritation, I collapsed my umbrella, opened the door, and stepped inside.

My first impression was of gloom. The small foyer of dark wood panelling and floorboards made darker by the storm and the hour. It smelled of damp and wax and something richly, unpleasantly sweet, like overripe cherries. A chime clock ticked on the wall immediately to my left, the swing of its brass pendulum a glint of light in the gloaming, and beside it a panelled door stood closed and—strangely— padlocked into what I assumed was the main floor suite which the man Baxter had mentioned. I wondered what could be behind such barricading. Across the foyer, a second, smaller door, flanked by brass-potted palms, was set into the wall beneath the stairs. This door was not padlocked.

Apart from these, there was only an iron coat stand to

my right and the stairs, banistered and covered in a richly filigreed ruby carpeting, which curved up and to the left into the darkened second storey.

I confess I was dismayed to find the house divided into two, possibly three, apartments. Surely I had been given the impression over the telephone that my gentleman employer was the owner and sole occupant apart from the recuperating relative. Already our conversation of only a few hours ago had taken on a hazy, gilded quality, as of something that had happened years previous, or that I had once dreamed. But I was exhausted, preoccupied, and my memory had never been good, as Jane had frequently pointed out. He might have mentioned it, after all.

Either way, it appeared no one would be coming down to greet me. I deposited my umbrella upon the iron stand and, after wiping my soaked shoes pointlessly, mounted the groaning staircase.

When I reached the landing, the air changed.

I do not know how else to describe it. It darkened, became more dense. The carpet grew unpleasantly thick beneath my shoes, a swollen thing. I paused, disoriented, off-balance, and gripped the cold banister to steady myself, the wax sticky on my palm. My sodden clothing chafed against my skin, and I unbuttoned the collar of my overcoat. I shut my eyes, breathed. Pricks of light raced behind my eyes like mad, blue constellations. I could almost feel the bracing, elemental rush of wind and rain beyond the papered walls.

It was a long moment before I regained my equilibrium, and I put this off, quite logically, to the storm and the absence of windows on the landing, and to my fatigue and light-headedness at the lack of a decent meal in many days. That I had not collapsed before now seemed miraculous in itself. I hoped I was not coming down with something.

Still, though I was not a superstitious man, I was aware that I had always been rather . . . impressionable. Easily swayed, Jane once said. The man Baxter's face came back to me, abashed as he mentioned his wife, the upstairs tenants. But I had detected something else there, too. A question in his gaze, and in the bleached gaze of the boy as well.

I gripped the banister more tightly, moved from the landing slowly upward, feeling that weightiness, as if it were pressing me back. A door stood closed in the shadows above me and I climbed toward it, sliding my hand along the nicked banister, my valise thumping against my knees. I hesitated on the upper landing only an instant, then raised my fist and rapped soundly, the noise ricocheting around in the darkness. My trousers clung wetly to my shins and I shivered and rapped again and, inexplicably, looked over my shoulder down the staircase. At last, hearing no sound from within and being, after all, expected, I opened the door.

I was hit, first, by a wall of bad air, as if neither door nor window had been opened in weeks. As if the rooms had sat long empty, the air unstirred by even the slightest movement. An earthy smell, not altogether unpleasant, flooded over me, mixed with that same musky sweet odour and even taste of old cherries. It filled my throat, recalling to me an orchard I must once have known as a child, the plump, rich fruit warm and soft from the sun. But as soon as I grasped for the memory, it was gone, as is the way with memories. Like ghosts, they can only be glimpsed from the corners of the eyes.

From where I stood in the doorway, the apartment seemed darker than had the main floor foyer. I recalled that from the outside I'd seen all the curtains pulled shut against the streetlamps and whatever scant grey light the sky yet held. That heaviness of air seemed denser there, weightier, as if the darkness were caused not merely by a lack of light but by the presence of something else.

I noticed, then, a panelled door down a couple of steps at the end of the front hall, set a little apart from the rest of the suite. Though the door was shut fast, a light shone dimly from beneath.

Hello? I called out. *Sir? It's Arthor Crandle.*

Only the wind and the rain outside. I stepped into the apartment, dropping my sodden valise with an intentional clatter, then rapped my knuckles in brisk manufactured annoyance against the wall where I stood waiting.

Hallo! I called again.

Still, nothing came. I could imagine only that my employer was asleep or had stepped out. I walked to the end of the hall and, descending the steps to the lighted room, rapped soundly there, just to be certain. My wet clothes hung heavily from my shoulders and hips as I waited. I cleared my throat, watching the dampness spread out under my shoes in the weak light.

Then, as I waited, an unpleasant thought: the unnatural, studied silence coming from the other side of the door was neither that of someone having just gone out nor of someone at focused work or even in deep sleep. Rather it was the stillness of someone's strained listening just on the other side. Watching, perhaps, through the crack there.

I felt a shiver run through me that was not the cold.

How I wanted, in that moment, to leave. Even as I thought, *My god, what things we do for . . .* not love, certainly. I knew very well it was not love which had driven me there, nor hope, nor even obligation. Desperation, certainly; but more than that: it was grief. A much fiercer and lasting kind of loyalty in the end.

A floorboard creaked behind me, and I turned in relief, expecting to greet my new employer.

But there was no one, only the open door through which I'd just come, out of the wet blackness, and my own shining footprints across the floor.

It was then I noticed the pedestal table in the entranceway. It bore, beneath the small light of an exquisite emerald lamp, a note weighted down, from heaven knew what phantom gusts in that still and airless place, with a human skull of such craftsmanship as to look quite real. I stepped toward it and, repressing an inexplicable urge to poke my fingers into its empty eye sockets, I plucked the envelope from beneath it with hands made unsteady by the cold and the strain, and by many weeks of having slept little and eaten less.

Welcome, Candle, it read.

WHAT IS IT IN US which blinds us? Standing there in the front hall, I felt a chill spread slowly over me, like a palm cupping cold marble, or a window left open to an autumn night. But for the wind and rain lashing outside, the house was eerily still, eerily silent. And yet I told myself it was only sleep I needed. A bed, warmth, rest.

I followed a set of creaking stairs from the front hall up to the darkened second storey, clutching his letter, my valise bumping noisily against the walls of the narrow stairwell. At a small landing I found two doors and opened one. I felt for the electric light but when I punched the button, nothing happened. From what I could make out, the room appeared to be empty except for a few boxes against the wall and an antiquated cornbroom abandoned in the corner. I closed the door and opened the other.

When I found the button this time, the bulb in the ceiling buzzed and crackled with a thin orange wire, then flared with light. I raised a hand to my face, blinking, and carried my dripping valise inside.

It too seemed little more than a large storeroom, low-ceilinged and grimly furnished. Behind the clutter of more cardboard boxes I could see a cast-iron bed, narrow and sagging and so short it would surely only allow me to curl up like a foetal cat or drape my ankles painfully across the foot rail. A washstand with blue-flowered enamel basin and pitcher stood beneath a darker oval on the far wall where a mirror or a picture must once have hung; but all this, too, and the chest of drawers, even the lamp on my bedside table, had been built in miniature. I thought of Alice, having stepped through the looking glass. I reached out and turned on the lamp, which glowed with a rosy light. Certainly the room must once have been used by, intended for, a child.

Yet clearly it had not been used so in quite some time. My shoes scraped the bare floorboards as I pushed aside sealed boxes thick with grit; even the folded bed linens, when I lifted them from the cold radiator, smelled musty from long disuse. The saving grace: the monitor roof boasted windows which, though smudged and fly-specked, afforded a nearly panoramic view of the city. Below one of these sat my desk. I regarded its stacks of manuscripts and correspondence without enthusiasm, then leaned toward the glass. Past my ghosted reflection I could see the university observatory glowing bluely, as if a celestial creation fallen, and beyond that the hilled Providence skyline, domed and steepled, and in the distance, on the edge of the silvered river, a building more striking still: dark and sprawling, its gloomy peaks and dormers lit but dimly through the rain.

As I stood watching at the window, a light in one of the dormer windows went out, and I was caught by melancholia, as I have always been at the sight of a light going out across a vast distance, like the sudden, cold extinguishing of a star.

The light came on again, only to be put out a second later. This flickering continued nearly a full minute, as if someone there were sending a signal out across the darkening city, through the storm; as if someone were seeking a reply; and I almost felt, in that moment, in that cold room with the wind and rain raging outside, that the someone being signalled was me. But then the light went out and stayed out. I waited some time but it did not come on again.

Before me, on the chipped windowsill, the desiccated bodies of flies lay thickly. I touched one with my thumbnail, lightly, and it crumbled to dust. I turned from the window and, putting out my own lamp, pulled off my wet shoes and socks and trousers and climbed into bed in my shirt sleeves, too tired even to bother washing up. From the bed, I could still see out the low window to the dormered building that had so caught my interest. I waited a few moments to see if the light would come on, but there was nothing. It occurred to me then, that, though my attic room was practically ringed with windows, all of the furniture—the bed, a small, dingy armchair, the desk and ladderback chair—were oriented toward this window, this view. It gave me a queer feeling and I made a mental note to rearrange things to my own taste in the morning.

I said a quick prayer, as had long been my habit, against the suffering of loved ones and for my own failings and for the unhappy intersections between the two. There had been a time in my youth when prayer had brought me actual comfort and so I'd continued the ritual—out of a kind of familiar obligation, as was sometimes the way with habits—long after I had lost faith in it, when it left me only as exposed and unmoved as the solitary, ordinary, lonely bedtime ritual of removing one's own clothing.

Thus have you also been cast off, Crandle, I told myself, and closed my eyes.

But I could not get comfortable. Apart from the smallness of the bed, the room was cold and I lay shivering and sleepless beneath the musty, too-short blankets, finding myself staring out across the city through the window, listening to the rain batter down upon the shingles above my head, and the house creak and shift in the high wind. When I held a palm to the wall, I could feel a draft seep as through something porous, as if the wall were not plaster but skin. The starched sheets chafed, the pillow lumped unpleasantly.

It was then, as I tossed about seeking comfort, that my hand came upon a small, hard object beneath my pillow, and I pulled it out and turned on the lamp. In my palm lay what appeared to be a triangular chunk of concrete, which I took at first for a broken bit of sidewalk or building masonry. And yet, as I turned it beneath the lamplight, I found it to be curved smoothly on one edge, polished but for its broken side, and all in all it gave the sense of something vexingly familiar—some exceedingly common thing—though just what somehow eluded me. I put out the light again and lay back against the pillow, rubbing my thumb against its smooth side as if it were a talisman. Possibly it had been so once, placed there as a charm against darkness for whatever child had inhabited that room. A charm against loneliness. It seemed terribly sad to me that the charm was still there, the child long gone.

At last I began to sink into sleep, down and down, with that sense of dark plummeting, as I imagined dying might feel.

I WAS STARTLED AWAKE. I knew not how long I'd slept, if truly at all, but a sudden thought brought my blood ripping hotly into my veins, startling me into the unfamiliar dark.

I switched on the bedside lamp and looked at the stone in my palm, the skin there welted red where I'd clenched it. I rubbed its smooth edge with my thumb.

A piece of gravestone.

I turned and turned it in my hands, and at last put out the light and lay listening for some time to the storm outside. The rain tapped at the windows; the wind creaked and whistled at one corner where a pane was loose from its caulking. Across the city, the light did not come on.

Finally, I closed my eyes. The stone radiated a deep and abiding cold which would not warm in my clenched palm. Though its presence might have been chilling to some, I found it only sad, as Jane claimed I found all things. And I suspected she was right, without having the power to change it, that melancholy I had known all my life, and which too must be a gift of God.

2

I AWOKE TO A ROOM filled with the pewtered light of a coastal morning, turning the walls a velvety lilac blue. The close, musty air felt rinsed after the storm. Beyond the windows, mourning doves shifted and sighed in the dripping branches. An automobile hushed past on the wet street. Somewhere, a child bounced a rubber ball against the sidewalk with a muffled, metrical regularity that set my teeth on edge.

I felt tired; a faint chill still lingered around my bones. My eyes ached at the backs of their sockets. But I had slept. And under a roof, and in a bed. I intended to write Jane first thing and tell her I was well situated and that I would soon be in a position to send money, likely that very day. I was not such a fool as to hope it might mean anything to her; hope, as they say, is the worst of all evils, prolonging only torment.

I lay awhile beneath the covers, turning the stone over in my palm. I was surprised, in a way, to find it still there. The house below me was silent, and though I listened for movement there was nothing. Beyond the windows, the city lay spread out in a misty, grey light, the observatory dark and somehow disenchanted—or was it unenchanted?—at any rate ordinary, and the sprawling, dormered building in the distance, which had so captured me the previous evening, quite ordinary too in a handsome, rather gothic, somehow forbidding way. I studied its four storeys of red brick, choked in ivy, its chimneys puffing great gallows of mauve smoke into the cold, and only with great effort could I tear my eyes away.

The view was, as my employer had promised, splendid; the house situated on the very crest of College Hill. The lower town spread out before me on three sides, the narrow colonials and Georgians huddled together beneath peaked roofs, watercoloured, chimney pots smoking, the trees leafless and profound, still black with rain. The mercurial river coursing flat silver into the bay. The spires and pinnacles and belfries of the downtown proper, stately and ornate as the Orthodox crosses of Old Europe. Beyond, the rolling countryside cobwebbed in the early light. I wondered that my employer had not taken these rooms for his own use.

I recalled, then, his letter. I plucked it from the bedside table and opened it. It was a long letter, at that, and written right up to the very edges of the bright orange pages, with no margins even to break the eye. If handwriting is, indeed, indicative of character, then his cramped, nearly illegible scrawl filling every inch of the page said a good deal indeed.

He was an odd sort, to be sure, writing in a kind of baroque, formal tongue, and I had the distinct sense, when reading, of having received his letter out of the distant past. In addition, he was not one to use five words when fifty would do. No point in repeating all the remarkable detail the note contained; important only that he left a tarnished, silvery key (presumably to the front door), long-winded, formally polite instructions as to the general management of the house, a list of errands and a veritable treatise on the work I would—and did—find awaiting me on the desk.

It occurred to me then that he had not yet given me his name. Nor had he mentioned it on the telephone. I flipped to the last page of the letter. He mentioned an aunt, Annie, currently convalescing, said something about *we Phillipses*, but as to his own name, he'd only scrawled something that looked like *Ech-Pi*. I tried to make sense of it, but no matter how long I looked, the letters did not mutate into a recognizable name.

Ech-Pi. Imagine.

I wondered if I would meet him that morning, though his letter had given me no reason to believe I would, neither that morning nor any other, as he claimed he kept inconvenient hours, sleeping—when he was able—by day, and working all through the night. He wrote further that he had been unwell for some time and had not much left his rooms, and suggested that our communication should be epistolary until he was feeling well enough to meet. He claimed, in fact, that he preferred it so, as one never really became acquainted with another until they had maintained a correspondence. Still, I could not help but think we should cross paths, and likely sooner than later.

He had, however, left no money for my promised advance. I read again his insistence that he not be disturbed, under any circumstances. And I thought, rather peevishly, that if he wished not to be disturbed he might have delivered on his assurance.

I rose and dressed quickly in the cold room, in my one spare suit of clothes, a light summer suit ill-matched to the morning's damp, my good jacket and trousers hanging like a doppelgänger in the window to dry.

I stopped.

Surely I'd not hung that suit the previous night. I recalled distinctly dropping my wet clothes to the floor and climbing, weary, into the cold bed. I could still recall the sound of my belt hitting the floorboards heavily. And yet there they hung, neatly, by the window. I could only imagine I must have been more exhausted than I'd supposed, to forget. Then again, such an habitual act could hardly be memorable.

I folded the letter into my trouser pocket with the key and made up my bed. After a second thought, I pocketed the piece of gravestone as well. Before venturing downstairs to find the bathroom, I paused a moment at the door to look back at the suit, hanging before the window, turning slowly in the blue light.

IMAGINE MY ASTONISHMENT, upon clicking on the overhead bulb in the cramped bathroom, to discover a claw-footed tub filled nearly to the brim with trash.

Not the usual household trash of the muckier sort, but rather candy bar wrappers and the emptied boxes of other confectionary, chocolates and gumdrops and sugary lozenges. I rifled straight through to the bottom of the tub, so confounded was I by this perverse collection. Nothing but candy wrappers.

After more rummaging about, I found beneath the sink some paper bags and filled several and twisted them shut and put them aside and rinsed the tub. The rest of the room, too, was in a state of what Jane would call disgrace: dust balls skated along the baseboards; the sink rimed with the powdery residue of old tooth polish; bits of toilet tissue littered the floor like ticker tape. Off-putting, to say the least. Nests of grey hair clung to the edge of the wastebasket like spiders. Fingernail scissors rusted on the lip of the sink. Everywhere a stench of unwashed underclothes. With some effort, I cracked the sticky window to the morning air, the sill there peppered, too, with a winter's worth of flies. I recalled the doubtful gaze of the clerk at the agency: *hisskeeping*.

I washed my hands and face in the icy trickle from the tap—the drain gave off a sour odour of old spittle—and only then did I notice no mirror hung over the sink. I peered about, dripping, my eyes stinging with water. I dried my face on a crumpled towel, then dug around back in the cabinet for one of those ladies' hand mirrors, which are used, I am told, chiefly in the viewing of the back of one's head; but none was to be found. I ran my fingers cursorily through my hair. A quick palm across my jaw told me I was in need of a shave. It was liberating, in a way, to know I was in a position where no such thing would be necessary. What could my appearance possibly matter to a man who would not meet me?

THE KITCHENETTE PROVED no better than the bathroom, the counters covered in a greasy film, likewise the floor, the soles of my shoes sticking unpleasantly. A table in the corner was lost in stacks of books and papers and unopened mail; against one wall a pile of cardboard boxes and empty tin cans, their tops flipped open like razored eyelids; a pair of dirty galoshes leaned by a door leading to a rickety exterior set of stairs; the wall above the range so spattered with cooking oil it shone.

Oddly, though, there was not a dirty dish, or cup, or spoon to be seen. I found the pots and crockery all clean and put away neatly in the cupboards, which nevertheless stank of damp and too-few openings. On the door of an ironing closet hung a calendar, issued by the Insurance Company of Providence, depicting the gateway arch in Federal Hill with its famous *pignoli* cluster dangling obscenely. The month showing was February and I flipped the pages forward to April, feeling uneasily as I did so that I was violating some kind of inexplicable order. I shut the closet only to open it a second later and flip them back to February again. When I turned on the faucet the pipes banged and lurched, and a thin, spitting foam of grey water spattered into the sink. I located the kettle in a drawer beneath the range and filled it and put it on to boil. But upon closer examination of the cupboards, I could detect not a single leaf of tea, nor any food at all besides a few unopened tins of Zocates and chili con carne and Protase and an ancient can of cocoa ranged unassumingly next to a line of spoiled-looking jellies—or so I imagined they were—with unlikely labels, handwritten: dandelion, stinging nettle, hawthorne. I pushed the dusty preserves and the tinned bread and meat to the back and opened the cocoa, struck by an earthy, wet-wool smell, not altogether unpleasant but certainly not chocolate. I spooned it out in clumps. The kettle shrieked and I poured out the steaming water. In the small icebox I found a crusted tin of condensed milk of questionable date and poured a bit of that in as well and stirred, my spoon clanging against the sides of the cup like a cathedral bell in the silence. Finally, I sipped the concoction and, finding the odour worse than the taste, which could perhaps best be described as faintly mushroomy, I took the cup and went to the front hall, pausing there a moment in the gloom. The light shone from beneath the study door, as it had the previous evening, but I could detect no sound of anyone stirring within. I returned with my cup to the kitchenette and wiped off a seat at the table.

From the window I could see across a good-sized, overgrown garden to the yellow boarding house, temporary home of Baxter and James, as if they were partners in law. A low, glossy hedge in need of trimming and, between the two properties, a charming shed, the roof of which appeared to be—astonishingly—covered in cats. Creatures of various colorations and markings, sitting with their tails curled round them or prodding the eaves or patrolling the roof with serious, studied airs, like dancers just taking the stage. I counted some dozen of them. As I watched, a broad-shouldered silver tabby scaled the barren trellis up the side of the shed, then coiled himself just below the lip of the eaves, watching the others, tail twitching. When he pounced, the rest scattered. I knew that sort well. I'd never cared for the beasts. There was something about them so alien, so cold. Looking into their eyes, I saw no connection and knew very well they would gladly slit me open and eat me steaming from the inside out, then sit mildly wiping their gory muzzles.

Turning from the window, I sipped my cocoa and, taking up pen and paper, began my letter to Jane.

I SPENT THE REMAINDER of the morning with shirt sleeves rolled tightly past the elbow, carting out trash and cardboard boxes and newspapers to the bins at the back of the yard. The level of grime I discovered once I began exceeded all my expectations, even given that my employer had been on his own for some four weeks, according to his letter, and that he was a writer, with a writer's habits. I swept dust and debris from the floors and, getting down on hands and knees, vigorously scrubbed every inch of the kitchen and bathroom with a stiff brush and buckets of hot water and a yellowed cake of lye soap on a saucer—which I had at first alarmingly put aside as a bit of margarine for my lunch—and which left my hands puckered and raw, and my fingertips thoroughly bleached of ink stains. I scraped crusted food from the kitchen counters with a metal spatula, and hacked at the rusted film in the sink. A black, hard-shelled, antennaed thing crept up horribly out of the drain, groping blindly, and I cranked on the hot water, watching it flail in the vortex until it was flushed away. I screwed the plug in tightly, then turned my efforts to the greasy range.

All morning I scraped and scrubbed and polished. I ran over the furniture with a damp cloth. I shook carpets out the windows with a sharp snap. By noon I had managed to improve most of the apartment, leaving untouched only my employer's study and another set of rooms behind closed doors across the front hall. These I assumed belonged to the lady of the house, the aunt he had mentioned in his letter. I pushed all of the curtains open and punched on every electric light and pried the windows up to the sea air. And still the place felt stale and dark.

One small delight: I discovered, after clearing away some of the kitchen clutter, three pots of primroses on the windowsill—yellow, magenta and orangey-pink—and I was so pleased to find them there, still blooming in spite of their miserable surroundings, it was as if I'd discovered the first crocus of spring breaking through late-lingering ice. I crumbled off all the dead leaves and blossoms and watered them until liquid ran like steeped tea from their pots.

But, I will confess, all morning as I moved about the apartment, I found myself looking now and again over my shoulder at nothing. I could not quell a strange feeling: that something—someone—moved through the rooms with me, just ahead of me. That I was not alone in that apartment.

As, of course, I reminded myself, I was not.

I rattled about a good deal while I cleaned, taking comfort in the loud, ordinary noises, the sloshing and scrubbing and clanging, and thinking surely, sooner or later, to rouse my employer from his chambers. But the study door remained closed, and though I paused often as I passed through the hall, I heard nought.

IN THE AFTERNOON, after posting my letter to Jane in the red-enamelled box outside the front door, I dug with reluctance from the pile of papers on my desk the manuscript I'd been instructed to proofread and type. It amounted to only a few pages scrawled across with the same cramped, crippled script, which, on a second viewing, I seemed to have little difficulty making out. I was no great reader, but something in the opening lines caught me and instead of typing I sat at my desk reading.

It was a sort of a horror story—or it began like one, anyway—about a young chambermaid, Aralyn Eakinns, the only child of a reclusive and aged New England fisherman,

Oakley Eakinns. Aralyn had come to Providence shortly after her mother disappeared under mysterious circumstances, Oakley claiming the mother had *run off to Philadelphy or somewheres as she always promised she would.* Aralyn found work in a local hotel—elegantly carpeted and crystalled—down on Benefit Street near the waterfront. She was not a favourite among her co-workers and employers. A certain standoffishness, a certain haughtiness, hardly appropriate in a girl of such humble origins, was found distasteful, offensive. They found her cold, in every sense; her fellow chambermaids, brushing against her as they stripped the bedclothes, felt an inexplicable repulsion. They went out of their way to avoid her.

And more: Old Oakley would turn up there at the hotel each night, smelling of cinders, and sit in the lobby beneath the chandeliers, waiting in his work clothes on the finely upholstered rose settees, his muddy boots planted firmly on the silk carpets, scratching absently at the knees of his dungarees, watching everyone with a cold, bulbous stare while they pretended not to see him, and waiting for Aralyn to finish work so he could take her home.

Aralyn, seeing him there, would stop suddenly while passing through the lobby and stare coldly back. The other employees exchanged glances, watching from their corners, until finally Oakley bared his broken teeth at her and said, *High time you come home.* Then, nodding once, he rose and disappeared out the glass doors into the Providence darkness. The hotel manager was infuriated by them but would never have dreamed of inviting either of them, father or daughter, to leave.

It surprised no one when Aralyn, black-haired and bewitching, married into money. A frequent guest of the hotel, Mr. Harris Wolfe, a California businessman not much younger than Oakley himself, whisked her away to a life of sunlight and blue pools and caviar—this latter a delicacy for which Aralyn had a particular taste—far from her dreary, questionable New England roots and a life of toil and decadence, a word my employer seemed overly fond of using, along with "eldritch" and "unknowable." The other employees of the hotel were not sorry to see Aralyn go, not least because they would no longer be forced to suffer Oakley's objectionable presence.

And yet, though Aralyn was gone, Oakley continued his nightly visitations, stepping through the glass doors, trailing ribbons of fog, to sit staring an hour or two under the rose light of the chandeliers, before rising, announcing to the room, *High time she come home*, and disappearing back into the night.

Or so began the tale.

Though I had never been one for such nonsense, this story quite captured my interest, or fancy, call it what you will. I knew the hotel to which my employer referred on Benefit Street, which cut across College Hill west of the university, a street of red brick colonials and the aforementioned hotel, among others, frequented by moneyed tourists and businessmen. He certainly spun an engaging yarn, and I confess I was uncertain from how he told the story what to take as truth and what fiction. Since there was such a hotel, perhaps there was such a family also.

I set to focused work typing the pages, losing myself in the slow rhythm of the keys and, again, in Oakley and Aralyn. When at last I looked up and out the window over the misty garden, I felt, from having sunk myself so deeply into the story, remote, disconnected, as if I were not of the world. Beyond the box hedge, the man Baxter and his son had come out. The boy in his crimson scarf played with one of the shed cats on the grass while his father, in an overcoat, sat frowning on the steps, smoking, circling items in what I assumed was the help-wanted section of the paper. I rose and stood at the window. My heart went out to them.

The muffled creak of a screen door, and father and son were joined by a woman with a grey woollen wrap thrown about her shoulders. She looked pleasant, apple-cheeked, hardly a madwoman. I watched as she walked up behind Baxter and draped her arms about his shoulders, her chin resting comfortably on the top of his head. My hand went on impulse to my heart, as if it could still what swelled brutally there.

The man Baxter, perhaps alerted by my sudden movement, looked up sharply and I stepped back, out of the window. I cannot say for certain why I did so, nor whether he had seen me there, but he rose and took the woman's arm. *James*, I heard him command, and his wife, amused, puzzled, said, *What is it?* their voices so faint and brittle through the windowglass, they might have been speaking out of a former age. The boy, James, rose heavily and followed his parents, glancing back once with that unnerving gaze, directly up to the attic window behind which I stood, before disappearing inside the boarding house. Only the cat remained, abandoned there in the long grasses, looking perplexed, too, at the sudden departure.

And I felt, for no reason I could explain, as if I had been caught at something despicable.

3

I SAW HIM, my employer. I felt certain of it.

That night as I drifted into sleep, curled on my side, my hands pressed between my knees for warmth, he was there, bending close over me in streetlight, to see were I asleep or not.

I sat up in alarm, the bed coils shrieking beneath me.

Of course, there was no one.

And yet I had seen him. He was tall, about my height and build roughly, perhaps a little on the thinner side, a little on the older, with broad shoulders and a long, aquiline face. The vision was so strong I could even describe what he wore: wire spectacles, a heavy cardigan buttoned up over a white shirt. About the collar, or whether or not he wore a tie, I could not say.

I turned on the table lamp and climbed out of bed. The floor was cold. I opened the door upon the dark stairwell and paused there, listening. Nothing. I stepped onto the landing and opened the adjacent door. Just the old cornbroom and the boxes and an odour of dust and liniment. I closed the door again and went back to my room.

Still, the sense of someone having been there—the sense of *him* having been there—was so strong I dressed hastily and went down to the kitchenette, as if I might find him there, perhaps making a cup of cocoa, saying, *Ah, Candle, there you are. I hope I didn't waken you, but I did so want to meet you. I'm feeling quite well, you see. Care for a cup?*

But the second floor, too, was dark. Only the light shining dimly from beneath his study door. And that presence, a slight stirring of the air around me, as if someone, something, moved there in the darkness. I scarcely knew what to think of it, whether it was the place or my own unreliable perceptions.

About the nightmare—my employer in my room—I knew not what to think, either. I was beginning to wonder if it was not a result of reading that story, an eerie conjuring of Oakley Eakinns, though there was nothing of resemblance between the two. Still, there was something haunting in Oakley's refrain, *High time you come home*, which ran through my head in endless, unwanted repetition.

I returned to bed, locking the door to my room behind me. But I could not sleep and I rose again and stood instead for some time staring across the city to the lightless dormer window, Oakley's refrain still ringing in my head.

IN THE MORNING, a fat white envelope lay waiting on the pedestal table in the front hall. I carried it to the kitchen and sat down to read it over a cup of that detestable cocoa—the only thing I seemed able to stomach—made slightly more palatable by the addition of several teaspoons of sugar scraped from the bottom of a cracked porcelain bowl so palely blue it resembled bone. I made a mental note to go out to the shops to purchase more, along with a few other items that were wanting. Already, I felt foolish for my over-reaction to the dream of the previous night. A brisk walk in the fresh air would do me good.

The letter looked to be another long one. Tucked inside the envelope I also found a smaller envelope. This I took, with some relief, to be my advance, which I intended to post to Jane immediately. I put it aside for the moment and unfolded the letter.

It came to five pages, slightly shorter than his previous missive, though the handwriting, cramped and nearly illegible then, had deteriorated substantially. He noted this himself and begged my tolerance, explaining it away as the result of long hours at work the previous day. Were he to strive for greater legibility, he claimed, he would not complete the many letters and manuscripts he wished.

He was, oddly, both the most courteous (my eerie dream more foolish still) and the most thoroughly snobbish person I'd ever—I could not say met—become acquainted with. He was all exceeding politeness but referred often to his inability to go outside not only because of his illness and the dreadful cold but, worse still, *the miserable burgeoning rabble which throng the streets and shops daily.*

He inquired as to whether I had made any progress on the typing of his manuscript and his correspondence, adding that he hoped I would not trouble him but simply post the letters as I finished them, for he trusted to my accuracy. He advised again that I leave the typed pages on the hall table, forbidding me to knock at his door under any circumstances. He wondered also if I would be interested in *a rather tedious project which I have lately undertaken with some regrets.* This project, it seemed, was some sort of book of grammar, a kind of ghostwriting which he told me made up a good deal of his income, though he spoke of it as a favour, or a hobby, rather than actual gainful employment.

He apologized, too, at length for the lack of heat in my quarters and complained himself of the unseasonably cold temperatures, assuring me that once spring arrived, as it surely would any day, I would notice a distinct change in the atmosphere of my attic room *as the sun strikes there quite clear and bright, with a honeyed, bee-buzz warmth, for the greater part of the day, making it so pleasant I almost wish I'd arranged it for my own use.* I read this line twice, marvelling that a grown man would use the phrase "honeyed, bee-buzz warmth." But, then, he was a writer, after all.

He advised, in the meantime, that extra blankets could be found in the linen cupboard just outside his aunt's room. He wrote:

> *My good Aunt Annie, as I believe I have mentioned, is*
> *likely to remain in hospital another two weeks, and since she*
> *has, for some time now, been my most doting caretaker, I*
> *feel her absence keenly, as you might imagine. In fact, she is*
> *almost as a second mother to me, only more, how shall I put*

it, at once more demonstrative and more combative. I mean this in only the most affectionate sense. That she is not one to take things sitting down, as the young folks say nowadays. That she is not easily bruised, as it were; an anomaly among us Phillipses, it would seem. You see she is the younger sister to my mother, the latter by far the more sensitive of the two, though there seems in us all to be bred a streak of what I can only call the unusual; the inevitable result, perhaps, of a pure and unvarying bloodline. You will, of course, meet her in good time, my aunt, and then you may see for yourself what I mean when I say she is a bit of a Viking—that Nordic blood!—although her illness may have temporarily doused some of the fire in her, as mine has in me.

As to my mother, perhaps a word here is in order. I beg you to understand that all the damage wrought on a sensitive and artistic temperament such as hers—among other qualities and accomplishments, she is a painter and pianist of no little skill and has an impressive writing and speaking knowledge of French—has left her also unwell. Her, shall we say, highly refined, aristocratic nerves have for the moment gotten quite the better of her and so she has been advised a period of complete rest while she recovers her equilibrium, as it were. My own unfortunate illness, this grippe I have been battling most of the winter, now the worst it's been, along with the insufferably cold weather, has kept me this week from my accustomed visits, and she must be speculating at my absence. I wonder if you would consider paying her a call and explaining the situation? I have outlined the matter in my letter, but

Mother has always been a worrier and will no doubt jump to grim conclusions if the situation is not explained in propria persona, *or as close to it as I can manage! I have, you see, rather a history of—well, "nervous breakdown" smacks of the hysterical!—perhaps "nervous disorder" captures it best, and I was for a long time in my youth subject to my own confinement—but enough; suffice it to say she will worry. I grieve mightily at my own unavoidable absence and would consider your visit a great favour in addition to taking it into account as, shall we say, your services rendered.*

You will find when you meet her, no doubt, that she is striking, even given her age—which in itself is not considered "old" by any stretch of the proverbial imagination—her complexion not outmatched in whiteness and purity, and her features being rather inclined to the aquiline, the noble, retaining their good qualities no matter the advancement of age.

At any rate, I do believe you will enjoy meeting someone of her position and calibre in society, and I dare say you might spend a pleasant hour or two in her company should you see it possible to spare the hours from your work here. She is not one for games of cards or other such imbecile amusements, nor is she much inclined to conversation, but we have on her best days spent many a pleasant hour at the little park along the river in companionable silence.

He reiterated that he would be much obliged if I would make the letter a priority.

There was, however, no mention of advance or salary.

I upturned the outer envelope onto the table, and a thin fold of bills clipped together, hardly enough for the shops, slid out. A note accompanied this: *To be used for postage, foodstuffs, writing supplies, et cetera.*

On the reverse of this note, ink sketches of strange, insect-like creatures, emaciated and many-legged, with terrible, grasping mouths. Not a penny toward my advance.

I crumpled the note into a tight twist and flicked it from the table in irritation. It slid beneath the range. I sat staring into my cocoa a moment. Beyond my irritation, something about the letter made me distinctly uneasy. I could not put my finger on just what it was. In part, the mention of a nervous disorder, certainly. That image—premonition, vision, nightmare, call it what you will—of him bending over me in the darkness of my attic room came back to me. But there was yet something more, something troubling, about the mother.

I reread the letter, looking for clues to my unease. Finding nothing, but not finding comfort either, I rose from the table and, getting down on hands and knees, wedged my fingers beneath the range, feeling around until I retrieved the clotted, soiled paper. Smoothing it against my knee, I folded it and his letter into my pocket, along with the letter for his mother, and stuck the few bills into my wallet. Beyond the window, it had begun to rain hard again. The letter would not be delivered that day, at any rate.

So, too, did I feel not a little resentful that already he

required more of me while not holding up his end of the bargain. On the back of the torn envelope, I scrawled a hasty note inquiring again about the advance. After swilling the last dregs of my detestable cocoa, I rinsed my cup and put it away.

I WAS COMPELLED, upon returning to my room, to switch on the desk lamp as I worked, though whether because of the lowering skies or the black rain or my own uneasiness I could not have said.

I pulled the letter for his mother from my suit jacket. I stared at the envelope a long while. Finally, I took a letter opener from the drawer and sat tapping it on the desk. But I could not; it would be unforgivable. At long length, I dropped the envelope on the desk and rose with the letter opener. The boxes stood there along the wall. I confess I hesitated. I had never been one to pry into the business of others. If anything, I had been too much inclined the other way. *You lack interest*, Jane had often said, quite unjustly, I thought then, *in anyone other than yourself.*

Taking the first box, I slit it open. Papers, old pamphlets and circulars, anonymous memorabilia; insignificant, uninteresting. The same true of all the boxes. Nothing; though what I thought I might find I could not have said. The last two boxes in the corner were unsealed and I pried open their lids to discover magazines with grotesque cover illustrations: enormous, fanged serpents and tortured

spectres, winged demons and vampires hovering over cow-
ering, shrieking ladies in scanty dress.

Putting them aside, I surveyed the mess I'd made of the
room. I stacked the boxes all up against the wall again and
put the magazines on my desk. Then I recalled the other
boxes in the adjacent room. After pausing on the landing to
listen—for, though it was unlikely, I did not relish the idea
of being caught prying into someone else's belongings—I
stepped across and entered the lightless room. I opened the
first box. Then the second, the third. I did not stop until
they all stood open on the floor around me. Every box was
the same: women's clothing, the aunt's, I assumed, dated as
they were to my eye, but of good quality, silks and velvets
stiffened with age and disuse. A faint, stale odour of lavender and liniment filled the air. I felt queer standing there
among those garments. Guilty, but something else as well.
What is it you're looking for, Crandle? I asked myself. Having
no answer, I hastily stuffed all the clothing back into the
boxes. Then, feeling disgusted at myself, I closed the door
behind me, intending to make a quick trip out to the shops
for packing tape to reseal the boxes before my trespass was
discovered.

But, to my astonishment, it was almost four o'clock—
where had the hours gone?—and the shops would soon be
closed. I returned to the kitchenette with its bright row of
primroses and opened a can of chili con carne and heated it
on the stove. After eating a few bites while staring out the
window at the cats on the shed roof (they seemed to have

multiplied), the food did not taste good and I did not feel particularly hungry. I left the remainder in a covered saucepan on low heat on the stovetop for my employer to help himself, as I supposed was expected, though he had not said as much, and went directly upstairs for a few more hours at my desk.

And yet, as soon as I settled, I could not shake that image of him bending over me in the darkness. I rose and, feeling the fool, locked the door to my room.

THE STORY OF ARALYN and Oakley Eakinns unfolded as I read and typed and read some more. Several years passed at the hotel. None there had seen or heard from Aralyn. Oakley continued his nightly visits without fail. Then Oakley disappeared, too. At first, no one noticed his absence, so accustomed were they to his presence; the great irony of the familiar and the reviled. And, because of this late notice, there was some dissension as to just when his visits had stopped. Some claimed it had been more than a month, some a week, two at the most. One girl who worked in the laundry swore she'd seen him there just the previous night, owl-eyed and reeking of cinders, as always. But she was a known teller of tales, and scarcely to be believed. Then they heard he had been seen that previous Sunday, out on the bay. Boys who frequented the docks to smoke and throw stones at the pilings for a nickel a strike claimed to have seen him row out in his little, rotting boat around nightfall, just as the late November frets were beginning to drift in over the water. He seemed to be toting something in his boat, something wrapped in a white sheet, the corner of which hung over the prow, trailing in the black water. It looked, they claimed with typical adolescent imagination, like a body. One of the boys had called out as much to old Oakley, jocularly, some nonsense jibe. The old man had turned upon them then, teeth bared, a gaze so ominous as to silence them all and send them home, one by one, early to their lighted houses. Oakley's boat was found by a small fishing tug at dawn the next morning, drifting empty in the murderous, icy tides.

Aralyn appeared at the hotel not a month later, imperiously, decked in jewels and furs as black as her hair. Her husband did not accompany her; she made hasty excuses, ordering dishes of caviar, which she ate with great relish, downing goblets of water as if her thirst could not be quenched. Her colour, many remarked, was not good. She had aged, markedly, paled and shrivelled under that west coast sun. Her lips had taken on a greenish tinge. Her breath stank of the sea. Her former co-workers were hardly welcoming, distant, uneasy at her sudden, glittering appearance, casting glances through the glass doors to the Providence night, half expecting Oakley to step through at any moment, wreathed in sour sea-mist, announcing in a watery voice, *High time you come home.*

But he did not. There was only Aralyn, alone in the centre of the dining room, draped in furs that could scarcely be called glossy, as if they'd been cut from animals left dead sometime in the black of the woods, a silver dish of caviar before her, white hands placed palms down on the table, waiting for her former co-workers to fawn over her, as she seemed to expect they would. But, instead, they ignored her, were repelled by her. She grinned, finally, her teeth blackened with roe, and, in a rage, turned over the dish of caviar, the silver, the crystal goblets, and spat a dark curse upon the hotel and all who worked or slept within its finely papered walls, before blasting out the glass doors into the night, gone, some said, to find Oakley.

The telegram arrived the following morning. From a Mr. Wolfe of Windsor Hills, Los Angeles, California, inquiring as to whether anyone at the hotel had heard from his wife, Mrs. Aralyn Wolfe, missing this past month.

Though the story was indeed gripping, I could not say I liked it. It was not good. And yet I was compelled by it nevertheless. There was something about it so haunting, a certain desolation that rang quite true.

But dark, dark. I rose and took up a handful of the magazines and flipped through them. I could not help but wonder at the kind of imagination—the kind of man—who would not only read but write such, well, I scarcely knew what to call it. Horror, I supposed. But not quite that, either. There was something about the world he depicted, the coldness of it, the meaninglessness, which disturbed me. There was nothing of humanity in it. Nothing of goodness. Nothing of hope. There was something dreadful and empty at its heart and, therefore, I imagined, at the heart of its author.

To be the creator of all that hopelessness—well, how could one live with oneself? Darkness, I knew too well, begat only darkness. One way or another.

MOST PECULIAR: working on the story of Aralyn and Oakley, I began to lose track of the passage of time. I settled in to my work, then lifted my face to find an hour, two hours, had passed. Later, what felt to be hours would be minutes, moments.

I put aside the manuscript and turned to the typing of his correspondence, formal, self-deprecating letters filled with my employer's obvious insecurities and with sophomoric references to, and whimsical drawings of, the cats I'd seen lounging on the shed roof, a society he'd dubbed the Kappa Alpha Tau (KAT). Such playfulness hardly seemed possible in such a man. It made me feel, again, that my uneasiness had more to do with my own precarious state of mind than with this man I had not met. He was a mystery, certainly. A recluse. He was ill. But he was, it seemed after all, not really frightening.

HIS CORRESPONDENCE SOLVED one mystery, at least: among the various pseudonyms used by my employer—Grandpa Theobald, Lewis Theobald Jr., Augustus T. Swift,

Lawrence Appleton, John J. Jones, Humphrey Littlewit, Archibald Mainwaring, Henry Paget-Lowe, Ward Phillips, Richard Raleigh, Amos Dorance Rowley, Edward Softly, Albert Frederic Willie, Zoilus and the puzzling Ech-Pi—was his actual name. Not Ech-Pi, but H.P. Only that. Howard Phillips Lovecraft.

So ordinary. And sad, also. As the solving of every mystery must necessarily be.

FINALLY, PUTTING ASIDE my work, I gathered up the few finished pages for my employer, and stood and stretched and made my way downstairs.

Halfway down, I was hit by a foul, charred smell and I recalled the chili I had left to warm on the stove. I found it untouched, burned thickly to the bottom of the pot. I began to scrape the mess out into the trash and then, changing my mind, pulled a chipped bowl from the cupboard and, depositing the remains there instead, carried the bowl to the window, thinking with some amusement of that saying I'd once heard: that if you fed a dog, it would think you were a god; if you fed a cat, it would think it was a god. The cats were there on the shed, godlike, despite the darkness, and I tapped the spoon against the bowl. They glanced up at me, not with charming playfulness as in my employer's drawings, but with obvious loathing. I shivered and set the bowl on the roof, closing the window.

It was after midnight, I noted to my surprise by the

clock in the kitchen. According to his schedule, he should be awake and working. I took the typed pages back out to the hall. My note inquiring about the advance still lay untouched there on the pedestal table. The light glowed from beneath his door, as always.

On a whim, I went out the apartment door and down to the darkened courtyard. I stood in my shirt sleeves, shivering, and looked up at the second floor. Though there were windows there where windows should be—at the corner at which I placed his study—all were black. Surely, even with heavy draperies pulled shut, my employer's light should show through at that hour. I slowly circled the entire house: there was the kitchenette, the rear door leading out of it and down a set of rickety stairs to the garden, the frosted bathroom window, another set of windows which must belong to the aunt's rooms, and then back around again to the front and the lightless windows of my employer's study.

I returned inside. That feeling of heaviness, that stirring, met me on the landing and followed me upward and into the apartment. Eerily, the light still showed beneath the study door. So unnerved was I by this, and by my lingering fear—irrational though it was—that perhaps he had been in my room that night after all, that I determined, in spite of his forbidding it, to knock. As I approached the door, I heard, or thought I heard, a faint scratching coming from beyond it, so soft it could have been a branch against a window, a gust of wind.

I felt an irrepressible shiver. I raised a fist. And I knocked.

Something dreadful shot through me, a chill, as if emanating from the wood of that door and passing in a current through my knuckles, up my forearm, down the left side of my flesh. I stood like that, stunned at the force of it, my fist still raised, my blood loud in my ears.

I waited, heart pounding. There was nothing.

When at last I turned away, my eyes happened to settle upon the door to the aunt's room. Something, that cold weightiness, seemed to be leaning out from that space, leaning toward me. On an impulse, I crossed the hall and tried the handle.

Locked. As I somehow knew it would be.

What could I do? I placed the pages with my note upon the hall table, clicking off the emerald lamp, and made my way back up the narrow stairs, feeling myself eaten up by the darkness as I went.

TWO

I

ON THE THIRD MORNING, I was forced, finally, from Number Sixty-Six and out to the shops to purchase some few necessities. I had slept poorly, again. Sometime, during the dark hours, I had awakened, gasping, to see that light in the dormer window across the city, flickering on and off, on and off. I rose and positioned my bed so as not to face it. Then, the light seemed to filter in, fill the room. I turned my back upon it, the covers up over my eyes to shut it out.

Finally, just before dawn, I rose and dressed in my suit and shoes and sat on the bed, turning and turning the piece of gravestone in my hands, waiting for the hour at which the shops would open.

At eight o'clock I went downstairs, past the lighted room and out the apartment door. Once outside, I made a point of stopping again in the wet, cobbled lane and looking up. All the windows on the second floor, again, were dark. The drapes still pulled, tinged crimson by day, but lightless nevertheless from the inside.

From the outside, in daylight and fresh sea air, and with the ordinary sounds of sparrows rattling the tree branches, and pedestrians passing on the street, and the steady hammering from a building under construction across the lane, the house seemed quite benign. I could almost laugh at my fears. The air already seemed to be doing me good. I certainly felt better, clearer. I wondered at the simple possibility of blackout curtains at the study windows.

As I stood speculating, an elderly man in an overcoat stepped out of the house at the far end of the lane, toting with him on a leash a small dog the precise colour of the overcoat. It minced along on the wet cobblestones, as if loathe to dampen its paws, shaking its body dry periodically, though it was not raining. I wondered with dark amusement just how many such dogs would be required to make such a coat. I thought of the cats on the shed roof, how they would devour the creature.

The man was almost upon me when he glanced up with an air of angry surprise.

Good morning, I said.

He looked affronted. I had often heard such things about older, dying, aristocratic neighbourhoods, no one deigning to speak even to their own neighbours on the street lest they address someone beneath them. I had little patience for such posturing.

I wonder, I said, *if you could point me in the direction of the nearest shops.*

The dog sniffled about, ogling my shoes. I repressed an urge to boot it aside. The old man shot me a quick look, almost hostile, as if perhaps he'd read my thoughts, then looked swiftly away, frowning.

Come now, Daisy, he said, and tugged on the silvery leash. *Just keep going the way you are?*

He phrased it as if it were an angry question, and did not look up at me, giving the impression he was still addressing the loathsome Daisy.

You'll come upon it in another few blocks. Everything you want there, I should suppose.

I thanked him and wished him good day and began to turn away, but he said, grudgingly, *There's something in particular, some special item, you're seeking?*

No, indeed, I said, *just the usual things. Any department store should do.*

He hesitated, as if he would say more, and then gave me another irritable, I would even say furious, look. He said, *I hope you will beg my pardon.*

Yes?

Have you not been down there?

It's rather early. I suspect they don't open until after eight o'clock.

The old man continued to glare.

Come along, Daisy, he said, finally, and frowned deeply, rattling the leash and startling the dog from where she squatted peeing on the cobblestones next to my shoe.

I stepped with pointed care over the puddle and went on my way. When, a few steps on, I happened to look back, the old man still stood in the lane, glaring after me. Or at least, I thought he did. But then Daisy emerged, that vile little beast, kicking up some leaves over the steaming pile she had left beneath the elms, and they moved on.

THE AIR WAS SILKEN and fresh after the rain, though the cold yet held the bite of a New England winter. I did feel better, though still chilled, weakened. It was only to be expected. I descended College Hill in search of the commercial district, down and down, past students on their way up to their morning lectures, bundled in their tweeds and corduroys and woollens, scarved brightly in the current fashion. The boys, absurdly young, carried themselves with an important air, nodding to me, pink-faced under their tilted caps, man to man, while the few lone girls stared hard at their sturdy shoes as I passed, clutching books to their chests as if I might wrench them away; in groups the girls chattered and fluttered and did not notice me at all.

The crowds thinned the farther I walked from the university, winding down between rows of colonial houses, whose square edges and strong, deep reds and blues were softened in the misty light. An automobile passed now and again, looking coldly bestial, mythical, as if it had just lumbered in from some other place, studded with night rain and chugging plumes of exhaust. A familiar radio show played from a kitchen window cracked to the morning air, Vivian someone or other—Jane would have known—as the insipid Mary Noble, the worst of the soaps, until I realized it was only a commercial for Lux toilet soap. It all sounded the same to me. Still, there was a friendliness in the filtered household sounds, the clatter of dishes; the smell of coffee, bacon; the electric lights shining through the many-paned windows like the chambers of gilded hearts.

As the houses grew shabbier and finally gave way to larger brick storefronts and businesses, I passed now and then an archway leading into what appeared to be solitary courtyards which still held the detritus of a long coastal winter in their corners, rotted piles of leaves and dirt still dreaming darkly against the cobblestones.

Altogether a charming neighbourhood and one I thought I would enjoy occupying while I was there employed. I considered how well Jane would like it and, before I could stop it, a picture flashed before my eyes, of Jane and I strolling those streets arm in arm, Molly trotting ahead in a little red raincoat. I gasped with the shock and pain of it. Stood a moment in the street, openly gaping. Two girls in thick, bright cardigans shouldered past me, giggling, and I roused myself and walked on, breathing deeply of the cold air to steady my thoughts.

Of hope, there was none. Only atonement. If there was such a thing. Money. How ill-matched to my sins. But what else was there?

And yet I had not even that; could send no money if no money were forthcoming. I wondered, then, for the first time, at my employer's financial circumstances. The shared, worn accommodations, the dearth of foodstuffs. It all pointed in a certain direction. Still, I knew it was not unusual among his class. Thrift and economy as well as a certain cultivated shabby gentility were highly prized traits among New England aristocracy. It could just as easily have been that he was well off indeed. Impossible to know.

I heaved a great sigh in the cold air and, taking my gloves from my overcoat pockets, rubbed fruitlessly at the inky tips of my fingers, making a note to purchase another cake of lye.

BY THE TIME I returned to College Street with my purchases, the sun was bright and my spirits from the air and exercise somewhat improved. Still, I was not eager to return to the dark, oppressive atmosphere of that lonely apartment, my mysterious employer. I pulled open the front door and was hit by that scent of old cherries, though not nearly so strong as on my first arrival. I was thinking how quickly the strange becomes familiar, when I stopped short.

A young woman in a pale blue velvet cloak and bobbed yellow hair stood on the landing, a white handbag on her wrist, apparently deciding whether or not to go up. She held a key in one gloved hand and a white leather travelling case sat on the floor at the foot of the stairs beside a fully opened umbrella, still lolling fatly against the floorboards, as if she'd only just set it down. She half-turned as I came in.

Gracious, she said, *you startled me.*

Good morning, I said.

Thank goodness you're here.

She came down the stairs as she spoke, walking directly to the padlocked apartment door, her heels clacking against the polished boards.

This lock has me fit to be tied, I swear.

She stuck her key into the lock and banged it uselessly against the door frame.

Helen left this . . . key . . . for me, she said, addressing the lock, *under one of those palms there. S*he gestured with her head to a potted palm, soil tipped out on the shining floor. *But I can't get the darned thing to work and I've been trying ever so long.*

She pushed a curl back from her forehead impatiently with a gloved hand as if to demonstrate how long she'd been trying. Her fair cheeks were flushed, as with embarrassment or from the outdoors. *She said she'd be here. I might have expected as much from her, from Helen.*

Helen?

She's unreliable that way. That's why I told her to leave a key. Just in case. Not that it's helped any. She probably left the wrong one. I don't know her all that well, actually. The sister of a friend back home. She was always, you know. She waved her hand in a meaningless gesture. *It seems just the sort of thing she would do. Bit of a nut, even back then.*

She straightened and lifted a gloved hand abruptly to her mouth, looking at me over her shoulder.

Oh, I shouldn't have said that. How terrible of me. But, really, it's so vexing. I don't know what I am to do. She said she'd be here.

I fished from my pocket the key my employer had left me.

I have only this one, I said, by way of apology.

Obviously misunderstanding, she waved me toward the door.

Please, she said.

I hesitated, opened my mouth to correct her, then

came forward and slid the key in with an air of embarrassed indulgence.

The lock fell open.

I stepped back in astonishment. The woman clapped her gloved hands together in delight.

Oh, bravo, she said and, flinging the door open, stepped past me in a faint waft of green apples.

The suite, from where I stood blinking in the doorway, seemed bathed in light, though the day was overcast and the draperies drawn, and this I put down to the rich green paint of the walls. Almost everything in the main living room was some shade of green: the pale upholstered sofa, the bright rug, the draperies, the row of elvish ferns in their pots along the window, even a large, coarse—to my eyes—marble effigy of a horse which reared crazily on the mantle. All in greens. The light itself was green.

I must have stood staring with something like amazement, for the woman turned to me and said, *It's very . . . fresh, isn't it?*

She pulled the draperies open with a grand gesture over the main window overlooking the lane, loosing billows of gold dust that turned lazily in the light. She blinked her eyes prettily, then tilted her head back and laughed, as though she'd done something extraordinarily clever.

Well, she said, beaming a smile at me, *thank goodness you turned up just now, is all I can say. Talk about timing.*

She crossed to the other window and pulled the draperies open there as well with a dramatic swish.

It's wonderfully bright and spacious, but I'll confess it could use a decorator. All this green could make a gal go stark raving out of her mind. I don't know how Helen can stand it. Like living inside a bottle, isn't it? Like a genie. Pretty in a way, though. If you blur your eyes up it's like sunshine. But crazy, too. You know what I mean? But what am I saying, you must think I'm a madwoman. Flo, she said, then flung up a gloved hand and laughed again. *Gracious, I'm so rattled. It's amazing what one little locked door can do to a person.*

She took a deep breath, making a self-conscious—perhaps too self-conscious—effort to collect herself.

I'm Flossie, Flossie Kush. I'm the one staying with Helen. Obviously.

Helen.

This is her flat, isn't it? She said she was subletting from a Mrs. . . . oh, something to do with farmers . . . Shepherd, that's it. Mrs. Shepherd? While she's in Europe? Can you just imagine? What a place. Europe, I mean. That Adolf Hitler, the big bully. I knew boys just like him from first grade on. Babies, every one, and bullies because of it. Please, do come in.

You're not a supporter, then, I said, stepping into the room.

Goodness, is anyone? They're supposed to be so cultured, you know, so intellectual, those horrid Germans. They call us vulgar? They call us loud? Philistines, they say, Americans, you know, but really they're so awful and following that terrible man and his hateful ideas. He's almost as bad as that Reverend so-and-so everyone's so crazy about back home, Coughlin or whatever—do you listen to that radio show of his?

I'm not sure I know it.

Oh, but you must have heard of him. The Little Hour of the Golden Flower? *Or* The Golden Hour of the Little Flower, *I'm never sure which. He's not a German, of course, but he might as well be, he's just as bad. The things he says about those poor boys in, whatever, Scottsboro.*

Scottsboro?

Oh, you know. Those negro boys accused of, well, I shouldn't say—she lowered her voice—*rape. You know, down there in Alabama? I'll tell you those boys were lynched, that's what that was, only it was the courts that did the lynching. But to hear old Reverend Coughlin tell it. I'm surprised you haven't heard him, he sure makes himself known. We should just ship him off to Germany, too, that's what I think. You know I can't even picture it there, everything that's going on now. It's just about the last place I'd want to be, that's all I know.*

Alabama?

Silly. Germany.

Oh? Why is that?

Kush, she said, as if I should have known. *My surname. They wanted me to change it, of course.*

They?

No one wants to hire a Jew actress. That's one thing they were clear on.

You're an actress.

That's funny, you didn't say, "You're a Jew." Some do, you know. Well. Anyway. Trying. To be an actress, that is. Trying not to be a Jew. She laughed without humour. *Not really. On the outside, I guess. You know how it is.* She plucked at the hem of her cloak.

What was it? Before?

What was what?

Your name.

Kushner. Can you imagine? Florence Kushner? They wanted me to change it to something more delicious, they said. Delicious, imagine. Something like, oh, I don't know, one of them suggested Arabella del'Aqua. That one stuck with me, I can tell you. What a laugh. So now I'm Flossie Kush. I don't mind it. Only that I went on a cattle call once—do you know what that is, a cattle call?

I'm afraid I don't.

No, I didn't either. I hate the term. Not very flattering. It's like an audition, but it's open to, say, dozens of girls, hundreds. I guess it's open to anyone who wants to go, and you stand around waiting all day, biting your nails, like cattle, I guess. Though I think that's downright insulting, not just the name but, you know, all of it. Anyway, I went on this one and do you know this woman had the nerve—oh, but I shouldn't say.

Shouldn't say what?

She looked around dramatically, as if to check would she be overheard in the empty apartment.

She had the nerve to say, "Oh, Flossie Kush, is it? Sounds about right for the French market."

French market?

You know, she said, lowering her voice, *you must have heard about those kinds of pictures.*

I see, I said. *Yes, of course.*

Europeans again. Just like I said. Well. I'd like to say I gave her a piece of my mind.

Didn't you?

I needed the job.

I know about that.

Do you?

Did you get it?

She stuck her tongue out charmingly. *It was for, I don't know, cat food or something anyway. So who cares.*

You could have changed it to something else, I suppose.

The radio commercial? Oh, they don't let you do that.

Your name.

Oh. Like what?

I don't know. Anastasia Uppington Arabesque. The third.

That's a laugh. Can you imagine having to go around with a handle like that. Anyway, I've come to like Flossie Kush. It suits me, I think. Better than old Florence Kushner, anyway. From Miami.

Ah, Florida.

Indiana.

A Midwestern girl.

And how. Do you know it? Miami? There's a college there. A pretty good one, I guess, if you like that sort of thing.

Don't you?

My father wanted me to go. I had other ideas, I guess. She shrugged and fiddled with the hem of her cloak again, then looked up at me suddenly. *But here I am rattling on. You must have some papers for me, or something? And a key? One that works? Helen said you would.*

She lifted the white handbag from the sofa and rummaged through it. It was dirty and worn across the bottom, as if it had spent a good deal of time waiting on floors.

Do you have them with you now? she said. *The lease, or whatever you call it. I only plan to be here a couple of weeks or so, but Helen said Mrs. Shepherd was a stickler for that sort of thing. Germany's the place for her, I guess. And a key, of course. I'll need that. I have a pen in here somewhere. It's like a good omen, you know; if I carry a pen around, someone somewhere's going to ask for my autograph. You know, someday. That's what I think, anyway.*

It occurred to me then—I'll confess I was a bit slow—that she had taken me for the landlord.

I'm sorry, I said, *you must have me mistaken . . .*

But I wasn't quite sure how to finish. Had she mistaken me for my own employer? Was he subletting on behalf of this Mrs. Shepherd? Or had she confused me with someone else entirely?

I have you mistaken? she asked, looking up from her handbag and tilting her head. *Don't you live upstairs?*

Yes—well, no.

She straightened then, slowly, and the smile faded.

Well, which is it? Yes or no?

Forgive me, I said, feeling the heat rise to my face. I'd always been terrible in such situations. *I have not introduced myself.*

That's all right. She looked sideways at the open door behind me.

I . . . I do live upstairs. My name is Arthor. With an "o."

Orthor?

I spelled it. Then added, *It's Irish.*

You don't sound Irish.

My parents.

And you live upstairs? With your parents?

No. I mean, yes, I do live upstairs. Not with my parents.

Alone?

I don't know why I said it. It seemed simpler, I suppose, at the time. Easier than explaining the odd situation, and one I had so little information about. Perhaps I was embarrassed. Perhaps I did not want to feel as if I'd been caught in a lie, though what followed was, of course, far worse. Who can say why one does anything.

Yes, I said. *Alone.*

There is some saying or anecdote or proverb I'd heard somewhere about the first lie being the hardest. Certainly, that lie was not my first, nor even the first to which I'd admitted, and in truth it came out very easily indeed. It caused me scarcely a pause.

I see, she said, though the look on her face made it clear she did not.

Perhaps, I said, *you spoke with my . . . colleague?*

Your colleague?

Yes.

But, she said, *you are the one leasing the apartment? On behalf of Mrs. Shepherd? Alice Shepherd? That's what Helen said.*

Mrs. Shepherd, that's right.

You do know her?

Not what you'd say personally. She is fond of green, I am told.

She stared at me from across the room. She did not smile. She glanced again toward the open door.

Allow me to explain, I said, stepping forward.

She snapped her handbag shut and I could see I was causing her some distress.

This must seem confusing, I said. *I am not expressing myself well at all. Forgive me. Mrs. Shepherd is a friend.*

I thought you said you didn't know her.

A friend of a friend. Of . . . my aunt, actually.

Your aunt.

That's right.

And where is your aunt?

She's . . . in hospital just now.

Oh, she said, looking a little relieved. *I think Helen may have mentioned something about that.*

Rather a bad case of the grippe. No easy thing for a woman her age. So I've been managing her affairs. While she is incapacitated.

She doesn't live here then, your aunt?

In fact, she does.

But you said—

That I live alone? Well, as you can see, at present I do.

You live with your aunt usually, then? When she is well?

I laughed, as if it were an entirely understandable though quite clear error.

No, not usually. Not when she is well. I'm here only while she is in hospital, to manage her affairs, as I say. And then perhaps for some time afterward.

But . . . the colleague?

She's not as strong as she once was. Aging, you know.

But, she said, softening, *she is on the mend?*

I hope so, yes. She seems to be. Only one can never tell with these things. Strong of mind, not so much of body.

I marvelled at myself. How easy it was.

She seemed to consider. Then she said, again, *But the colleague—*

Did I say that, did I say colleague?

I believe you did.

A misunderstanding, then.

Well, Helen—

Indeed, where are my manners; I've troubled you enough, certainly. I must let you get settled.

Not at all, she said, pursing her lips. She seemed to hesitate over something. Then she said, quietly, musingly, *It is going around.*

I'm sorry? I risked another half-step forward and this time she did not recoil.

I say, she said, raising her voice louder than necessary, *it's going around.*

What is?

The grippe.

Ah. Yes. I smiled. Charmingly, I hoped. *For a moment, I thought you meant this conversation.*

A pause, and she studied me, and then the corners of her lips curled up into a smile, and she pulled off her gloves and, after an almost imperceptible hesitation, stepped forward and offered her hand. It was like a scene from the pictures.

Pleased to meet you, then, she said, *Arthor . . . ?*

Crandle. Arthor P. Crandle.

Arthor P. Crandle. From upstairs. My pleasure.

I smiled, felt it twitch uncertainly. A nervous tic.

Might I ask your aunt's name? Is she a Crandle then also, Irish?

Gracious, no. Let's all be glad she wasn't around to hear that. It's Annie . . . Phillips?

Was it? I seemed to recall it from the letter.

The "P." For Phillips, then.

I beg your pardon?

Phillips. Arthor Phillips Crandle. She looked pleased with herself.

That's right. Phillips. Of course. I smiled again. She seemed, I thought, to be waiting for something, but I had no earthly idea what was expected of me. I had begun to enjoy our little charade, my little charade. But it occurred to me then how deep I had sunk myself and I panicked.

Well, I said briskly, uneasily. I made a sudden motion toward the door. It seemed to startle her. *I should be going, let you settle.*

But . . .

Yes?

About the lease, of course. And a key.

The emphasis she put upon the final word did not escape my notice, as I believed it was intended. She stood there with the grey light from the window silvering her pale hair, her slender silhouette.

No doubt, she said, *you would also like payment.*

Payment?

The first month.

I'm afraid I don't understand.

She laughed. *This apartment is a bargain. I assume you would like to receive some money from me. For the rent. Or do I give it to Helen? She was unclear about the details. So like her.*

I paused there in the doorway, considering the new twist. It was so neatly packaged, it seemed almost preordained, certainly fortuitous. Money, precisely what I needed.

Yes, I said. *Of course. The rent.*

She reached again into her handbag and counted the money out carefully and handed it to me. I thanked her and stood holding it out—it burned in my palm—as if giving her opportunity, as if urging her, to snatch it back.

I will need a key, she stressed again, leading me to the door. *What is it with these locks, anyway?* she said, lifting the one on the inside—a twin to the one outside—with the tips of her fingers and letting it thunk loudly.

I suppose you would have to ask your friend . . . ?

Helen.

Yes.

She isn't really a friend.

You said that. As to the locks, I can assure you they aren't necessary.

At the door, she looked pointedly at the key in my hand. What else was I to do? I hesitated, then held it out. But when she grasped it with her polished fingertips, I did not let go. I was seized with anxiety, the enormity of what I'd done. And then, to hand my key over, just like that—might I not need it myself? Might it give her access to the upper apartments? Might . . . ?

Her eyes flickered alarm again, or I thought they did, and I laughed uneasily, as though I'd hung on merely for a lark, and let go. So she would not see my embarrassment, I bent quickly to the sack of purchases I'd left in the foyer. Her travelling case sat there, next to her umbrella which lolled still, as if rocked by some phantom movement.

I picked it up along with the groceries and collapsed it for her with a winged sound.

Bad luck, you know, I said lightly.

She seemed not to know what I was talking about.

You've been to the shops, she said.

Just a few things.

Perhaps the next time you're going out . . .

Yes?

She looked at me meaningfully.

Would you like something picked up? I ventured.

I thought, she said, *I might join you. You can show me the neighbourhood. If it's no bother.*

What about Helen?

Oh, Helen, she said waving her hand. *But if it's a bother . . .*

Not at all. Well, I said then, awkwardly, taking my leave. *Welcome.*

When I looked back from the landing, she was still standing in the doorway, watching me. She smiled a little, or I thought she did, lit as she was from behind, her face all in shadow.

I RETURNED TO MY attic room in haste, my shoes banging on the old stairs. I felt terribly uneasy, aghast really, at what I had done below, the things I had said. I had the slight beginnings of a headache and I intended to dig out an old bottle of Aspirin I was sure I still had in my valise. But when I opened the chipped door to my room, I paused.

I had the distinct sense of someone having just been there. I crossed from the door to the windows, and then to the bed and back again, like a hound. It was nothing I could put my finger on, nothing out of place, nothing like my valise standing open where it had been closed, only that eerie sense one has of entering a room which another has just vacated.

I LEFT MISS KUSH'S money on the hall table for my employer, along with a note about the new tenant. I was no thief.

All right, I took only what I felt was owed me, promised me, as an advance. But no more. It was a small amount, very little, and I tucked it into an envelope to send to Jane.

I left that in the note as well, not about Jane, of course, but that I'd taken the few dollars. I was not so dishonest as all that.

I SPENT THE REMAINDER of the morning typing "business" correspondence—letters to fans and publishers and other writers—and I planned to give the afternoon over to work on the book of grammar, the ghostwriting project upon which I'd made no progress. In the evening, I would type his horror story.

It occurred to me only then the perversity of such a schedule, working on the horror story in the dark hours before going to sleep. Given my bad dreams and my general uneasiness since arriving at Number Sixty-Six, my own growing inclination to see, to feel, darkness everywhere, I determined to restructure my days. The grammar book, indeed, was dreary business, and sure to put me into a dreamless sleep.

I began another letter to Jane, enclosing the money and assuring her more would soon follow. Beyond that, I had little to write and I found myself staring at the page, so I signed off and sealed the envelope and put it aside. I picked up the chunk of gravestone and sat turning it, staring out at the glittering city. The dormer light there blinked on and off, on and off. I was becoming quite accustomed to it. I thought I must venture out when the weather was warmer and find out just what sort of building it was. I recalled then, with a ripple of remorse, the letter for my employer's mother. I had forgotten all about it. I stood, riffling through the papers on my untidy desk and finally plucking the letter from beneath a stack, intending to head straight out, but then the pages of the grammar book caught my eye, waiting there. I looked again at the directions he'd given me to his mother's. It appeared to be no short distance and I was feeling fatigued from my morning's outing. What was half a day more? I considered whether Miss Kush might enjoy such a walk as well.

I wondered how she was settling in to her green apartment below. In spite of my poor judgment, my foolish actions, I was very glad, indeed, to have her there, Helen or no. And who was this Helen, after all? Certainly I'd seen no signs of anyone else at Sixty-Six. The presence of others was quite welcome, though, and I felt I would sleep easier that night.

Still, I promised myself I would set Miss Kush straight about the situation at the earliest opportunity.

SHE WAS QUITE BEAUTIFUL. I don't believe I mentioned that.

2

MISS KUSH WAS LEANING against the balustrade on the landing the next morning as I went down to the postbox with my letter for Jane. Hands clasped before her, ankles crossed, she appeared to have been waiting some time.

She smiled up at me, her lips a shocking, glossy shade of red. The pale skin of her hands and throat luminous in the half-light.

Well, Mr. Crandle, she called, *have you come to keep your promise after all?*

My determination of the previous day to come clean about my foolish pretences flitted back to me and I paused on the stairs. Had I been so transparent, after all?

Miss Kush?

Miss Kush, she said, *sounds like some frumpy governess. Flossie. I insist.*

You are hardly. I cleared my throat. *Please, call me Arthor.*

I intend to. And I can see by your face you've quite forgotten your promise of taking me out to the shops.

Indeed, I had.

On the contrary, I said, slipping Jane's letter into my pocket. *Here I am.*

She smiled archly as I descended to the landing but said nothing.

When I reached her there, the hair all up my arms stood on end and I ushered her quickly before me down the stairs. When I looked back from the foyer, of course, there was nothing.

Arthor? Flossie said, giving me a funny look.

Just wondering if I'd forgotten anything, I said. And smiled. But, having said it, I realized that in fact I had forgotten something: the letter for my employer's mother. I had intended to go straight out with it after breakfast. Well, after lunch, then. And I would invite Flossie to accompany me. A pleasant thought. It was astonishing how greatly her presence had lightened the atmosphere of Sixty-Six.

The pale sky was clear and bright, and the air felt sharp and fine against my face as we stepped out, blinking, into the shining courtyard. I slipped Jane's letter discreetly into the red enamelled postbox. Flossie was watching me but pretending not to. I gestured for her to precede me into the lane and she smiled. The previous night's rain lit the trees spectacularly, the bare limbs flaring and glistening as the breeze stirred them.

It's like Christmas, Flossie said as we passed beneath.

I turned up the collar of my overcoat.

It's certainly cold enough.

At the end of the lane, we stepped out onto the street and into the violet shadows of the John Hay Library. Flossie wore the same pale blue velvet cloak in which I'd first seen her, with a matching hat and gloves, and had thrown, in addition, a silvery fur about her neck. Her nose was very pink in the cold air and, between this and the fur, she gave the impression of a friendly little rabbit.

Such a lovely morning, she said, *such a lovely street, and then there's that.*

What, I said, following her gaze, *the library?*

So cold, she said. And shivered.

A mausoleum of books, I suppose. I felt rather pleased with the sound of it.

It isn't very welcoming.

Rather dignified, though.

If you like that sort of thing. I prefer a bit of romance myself.

In a university library? Glass doors onto long verandahs? Gauze curtains stirring in the breeze? Wisteria?

And why not? A girl likes to be seduced by the building as well as the books.

She shot me a glance, expecting some particular sort of response, obviously.

Settling in all right? I asked instead.

Right enough. Only . . .

Yes?

Vexing that Helen hasn't turned up yet.

Hasn't she?

Flossie shrugged. *I suppose she's away.*

Traveller, is she?

I don't really know. Anyway, I'm sure she'll turn up soon enough. In the meantime, it's nice to . . .

Nice to?

I was going to say, it's nice to have the place to myself. But I would have been lying.

Would you have?

I hate to be alone. I can't bear it, really.

She said it lightly, but something in her tone had changed. A certain thoughtfulness settled over her.

We walked on in silence, out of the violet shadows and into the drunken April sunlight, descending. The antique city spread out before us, its black domes and steeples and great trees still dead with winter, the river a slow unwinding of light, and beyond it the bay, stretched out shining like a foil sheet. Flossie's pretty blue heels clicked against the cobblestones in a pleasant way and she chattered on as we wound our way down toward the commercial district. The houses began to give way to shops, and then the automobiles came steadily and the sidewalks buzzed with bundled housewives, toting their woollened young, gathering foodstuffs with an irritable, hungry, distracted air, as if just emerged from hibernation; scrubbed businessmen tapping spoons against coffee cups in café windows or shouldering past us, frowning importantly, overcoats thrown across their arms as if the cold could have nothing to do with them. Everywhere was movement, an air of things happening, important or ordinary. Only the rhinestoned salesgirls waited motionless in shop doorways, glittering sleepily, already checking the clocks.

We wove our way in and out of shops, and every one

held something of interest to Flossie. She astonished me with her vigour and enthusiasm. Packages accumulated in her hands as if by magic, and she displayed them all to me as if they were marvels, those charming unnecessaries: violet pastilles in a pretty little pewter tin; a hair comb inlaid with tortoiseshell; a pink glass jar of rose hand cream. In a jeweller's, she ran ropes of pearls through her fingers and hovered for what seemed an hour over a velvet tray of cocktail rings and held up at least a dozen pairs of earrings, turning her head to and fro in the rosy light of a looking glass, finally settling on filigreed silver drops with lemony stones that matched the colour of her hair. I thought of the plain silver cross Jane used to wear always around her neck, the way it had sometimes throbbed with the steady rhythm of her pulse as she slept. I wondered if she wore it still.

Flossie turned from the cash register with a smile.

Shall we? she said.

I held open the door of the jeweller's, noting that she was wearing her new earrings, glinting with sunlight as she stepped outside. These were no paste reproductions. I speculated at their cost. Certainly, she seemed to have no qualms about spending. Her family was obviously well-to-do. Footing the bills, as it were. Or someone was.

It occurred to me then that Providence was an odd place for an actress. I asked her about it.

You mean why am I not in Los Angeles or New York or some-where?

One would think even Bridgeport. But Providence?

She laughed, then fell silent awhile; musing, it seemed. We walked slower, negotiating passersby and the puddles on the cobblestones, and bumping pleasantly against one another. Flossie glanced discreetly at her reflection now and again in the windowglass and I recalled Jane remarking once upon this being the pastime of certain kinds of narcissistic women, *as if*, she said, *they could not be parted from their own precious image for even a moment. As if they might lose themselves.* Jane thought herself above mirrors, and it occurred to me to wonder only then, in hindsight, what she feared she might lose there.

I found this habit of Flossie's charming.

Finally she said, *It wasn't my career which brought me here, I'm afraid.*

I see.

We strolled on beneath the bare elms and shop awnings in silence. I hadn't intended to pursue it, but my curiosity got the better of me.

Might I ask? I ventured.

Where he is now? she said quickly, as if she'd been waiting for me to ask. *Oh, still here. In Providence, I mean. With someone else. In our bed.*

So you were married, then.

She gave me a funny look.

I see, I said.

You needn't be so shocked, she teased.

I'm hardly a prude in such matters. Though I confess it hadn't occurred to me.

So, anyway, she said, *that's why I needed the sublet in such an awful hurry. And Helen, I'd heard she was living here, and when I telephoned she'd sounded only too eager for a roommate, and so I handed him my walking papers. I swear my teacup hadn't even cooled and he had her all moved in. Well. So what. He wasn't worth it.*

But, I observed, *you're still here.*

She shrugged her silvery fur. *For now. I don't plan to stay. Just until I get my sea legs again. Do you know what I mean?*

I think so.

She eyed me from beneath the velvet brim of her hat.

What about you, Arthor P. Crandle? Got a gal? She grinned up at me, teasingly, and her smile faded. She brushed my sleeve. *I'm sorry, that was too forward of me. I forget not everyone wants to hang out their laundry. Nor look at anyone else's.*

She dropped her hand.

It's the Midwest in me, you know, she added after a time. *I don't mean to be rude. We're very direct. It's considered good manners there to just come out and say a thing. Otherwise you'll be thought sneaky, suspicious. I forget you New Englanders are . . .*

Sneaky and suspicious?

Reserved.

That too.

There is something to be said for discretion, I'm sure.

There is something to be said for all things, given one's perspective.

Yes, she said, and considered. *Except deceit.*

I glanced down at her.

Even that, I offered cautiously, *can be excused, or at least accounted for. In certain circumstances. Can it not?*

Not by my code.

The code of the Midwest?

The code of Flossie Kush.

It was my opportunity to come clean about it all. I knew very well it was then or never.

Sounds like a picture, I said instead.

Doesn't it. There you go. I am at least the star of my own life. As are we all, I suppose.

No, indeed.

No?

I think we are only the minor characters. Others take the best roles. The leads.

That's a sad thought.

You're right. It is. Let's talk no more of it. It's too cold for introspection and melancholy.

But I seemed to have genuinely saddened her, and I regretted my silly banter. I had never been good at what people call "small talk" and I feared I had spoiled the morning.

But I had not to worry long, for Flossie stopped abruptly in front of a shop window beneath a green and white striped awning.

Oh, look. Do let's go inside. My treat.

I peered through the glass. White tiled floors and little round marble tables and wrought iron chairs with backs like twisted hearts.

It's an ice cream parlour.

Oh, please, I'm almost frozen to death.

And so you'd like ice cream?

It'll make us feel warm. Like when you jump into a lake on a cool day. It's so much more pleasant than on a hot. The shock is not so great.

I don't swim.

You've never swum in a lake?

I've never swum anywhere.

Then you must at least have ice cream, she said firmly. *To make up for the loss.*

And, taking me by my overcoat sleeve, she pulled me inside, saying, *We'll agree to talk only of ice cream. Nothing of our personal lives. And nothing serious. It's too cold for talk of serious things.*

I agreed that it was.

Do you know, she said, unwinding the silver fur from around her neck as the door tinkled shut behind us, *they say in India everyone drinks only tea? Because of the heat.* She smiled up at me. *Doesn't that make good sense?*

I agreed that it did.

The shop was nearly empty. I placed our orders at the counter while Flossie selected a table at the very rear of the room and sat with her back to the wall, settling her handbag neatly upon her knees.

Perhaps they have a table in the ladies' room, I suggested, joining her.

She smiled up at me.

I always like to sit in the very back. Of restaurants, or street-cars, or theatres, or wherever. Do you want to know why?

Why?

Because I can never stand the feeling of someone's gaze on the back of my neck. It makes my skin crawl and I break out in goose-flesh, as if someone's just walked on my grave. I like to know always what's behind me. They say you can tell a lot about a person by where they sit in a room. Where do you sit, Arthor?

Wherever there is space.

I'm sure that's true. I bet that says something about you, too.

No doubt it does.

Do you want to pretend something?

I looked at her doubtfully.

You know, pretend we're visiting somewhere.

We are visiting somewhere.

I mean somewhere exotic. Like India. Or Paris. Or, I don't know, Singapore.

Not likely.

I spoke more loudly than I'd intended. A woman in a ghastly hat three tables from us turned and gave us a goggle-eyed look over her shoulder, then stood and primly changed her seat. Flossie took no notice.

Why not? she said. *It would be fun.*

I gave a half-hearted shrug. I had never cared for such games. There seemed always a hidden motive in them.

Flossie smiled and leaned toward me across the table.

Arthor. Don't you ever have any fun?

Not in a long while, I said truthfully.

She gave me a serious, searching look.

I think that's sad, she said, unhappily. *Oh, here's our ice creams.*

ROUNDING THE CORNER of the library, Flossie was chattering out some amusing little story, some nonsense about a two-headed calf named Calvin back in Indiana. I began to laugh and, happening to look up, stopped cold.

There, in the window of Sixty-Six, stood a man.

But not on the second floor where my employer's study would be. He stood in the window of my own attic room.

What is it? Flossie said, turning back to me.

Nothing, I said quickly. *Thank you, Flossie, for the lovely morning. Arthor?*

But I was already running ahead, down the lane, throwing open the door to the house and clattering up past the cold landing. I opened the apartment door and stepped inside and stood very still in the listening gloom of the front hall.

Nothing stirred.

The rooms felt heavy, muffled. Before me the hall stretched dimly down toward my employer's closed study door. I listened and then I heard, very clearly, the sound of footsteps passing slowly over my head. My eyes tracked across the ceiling.

I crossed to the foot of the attic stairs and peered up. I could see nothing, no movement, just the twist of the stairwell walls in shadow. After a moment I went silently up, my left hand curled into a fist. I paused at my door, then reached out in a smooth gesture and flung it open.

It was empty.

I stood in the doorway a moment, blinking, then walked slowly in, pacing the perimeter, peering behind boxes, scraping back the bed from the wall. Of course there was no one. At last, with nothing else for it, I stood at the window and stared out over the rooftops, my heart hammering in my ears. I could not think what had just happened. Or how. I pressed my palms against the glass, tried to pry the windows up or out; they were, of course, sealed shut.

On impulse, I pushed all the cardboard boxes into a corner and moved my bed back against the far wall, then shifted my desk so that it faced, not the window and the dormered building, but the room and the doorway.

When I had finished, I stood panting, wondering what Flossie would have thought to see me behaving like a madman. I had abandoned her in the street. I looked out, as if she might still be there, waiting, where I had left her. Of course, she was not. What she must think. A madman, indeed.

But I had seen him there in the window. Had heard those footsteps.

And yet more.

When I crossed the room and shut the door, the hair stood on end all up the back of my neck. Though it was light outside, the shadows hung heavily in the corners. I felt a thickness in my throat, as if I could not swallow: that presence I had felt always on the landing and the second floor, it had followed me inside.

It was in my room.

3

====

I ROSE LATE the next morning, exhausted, consumed by
a deep uneasiness, a creeping damp, in that attic which, I
realized with some shock, I had begun to think of already as
a kind of home. The presence was still there, though fainter
than it had been the previous evening. The sense of someone watching me, always. I had slept poorly, the door to my
room locked, though against what—whom—I knew not.
I'd had terrible dreams and when I woke periodically, gasping, the light from the dormered building across the city
flickered, filling the room with its cold, staccato light before
I sank again into exhausted, uneasy sleep, with the vague
sense of someone, something, moving in and out of the dark
corners of the room.

And another thing: I had begun to notice that upon
waking, I did not feel like myself, as if I'd spent my few
sleeping hours dreaming the dreams of someone else; perhaps that, too, a result of the manuscript, that eerie story,
or a symptom of the work at least, typing someone else's
correspondence, someone else's thoughts. I wondered if
there wasn't some syndrome or other which affected personal assistants or secretaries or even butlers or ladies'

maids; a sense of being you but not you, or, if you will, more than you. Crandle Syndrome. What an ominous, melodious ring that had.

I wrote my employer a short, rather imperious note, before I could change my mind, demanding to know why he had been in my room. Then I dressed in haste and went quickly out, dropping the envelope on the hall table without pausing as I had used to, and closed the apartment door softly behind me.

I had no great desire, anymore, to meet him.

ON THE LANDING: Flossie, in a startling crimson dress, on her way up. I was both pleased and dismayed. I found myself gritting my teeth, short of breath as I took her by the sleeve, steered her down to the foyer, away from that coldly suffocating presence which I seemed able to escape now only outside of the house or with Flossie, as if whatever was bright about her kept the darkness at bay. The daylight showed faintly through the leaded windows, glinting off the face of the big clock, its brass pendulum throwing sparks, counting in perfect weighted measure the accumulating silence between us. I ran my hands through my unwashed hair, then checked the self-conscious gesture and stuck them in my pockets like a lunatic farmer. Great god, what is one to do with one's hands?

Flossie watched me, frowning.

Is everything all right? she finally asked.

I assured her it was.

Yesterday . . . ?

Yes, I do apologize, I said, too briskly. *I felt quite unwell.*

The grippe?

I suppose it must be.

You don't look well, she said cautiously.

I told her I needed some air.

I'll go with you, she said, adding, before I could object, *Just let me get my mackintosh, it looks like rain.*

I waited impatiently in the foyer. The clock ticked. The grey light fell in through the windows. I felt the presence creep down the stairs, toward me, growing blacker. I rubbed my burning eyes, turned my back on the stairs, the skin up the back of my neck crawling. I stepped into the light from the window.

Ready? I called through Flossie's open apartment door, just to hear the sound of my own voice.

There was no reply.

Flossie? I called again.

I noticed then that the potted palms against the wall had wilted badly, their long leaves drooping out over the sides of their pots, browned and crumbling. Between them, the door in the stairwell. On impulse, and for no reason I could have articulated, I went up to it and tried the latch.

Of course, it was locked.

Arthor? Flossie said behind me.

These palms could use a watering, I offered unconvincingly, lifting a dead frond as if to take its measure.

She frowned at me deeply, seemed about to say something more. Something meaningful. To prevent her doing so, I said, *You look as if you're dressed for an occasion.*

She smoothed a hand across her silky dress, as if just noticing it herself.

I got tired of sitting around being frumpy. Then she added, *Anyway, a girl likes to feel she has a reason to be pretty.*

I opened the door and Flossie donned her absurd yellow mackintosh and we headed out into the lane. By Flossie's suggestion, we cut across the university campus, in the direction of Narragansett Bay.

You've not been down there? she asked.

Never.

It's so pretty. I go there often, just to walk and think. I guess it's the landlocked in me, the Indiana. I've always been drawn to water. I suppose we're like that, forever wanting what we don't have.

She trailed off. We walked in silence. She was subdued, and I did not feel much up to small talk, either.

The quadrangle was busy, coeds milling about in light spring jackets though the air was frigid, skirts blown tight across their self-conscious hips, bobbed hair whipping unprettily in their faces as they stood, too obviously ignoring the young men smoking along the stone wall, collars turned up to their softly indifferent mouths. We passed beneath the white dome of the observatory. Faces up there, dulled by windowglass, looking out at us like gods. I wondered what they would be doing up there, in daylight.

You seem troubled, Flossie observed after a while.

Not at all.

We passed out of the university grounds and took a side street leading steeply down to the waterfront. The bay spread out lightless before us, rippled and grey as an old skin. A ship made its slow way up to the horizon.

Finally, she said, *Well. I am troubled. In case you're wondering.*

Oh? I cast her a glance. *And why is that?* Though I did not really want to know.

Oh, you don't really want to know.

Nonsense.

She considered a moment.

Well. For one, it's the strangest thing. Helen . . .

Yes?

She still isn't back.

We paused on the corner to wait for a bicyclist to pass.

I'm sure that's not so unusual. Perhaps she's away, taken a trip somewhere, as you said.

I know I did, but I didn't mean it, not really. I don't believe she has.

Why not?

You'll think I'm foolish, but you know the other day? When I arrived? There was a half-eaten dinner there on the kitchen table. Just sitting there. A toasted tuna-fish sandwich. And an opened jar of pickles. The lid was there on the table, as if someone'd just taken it off. And a glass of milk. It's the milk that bothers me more than anything. No one just leaves a full glass of milk, just sitting there like that.

But you said yourself she is scattered.

I know. I thought of that too. But, her toothbrush . . .

Perhaps she travels with a spare.

But it is odd, don't you think? I mean, she did know I was coming. She even left that key under the potted palm, useless though it was. And she did say she'd be there. How could she have just disappeared? What if something happened? Something . . . bad?

Bad?

Bad things happen, Arthor. Especially to young women. Living alone.

You're jumping to some pretty serious conclusions.

I'm not jumping to anything at all. But it does happen. What about . . .

What?

Well, what about The Gray Man?

What grey man?

You know, that terrible Albert Fish. In New York.

Albert Fish?

Oh, surely, Arthor. Have you been living under a rock? It was all over the news last winter. He got the electric chair.

For what?

Oh, it's too awful. She shook her head. *Children . . . children . . .*

For heaven's sake, Flossie.

When they arrested him, he claimed to have children in every state.

I was confused. *What? Fathered them?*

Flossie's eyes glittered hotly. *Killed them. And . . . and . . .*

What?

Eaten . . .

She put a gloved hand to her mouth.

Oh, I said, for some reason annoyed, *surely not.*

He was insane, she cried, looking quite mad herself. *That's what they said; he'd have had to be, wouldn't he. It ran in his blood practically; half his family was in asylums. Albert, that wasn't even his real name; he'd taken it from his dead brother. His dead brother. And then all those children, he said there'd been hundreds. The things he did. And that first little girl he took, how he wrote the mother afterward, anonymously, describing what he'd, how he'd . . .*

Come now, Flossie, get a hold of yourself.

Oh, I knew you'd act like that. You always do, you men. As if such things were ridiculous even as they're right there in the papers, right before our faces, even as they are happening, every day, maybe, maybe even to Helen.

What is? What is happening to Helen?

I don't know, she cried. *That's just what I'm trying to figure out. It isn't easy, you know.*

Good lord, what isn't?

Being a woman. Alone in the world. To know there are people out there, like him, like The Gray Man. One doesn't know who to trust. Or whom. Neither of those. Albert Fish. Albert Fish! Who wouldn't trust a man named Albert Fish? I've seen his picture in the paper. He looked perfectly normal, perfectly sane. A bowler hat. That's what he wore. And a three-piece suit—

She took a deep breath, wrapped her arms around herself, as if to contain what boiled there.

Anyway, she said after a moment, more calmly, *that's one thing. That is bothering me. The lunatics of the world. How can it not? They are out there, Arthor. Living among us. And they look quite ordinary. Just like you or me.*

I thought of that figure in the window of my attic room, and paused there in the street, then quickly brushed the image away. Flossie stopped too and looked at me.

Arthor? she said.

No, indeed, I managed.

She stared at me a moment, then turned up the collar of her mackintosh against the wind and began walking again.

An unpleasant thought was building in me. I did not wish to entertain it. But I could not deny it. Flossie's phrase came back to me, *the ordinary lunatics.* Is that what she had said? I shut my eyes against the image of my employer in my attic window. And against the other thing, which had only just then settled over me like a chill: I was surrounded, it seemed, by absent women. The aunt, the mother, this Helen. There was only my employer, there in his locked room, forbidding me to enter. And an attic full of women's clothing . . .

At any rate, I said quickly, firmly, *there's no point letting one's imagination run away—*

Imagination? Flossie turned on me, outraged. *Arthor, it was in the papers. He stood trial. He was given the electric chair for it not three months ago. At Sing Sing.*

Well, really—

And what about Jack the Ripper? Is that imagination too?

What about him?

All those women. Just taken from the streets like that. Throats slit, hearts ripped out. Their hearts. They were gutted. Like animals. Gutted, Arthor.

But, Flossie, they were prostitutes.

A funny look crossed her face. Her cheeks flamed and she turned away.

I stopped short again, this time in the middle of an intersection, staring at her in astonishment. An automobile blew its horn and swung around me. Flossie stood on the corner with her back to me, her yellow mackintosh flapping noisily in the wind.

Flossie? I said.

When she turned, her eyes had welled up. Her yellow hair whipped across her face and she shoved it away.

I knew you would think that, Arthor.

I stared back at her. Another horn sounded and I stepped up onto the curb, next to her.

Not me, she said firmly. *Not me.* She looked me straight in the eyes. *You can believe it or not.*

But . . . your friend? Helen?

I don't know. I . . . I suspect. But I don't know. After a moment, she added, *And anyway, it's not for me to judge, Arthor. And not for you, either.*

We stood looking at one another in the street. It did not bother me, about her friend. But about Flossie . . . and yet I had no right. There was nothing between us. Nothing. And even if there was, even if there would be, I was, I reminded myself, still married. And more: I was not even who she thought I was. My god. What right had I to judge, indeed.

You won't throw her out, will you?

What?

Helen. You won't throw her out. If she is.

I frowned at her. I had no idea what she meant.

And then I remembered. Great god. She thought I was the landlord, the landlord. These deceptions—

You won't, will you?

I shook my head.

Can we walk? she said.

Yes, I said. *Yes, we can walk.*

I knew I should say something but, for the life of me, I knew not what.

After a while, she said, without looking at me, *Do you believe me, Arthor?*

And though I did not know what to believe, I told her I did.

THE WEATHERED BLUE and green canning shacks ranged like a shantytown along the water. Gulls circled and cried. A fine cold mist blew in from the sea. The islands out in the bay had blackened and the sky over the grey water swirled darkly. The black ship was still there, inching toward the horizon in the paradoxically heavy-weightless way only massive vessels built to float could. The air smelled of wet rot, of the bottom of the sea churned to the surface. There was an odd electricity, as if far out on the water, something terrible gathered and swelled. Flossie cast questioning glances at me now and again. I knew not what to say. About anything.

She lifted her head and breathed deeply.

That air, she said with obviously forced cheer.

Is putrid, I finished.

Instantly, I regretted it. Flossie looked hurt. I was not angry. Or, at least, I was not angry with her. I was angry, certainly, with my employer. Perhaps with myself. A familiar story. I felt the beginnings of another headache.

Flossie stopped on the boardwalk and looked down the beach, one hand shading her eyes, the wind in her yellow curls. The romantic pose was not lost on me, as I supposed was her intention. I pretended not to notice and peered hard out at the horizon. The ship I'd seen only a moment ago had disappeared. I scanned the bay but could find no sign of it.

What are those people doing down there, do you think? Flossie said.

She pointed to a small group standing looking at something on the sand near the edge of the foul water. Gulls cried and lifted and circled in the ruckus. Low waves rolled bleakly in. My eyes drifted out, past the shoals, to the low line of light along the horizon. Where had the ship gone? It bothered me. Gulls, something, wheeled erratically in the high wind, far out. I put my hands on the rail and the wood was damp and swollen and splintered beneath my palms.

Arthor? What are those people looking at?

I haven't the foggiest.

Flossie clicked down the rickety boardwalk and I followed. Her heels sunk into the sand at the bottom and she wobbled, taking my arm.

Perhaps we should go back, I suggested. *Something's blowing in. And you're hardly dressed for a day at the beach.*

She shot me a pointed look.

A girl's got to dress for something, she said, and I had the odd sense she'd said this already.

Then, slipping her shoes off, she set out determinedly in her stockings across the sand, flat-footed, like a child. Jane would never have done such a thing. I would not have done as much myself. I did admire her, I had to admit, whatever she was or was not.

I followed Flossie to the fringe of a strange, bedraggled crowd. Wet-looking, all of them, and sad, as if they'd been caught in a storm. A small, pale boy in faded dungarees and a woolly red sweater had picked up a stick and was prodding at something in the sand.

Don't, Stevie, a woman, presumably the boy's mother said; a bloated, equally pale, unpleasant-looking woman. She knocked the stick away. *You don't know what it is.*

I'm not touching it, the boy said. *Not with my hands.*

No, for heaven's sake, don't touch it, someone else put in.

That's right, keep well back, everyone.

What is it? Flossie said.

The strange crowd parted slightly to allow us to step closer. I stood behind Flossie, looking over her shoulder. A terrible smell wafted up, as of rot, soured flesh.

There, half-buried, lay what I at first thought to be an astonishingly large strand of kelp, bulbous and glossy and reeking. Sandflies hopped crazily upon its slick surface, the wet sand sticking to it there. Then I saw what it was, and my stomach lurched.

Is that . . . , Flossie began.

It's a tentricle, said the boy, Stevie.

Tentacle, the mother corrected.

Is it an octopus?

Can't be.

What then?

Beats me.

How long? Stevie asked.

Some fourteen feet, looks like, said a man in a battered homburg and spectacles. It was a moment before I noticed the glass in his spectacles was badly cracked on one side. I wondered if these were the "wharf rats" I'd heard about, who, having lost jobs and homes, lived in the abandoned canning shacks along the water or even, sometimes, beneath them. Certainly, they were a strange lot.

Impossible, said someone else.

Pace it out.

Not me.

I'm not going near it.

Look how it's buried there at the fat end.

Like maybe it's attached to something.

Oh, exclaimed the mother, *awful. I can't even think it.*

The slick flesh of the thing looked sticky, purplish, as if it were bruised. The smell was dense, a sour reek of earth overturned. But it was the bloated thickness of the thing that disgusted me.

What are those big bumps? Along the bottom there?

Suckers, said the boy.

Steven!

That's what they're called.

I'm sure they aren't, said the mother.

It's what they use to grab onto things, said someone else, *so they can move.*

The mother put her hand to her mouth.

Has anyone tried to pull it out? Flossie asked.

Stevie stepped forward again, as if he might do so, and the mother swatted him back.

Arthor, Flossie said, turning to me, *we should pull it out.*

What? I said, appalled.

The crowd looked at me. I lowered my voice.

What on earth for?

Aren't you curious?

Not enough to pull it out.

That's a good idea, someone said. *Somebody should pull it out.*

But you don't know what it's got, the mother said.

You think it's got something? Down there? asked a young woman, hardly more than a girl, in a bleached dress.

What? No. The mother paused then, frowning, considering this new possibility. She shook her head. *No. What I meant is, you don't know what it died from. I wouldn't touch it, that's all.*

Maybe it isn't even dead, someone observed.

Oh, it's dead, all right. The smell.

Well, we won't touch it, then, Flossie said. *We'll just dig it up a bit, won't we, Arthor? Just to see.*

Dig it up? I said in disbelief.

Again, the crowd turned to me. Stevie solemnly handed me his stick.

I repressed an urge to hit him with it. Instead, I took it and stepped forward. The crowd parted further to let me through.

I wouldn't, the mother said again. *You never know.*

I made a few weak stabs in the packed sand.

Watch you don't puncture it, someone said.

Puncture what?

Whatever's down there.

The crowd fell silent again, each variously imagining what might be down there. The gulls circled and screamed.

I scraped a little at the sand.

Oh, for heaven's sake, said Flossie and, dropping her shoes, she elbowed me aside. Before I knew what she was doing, she had grasped the end of the thing with a little mew of disgust and wrenched at it like she was strangling someone.

She's from the Midwest, I said to the crowd.

The man in the battered homburg stepped forward to help. Two more tugs and the thing came loose and Flossie and the man staggered backwards, dropping it in the sand. It landed with a sickening wet *thunk*. Flossie lifted her palms, stared at them as if they burned.

Why, someone said, *it isn't attached to anything at all.*

Not anymore, it isn't, another added drily.

I told you so.

That's right, he did.

But . . . what is it?

That's the question.

It's a tentacle, all right.

But gotta be, what now, sixteen feet.

More.

The man in the homburg poked it with the toe of a waterlogged shoe.

I wouldn't, the mother said.

Someone should alert the authorities.

Authorities?

Police or whatever.

So they can arrest it?

The university, then.

That's right, send it to college.

Someone's got to figure out what it is.

It's an octopus, like I said.

Can't be.

I know what I'd do, said the mother.

What?

But she said nothing more.

I couldn't stop staring at the thing. There was something too awful about it, beyond horrifying. Not just the swollen size, the heaviness, but some other quality, something . . . almost human about it.

It was then I noticed Flossie was gone. I turned to see her crouched down at the water's edge, swishing her hands in the sea, the hem of her crimson dress darkened with seawater. She looked very small and I could, for an instant, clearly picture her as a little girl, playing in the dirt of an Indiana cornfield, bright hair straight down her back, late again for supper. I felt sorry for my peevishness earlier. What she was or what she wasn't, it hardly mattered. And, then, I was not in any position to judge. What did it matter what any of us were or were not. I'd had enough of doubting. Enough of darkness. I needed certainty, light. She was the first glimpse of it I'd had in a long, long time.

That water's not any cleaner, I advised gently, coming up behind her. *You'd be astonished what they dump in here, those canneries.*

Then I saw she was crying.

ON THE WALK HOME, Flossie was quiet. The wind was up, ruthlessly, spitting cold drops that stung our eyes and faces, and we leaned into it, the sky black and rumbling over the water behind us. We walked quickly, in spite of Flossie's heels. I made some silly joke about them, to lighten things, though I felt heavy also. She didn't even bother to smile. The wind off the water buffeted against us, billowing her mackintosh out like a bright sail.

Better batten that down, sailor, I said, *or you'll float away.*

Still she said nothing, just wrapped her arms around herself, holding the coat to her waist, as if she thought I'd been serious.

Finally, I said, *Does it bother you, that thing back there?*
She shook her head.

Helen, then? Or are you worried . . . do you think . . . ?

I took her silence as confirmation. The image of my employer in the window of my attic room came back to me. The missing women. The boxes of clothing. I did not say it was troubling me, too. I pushed the thought away.

I want us to think well of each other, Arthor.

I do think well of you, Flossie. I told you.

I meant it. She nodded. After a few moments, she said, *There's another thing. That's bothering me. Something I've been meaning to tell you.*

I braced myself. Here it comes, I thought. The confession. She was, after all. Of course she was. It all made sense. Even as I told myself, *It doesn't matter; it doesn't matter.*

What is it?

The wind pasted her yellow curls across her eyes and she pushed them away and blinked furiously in the wind.

She said, *I met the next-door neighbour this morning.*

Next-door neighbour?

I can't remember his name. He has a little dog. Maisy, or something. Daisy.

Puzzled, I recalled the hostile old man in the camel overcoat I'd seen in the lane.

What about him?

He said, she began, *he said some funny things about you.*

I looked at her in surprise.

What could he possibly have to say about me?

Well, I'd just been asking him, you know, about Helen. He said he'd seen her around but not in a few days, and I said I was worried, that she was supposed to be here and then she wasn't, and I hadn't heard anything from her.

What does that have to do with me?

That's just it, Flossie said, looking uncomfortable. *He said—oh, I shouldn't even have brought it up. I wish I hadn't.*

What did he say?

He said . . . She gave an apologetic laugh. *He said—it's so ridiculous—he said, "If your friend's gone missing, I'd look for answers with . . . "*

With what?

"That monster."

Monster?

"The one who lives upstairs."

She stared back at me, embarrassed, yes, but I could see a question there, too. It took me a moment. I stopped abruptly in the street.

What, me? You must be joking.

I know, crazy, isn't it. I didn't even know what to say.

You didn't ask him what he meant by that?

No, she said, still hugging herself. *Why should I?*

I began walking and she followed. We'd crested the hill now by the university. The storm had cleared the lawns and quadrangles and paths of students. Elms twisted in the wind. Lights glowed in some of the classroom windows, as if it were evening. They flickered once, twice, and went out.

Oh, Flossie said. *The lights . . .*

Indeed, the sky had darkened ominously. I had darkened, too. What a day. And not half over.

Well, I said finally, stopping again, *you might have at least, I don't know, told him he was crazy. Or something.*

A sudden gust of wind whipped her mackintosh open with a wet slap and I stepped away from her.

He is crazy, she said, wrestling the coat. *Of course he is. I shouldn't have told you. You're not feeling well. I wasn't thinking, I'm sorry. I shouldn't have brought it up.* She laid a hand on my overcoat sleeve. *I thought we would just laugh about it. It's all so silly. A monster. Imagine.*

But she wasn't laughing either.

So, all that talk, I said. *Albert Fish. Jack the Ripper.*

She took her hand off my sleeve.

No—

I began walking again and she hurried after me.

Arthor, of course not. You must believe me.

But I did not. I did not. She'd wondered about me. Neighbours talked about me. It built and built until my blood roared. I only wanted to be away from her. Away from my employer. Away from everyone. And there was nowhere, nowhere.

It wasn't until we'd turned into the lane and the house, darkened, stood before us that it occurred to me, dreadfully. The realization stopped me cold.

It wasn't me the old man was talking about. It couldn't have been. Flossie only thought so because she didn't know there was someone else.

I wasn't the monster; it was my employer.

4

THE STORM BROKE over us, pelting icy rain before we had reached the doorstep. The entire street was dark, the electricity blown out. I left Flossie at her apartment door in an air of dread—mine—and apology—hers—and mounted the stairs without looking back, though I could sense her eyes following me. Entering the apartment in the afternoon gloom, I felt drained and miserable—all right, I felt outraged. And, for the first time, genuinely afraid. That, too.

Who was this man? What was he?

I punched the light switch, tugged the cord of the emerald lamp, but of course no lights came on. My note demanding to know why he'd been in my room lay, not surprisingly, untouched on the pedestal table. My hands trembled. Water seeped from my thin soles onto the floorboards of the front hall. I thought of my arrival, some days ago.

For the first time, no light shone from beneath his study door.

Standing there, I had the unmistakable sense, again, that someone had just left the passageway. *And who are you?* I wondered of the presence. *Are you him, too?*

I peered about but could see nothing in the grey light. As I entered the stairwell up to the attic, I had that same strange perception: a whisper, a rush of air, as if someone were just ahead of me on the stairs. The sensation grew so strong that I entered my attic room certain I would find someone—him, the monster—standing at my desk, or seated on my bed, waiting, regarding me with dark eyes.

Of course, again, there was no one. Only the storm outside, shaking and battering the windows and walls as if to peel them back.

It had become clear, finally, that I must confront him or leave. Leave, I could not. Where was I to go? Back on the streets? I would surely die there. I'd written Jane, twice, had sent her the money and had had no response. There was nowhere, no one. Outside, the storm raged. I knew I must confront him, must see him, see for myself what sort of man I'd become associated with. I feared the worst.

And yet . . .

And yet he'd done nothing. He'd failed to appear, yes; he was ill, and reclusive, by his own admission. He'd been in my room, yes; I'd seen him there in the window, but he'd touched nothing, as far as I could tell. Perhaps he'd come up quite reasonably looking for papers, some manuscript, a magazine from the boxes on the floor. Or, simply, for me.

But what, I wondered, about this Helen? What about the aunt? The mother?

My god, I thought then. I rose and riffled through the pockets of my suit jacket. I pulled out my wallet, the chunk

of gravestone. Where had I put the letter? Then I recalled I'd
left it sitting on the desk. There it was, itself a mystery: each
time I meant to deliver it, something distracted me, something stood in my way. As if forces were conspiring against it.
I turned the envelope over in my hands. The mother, surely,
would shed some light on the man. Perhaps that in itself was
keeping me. Perhaps I was afraid of what I would find.

I propped the letter against the chunk of gravestone
where I would be sure to see it in the morning. I determined
to let nothing stand in my way. I would go as soon as the
power was back up. I sat on my bed, staring out at the storm
and the city. The light in my room grew dimmer and dimmer as the storm raged and the afternoon wore on.

That monster, I heard Flossie say, *that monster*.

And there was that other thing, too, I could not account
for. That heaviness, that movement I'd first felt on the landing and which seemed now to follow me about the house,
upstairs into my attic room, wanting something. I felt it
there with me even then, a shifting in the shadows, a constant, terrible presence, like Oakley Eakinns and his refrain,
It's high time you come home.

Outside, the storm battered at the shingles, whipping the
branches of the elms against my window. What was I to do?

I HAD BEEN READING from one of the horror magazines
I'd found, the blue light of the storm spattering the windows, barely illuminating the page in a watery, shifting

light. I flipped the pages slowly—preposterous tales, all macabre ghouls and monsters and things returned from the dead. Hardly what I needed just at the moment, but there was nothing else, and I suppose I hoped, too, I might find clues there among the stories by my employer.

I read them all in the dim light until my eyes ached in their sockets. I could not say I cared for his tales, gripping though they were. His heroes were all unheroic. When confronted with horror, they only turned and fled. The world he depicted was hopeless, implacably bleak. And yet there was a familiarity in it, too. A truth I could not deny. I read on, not wanting to sleep. My eyes burned and I closed them a moment, to rest them, the blackness cool, inviting, it pulled me down, and down. Something was building, behind me, something that began as an idea, swelling, I ran and ran— and woke with a start, into darkness.

The attic, the windows, the city beyond impossibly black. I flicked the bedside lamp several times with something like panic before remembering the power was out. I sat up, rummaged about in the night table drawer, hoping for candles, but found only a button, a safety pin, dust.

Damn it, I said, foolishly, into the darkness.

The storm lashed at the windows, as it had the night of my arrival. The roof groaned. The loose pane in the corner rattled. I rose, groping my way along the damp walls and down the stairs, moving slowly.

As I neared the second floor, I could feel it, that thickening the presence seemed to do there that raised the hair on the back of my neck. It occurred to me that the presence was strongest when moving toward his study door, or away from it. I could almost hear it. A low, steady, almost imperceptible groan. I nearly spun a retreat to my room; but the idea of turning my back on the thing, the feeling, whatever it was, in that darkness, was worse than moving forward, to the promise of light, candles I remembered seeing in a utility drawer in the kitchen. I pressed on, palms against the warped plaster walls, the hairs all over my body on end, through the hall, the sense all the time that someone was just behind me, that if I were to turn around—

Steady, Crandle, steady, I said aloud.

I stumbled into the kitchen, fumbling along the cabinets, prying swelled drawers open with my fingertips and rummaging there—I could have sworn I felt breath on the back of my neck—nicking my hand on the blade of a knife, before finally grasping the candles, their waxen coldness unpleasant in my palm. But no matches.

The black feeling was all around me. I took the candles and, turning, knocked an empty tin can from the counter. It clattered impossibly on the linoleum, spinning and spinning in the darkness. And stopped. So suddenly it was as if by some hand.

I fumbled my way back out into the hall, moving too fast, the sound of my own breathing rising absurdly above the storm. I felt my way past the pedestal table, nearly upsetting the lamp there. I grasped the glass shade, setting it upright again on the table.

There, to my surprise, lay a reply to my note. I picked it up but could not see what was scrawled there. He had responded, at least. He was in there, in that black room, even as I stood rattled outside of it. I hesitated. Then, taking the dead candles and the note, I crept toward his study and paused, listening. That blackness, that oppressive air, I felt sure then, must be coming from that room, from my employer, from his being, whatever he was. *Monster*, I heard in my head, *monster*. My skin crawled and prickled as if the black air outside his door were alive. I recalled hearing once how the insane seem to radiate a terrible energy.

Raising a hand, I stood dumbly, unable to make contact, again, with that door. I was paralyzed, unable to go forward, unable to turn away, when a voice said, distinctly, *Come in.*

INSIDE WAS DARKER. The air so thick, so heavy, so purely bad, I felt strangled by it. I stood in the doorway, terrified— yes, I am not ashamed to admit it. At the far end of the room, the night lashed faintly behind pulled draperies. The silhouette of a floor lamp, a Morris chair, and someone— was that someone seated there?

So, he said finally, softly, *you've come to see the monster.*

I strained, peering through the darkness.

I've brought candles, I said, stupidly.

A long, terrible pause in which the house groaned around me. Then, *You will find matches in the table to your left.*

I reached down, found the table, and the drawer there, and fumbled about for the box of matches. When I found it, I struck and struck, but the match would not light, only flare up an instant and extinguish, as if pinched out. My hands were not steady.

Perhaps they've grown damp, he said.

It was a moment before I realized he meant not my hands but the matches.

I have little use for them, he said. *Nor candles. When the lights go out, I am content with darkness.*

I dropped the box of matches and they scattered across the carpet, soundlessly, as if they'd fallen and fallen into black, limitless space, as if, should I take a step forward, I too would disappear without a sound.

Leave them, he said. *You will find a chair there.*

I remained standing in the doorway, unable to move forward. That feeling of overwhelming—I hesitate to call it malevolence, but there is no more fitting word—hung heavily all around me, the strongest it had ever been, telling me not to go in. All my nerves stood on end, watching for any small movement in the room, my eyes constantly drawn to the faint blue light showing at the two windows, and the Morris chair there.

And then I saw him, his silhouette against the draperies, rising slowly, a gaunt figure, tall but hunched, crippled almost; just for an instant, darkness against darkness—I might have imagined it—and it was gone.

Forgive me, he said, weakly, *I had been writing a long while before the power went out. I am tired. It has been a bad time, these recent weeks.*

Sir?

Finances, my own poor health, my aunt. My work, of course. It builds and builds and yet I have no energy for it, no enthusiasm. I am tired, Candle. I must lie down.

A slow dragging in the darkness, as if he, whatever he was, had not the power to walk but only crawl. Some rustling, and then all, again, was quiet. Only the wind outside.

I have wasted myself, Candle, came the voice again, *at pen and paper. I have been writing since I was a child. Do you know how many books I've published?*

I shook my head stupidly in the darkness.

None. I wonder sometimes, had I made greater efforts, earlier on, to write something of importance, something meaningful.

Meaningful?

A story I wrote some time ago. I don't suppose you know it. Never mind. It matters not. In it, a character of mine finds a key which allows him to return to a time of childhood, where he was happiest. Do you see?

I think so. Though, of course, I did not.

He disappears from his adult life even while his relatives report that at the age of ten he gained the ability to predict the future.

Time collapses?

In a way. I thought that was important. Then. But it has all been drivel. I have of late been making certain attempts . . .

Yes?

A family saga. The inheritance of blood is, after all, inescap-

able. But then I have always been relatively indifferent to people, and so depth of character, or feeling, has been a problem for me.

To which I could quite rightly think of no reply.

Indeed, Candle. Indeed. But this new story, of blood, can hardly escape character.

Blood, sir?

Inevitability. There is a certain school of thought which explains all our monsters, our witches and vampires and werewolves, as a certain kind of insanity. Not that they do not exist, but that they do. That a demon is because he believes himself to be. An internal phenomenon, rather than an external.

Do you believe it so?

I know not anymore what I believe. I only want to write . . .

Yes?

Something . . . important. He paused. *And then again, it is awfully late. Forty-six is, after all, forty-six.*

That is not old, sir.

For some things, Candle.

He was silent a long moment, then said, *It is too late anyway for those kinds of regrets—*

He broke off as if he had lost his breath.

Are you very unwell? I asked.

More rustling and a rusty creaking, as of sofa coils.

I have been always unwell, he said, after a time. *A habit, perhaps, from childhood.*

A habit, sir?

That which is forced upon us early enough. They become our habits. For better or worse. I formed the habit of illness. And of reclusiveness. He paused. *I was considered, by some, monstrous then, too.*

I chilled, thinking of the old man's words to Flossie.

Why monstrous? I asked.

It was said I did not go out because I was too hideous, too terrible. I could not be looked upon.

Said, I asked, *by whom?*

My mother.

The storm lashed and lashed at the windows. The house seemed to tilt in the relentless wind.

A long silence, and then, *I'm quite unwell. Very tired, Candle. You will forgive me if I ask you to come to the point.*

The point, sir? I . . . wanted to see . . .

Yes.

. . . if you were all right—

Did you.

Your illness—

Very good of you. To have come. And how is she?

She?

Mother. Does she send word?

She . . . she's . . . she's well.

I cringed in the darkness. Was there nothing in me of truth anymore? I prayed he would not ask more. And he did not. The wind rattled the walls.

Do you need anything? I finally asked.

I feel, Candle, he said, *that I need so much that, were I to be granted my wishes, I would not know where to begin, and I would leave as I had come, with nothing.*

If you should need . . . , I began, for lack of anything else.

Ink.

Ink?

For writing. I will leave you another letter for Mother. She must be wondering. How is she?

She's . . . well.

Forgive me, he said. *I've already asked you that.*

I stood awkwardly in the darkness. I did not know how to leave. He was quiet again, a long while.

Things were not always so, he said, finally. *We . . . I . . . lost everything. Everything*, he stressed. *I lost everything. There was*, he mused, *a time when I was considered, too, quite a prodigy—*

He broke off then suddenly, with a stifled groan. I knew not what to do with myself and so only stood there, stupidly.

Forgive me, he said finally. *I am in a bad way tonight.*

He was quiet again then, a long time, and I realized, with no small degree of horror, that he was, in fact, weeping there in the darkness.

I stood awhile uncomfortably in the doorway. Finally I said, *I shouldn't have troubled you.*

When he did not reply, I knew it was because he could not, and wanting to spare him any further humiliation, I felt my way backwards out of the study, closing the door with a soft click behind me, wishing, as is often the way with doors, that I'd never opened it in the first place.

I HAD NOT EXPECTED so much. Had not expected to find him so broken. A monster, indeed.

That night I did not sleep. I rose and moved around restlessly in my attic room. I felt weary—sad, too—and I went to the window to look out over the darkened city, turning the piece of gravestone in my fingers as had become my habit and comfort.

I had seen into the heart of a stranger—a monster—and found it filled with such familiar longing and disappointment and despair that it might have been my own. How alike we all are. How broken. I could hardly bear to think about it.

But, more than that. Something had changed. I felt different somehow, I felt . . . alone.

Quite literally. That black oppressiveness had lifted, was gone. I was alone in my attic room. I breathed deeply. Outside, the storm was dying. The rain had ceased, though the wind was still up. Everywhere in the blue darkness, it seemed, things moved. A moon was there, showing sickly between the clouds as they split, its light filtering through the lashing branches as the darkness scattered and regrouped.

And I saw her.

A girl, down in the garden, passing quickly between the trees in a long white nightdress. I stepped nearer the window. But she was gone, disappeared it seemed, through the garden entrance to Flossie's suite. And yet it had not been Flossie, certainly. I was sure of that. I wondered if perhaps Helen had returned. She must have.

And so another mystery was solved. The sad pieces, it seemed, were falling into place. And yet there was no satisfaction in any of it. I felt the beginnings of another headache and wondered how I was to sleep that night.

I thought of my employer, weeping in the darkness below me, and of that malevolence I had felt shifting in the rooms there, in the front hall. It—whatever it was, that darkness—did not come from my employer, as I had thought. He was not its source. He was its victim.

I lay down upon my bed, pressed the heels of my palms into my eyes until the darkness blazed red.

THREE

I

===

THE MORNING BROKE bright and wet. A fine, clean light shone in through the windows. The horror magazines I'd been reading the afternoon before lay scattered at the foot of the bed and I gathered them up, their grotesque covers absurd by daylight. The previous day seemed a blur, a nightmare, all of it. The trip to the wharf with Flossie, the storm, the unhappy interview with my employer, the girl in the garden, Helen. The latter, at least, had been a welcome discovery. Though why she'd been out in the garden in such weather and at such an hour was certainly mysterious.

My head ached. I pulled the Aspirin bottle from my valise. It was empty, though was sure it had been nearly full when I'd taken some the previous day. I would have to go out to the shops for more. I tossed the bottle into the wastebasket and dressed hastily. Sticking a hand into my trouser pocket, I found an envelope. In all the night's upset, I had forgotten about the note I'd plucked from the hall table in darkness. It was a moment before I realized it was, in fact, not a letter from my employer, as I had thought, but my own letter, the one I had left for him. In the darkness, an easy mistake.

I WENT AT ONCE out to the chemists, still in a kind of fog, my eyes throbbing and my thoughts troubled, playing over and over the conversation I'd had with my employer. I did not wish to pry into his affairs. And yet it seemed to me something very wrong was at work in that house, something very wrong at work in him, around him. What had he said of his mother? That she had considered him too monstrous to look upon? No, I could not shed the feeling of pity I felt growing for the sickly man. To be despised so. I did not ask myself if there was something of myself I saw, too, in his misery. I felt ashamed, the things I'd wondered about him.

I did not feel up to the long walk to the chemists, after all, and the Weybosset was still closed, so I stepped instead through the swinging glass door of Woolworth's and was hit by an unpleasant mixture of smells: plastic and floor cleaner, coffee and sausages from the lunch counter at the back.

I made my way up the mopped aisles, my shoes squeaking against the washed linoleum still slick with suds, collecting what I needed: Lifebuoy soap, ink, a large bottle of Aspirin. A girl scarcely out of her teens, hair held back prettily from her face by a rhinestone pin, stood noisily filling a jar with jellybeans at the candy counter. She smiled at me as I passed.

Apart from the girl, the store appeared to be empty. I was spared the tedium of waiting in line. It diminished one, such waiting. I scarcely had the energy for it.

I set my purchases on the counter. A woman with a gold lapel pin in the shape of an angel—or possibly a moth—

waited there. The image of the pin was familiarly iconic somehow, as if it were the symbol for some well-known organization I should have recognized, like the Boston Red Sox or the Salvation Army, and this woman before me looked as if she might well stand ringing her little bell, part forced cheer, part grim determination.

Good morning, she said.

She shifted a box of Wrigley's out of the way and picked up the bottle of ink I'd just set down, dangling it between her fingers, like a mouse.

Well, I say, hardly nobody ever buys this old cheap stuff here. Dust on the bottle, even; look there. Now that's not a judgment, mind—we all need to save our pennies where we can—there's only a fool would spend extra on something meaningless as ink—that should be a saying, shouldn't it, meaningless as ink, like . . .

She flapped her fingers in the air, physically grasping for another figure of speech, then waved and shrugged.

Anyway, I don't judge you, not one bit. It's the spendthrifts, and I see a bunch of them. You wouldn't think it, the way things are, so many struggling, but there are the Haves and the Have Nots, same as it's always been. I see it all; I'm here every day just about, unless the arthuritis gets me down. That's why I do these nails, see.

She clacked the bottle of ink back down on the counter, displaying long, pink fingernails.

Oh, I know some would say it's, you know, furvolous, but I always think: Treat a thing right and it'll come back to you. Treat a thing bad, well, that comes back, too. Comes back even stronger. It all comes around. But I don't have to tell you that. You types know all about that, about how what goes around comes around, how every-thing does, all the time.

Types?

Oh, she said, leaning forward in a hot waft of some flow-ery cologne, *it's always in the eyes, you know.*

What is?

She waved her hands and laughed. *Oh, now, I'm just fool-ing with you. I can see you got ink stains all over your fingers, so you're either a writer or you work for one of them newspapers, and I sure hope you ain't that or I'll have to give you an earful. Are you?*

Am I?

A newspaperman?

No.

Well, good. You don't even want to get me started. Only thing worse than a newspaperman is a banker. The nonsense in those pages. This new technology, funny cameras, who knows what they can do. Anyway, you know what it means if something funny is in the papers.

No, I said. *What does it mean?*

Something else is going on they don't want us to know about, that's what. So somebody plants some silly story, ghosts or, you know, creatures.

Creatures?

Space monsters.

I must have given her quite a look. She had the good sense, at least, to look embarrassed.

Oh, well, she said, *they don't come right out and say that, of course. They don't say space monster, but just that it's inidentifiable. And we fall for it. They could pass off any kind of nonsense. Like that fly-girl.*

Fly-girl?

That lady pilot, flying all the way around the world.

Amelia Earhart?

What nonsense. And then, too, just the other day, right there in the paper, that thing they found on the beach, down at Narragansett.

I looked up at her sharply.

Some big tentacle or other. But, you know, awfully big. So now everybody's talking sea monsters. I mean, really. All that talk. It's been around since, she waved a hand, *just forever. But what am I saying; you didn't come in here just to visit now, did you? Say, you feeling all right?* She narrowed her eyes at me across the counter. *Here,* she said, picking up the Aspirin, *let me ring these through.* She punched some numbers into her till, carefully, with the pads of her fingers, so as not to damage her nails.

I'm all right, I said.

Not sick, are you? Lot of stuff going around.

No, not sick.

She stared at me, as if waiting for, expecting, more.

Tired, I said. *Rundown, I guess, is what you'd call it.*

Well, she said, *you know what they say about the man who was feeling rundown.*

She handed me the Aspirin, and I cranked open the lid and fished out the cotton batting and took two tablets, wincing at the sour, chalky taste.

Thank you, I said, screwing the cap back on the bottle and slipping it into my overcoat pocket.

Don't mention it, she said. *Feel better?*

As if the Aspirin were already doing its work. I nodded.

Now this, she said, and punched in the ink. *Can't have you leaving without that. I thought you said you weren't a writer.*

It's not for me, actually. Just the Aspirin; that's mine. The ink . . . I waved a hand meaninglessly across the counter. *I'm on errands*, I said, then paused. *For a friend.*

She must have sensed my awkwardness over the word, and I can't say myself why I used it. It was easier than attempting to explain a situation that was inexplicable, and she seemed just the sort to inquire.

But, she said, raising a pencilled eyebrow, *you've been in here before?*

No, indeed.

But I'm quite sure . . . that ink—

For my friend. My employer, actually. He is the writer, not me.

She neatly placed my purchases into a paper bag.

Well, she said, taking my money, *I just work here. I don't mind other people's business.*

Something in her tone had changed, and I felt I had put her off somehow, or offended her, though I could not see how.

Thank you, I said, inviting a return to her former cheeriness. But she did not respond. I tapped my fingers on the counter. *Normally I'm healthy as a horse*, I said.

All right, she said.

I picked up my bag, puzzled at her change in demeanour.

By the way, I said, *what do they say? About the man who was feeling rundown?*

Oh, she said, waving a hand again, not looking at me,

just an old joke. I hardly remember. Something silly. Never mind.

She busied herself rearranging things behind her counter, and I said, *Well. Thanks.*

Mm-hmm, she said.

At the door, I turned back, but she had already put up a sign on her counter that read, *Next till please*, and moved away to the back of the store, one hand in her hair, her black skirt swishing purposefully.

I'D SCARCELY SHUT the door of Sixty-Six behind me when Flossie popped her yellow head out from the landing. She was standing on a tasselled footstool, holding something in her hands. She looked fresh and bright. Swing music—I might have guessed as much—drifted through her open apartment door, the rich, toasted smell of fresh coffee in the air. She looked at me, I thought, a little warily.

It's so dull and gloomy on this landing, she said. *I thought it could use some brightening up. I hope you don't mind.*

We had not spoken since our strange, unhappy parting in the midst of the storm the previous day. No doubt she still thought I was angry. I had certainly behaved so.

She held out the thing in her hands for me to see. It was a small painting. The ocean impossibly green. Inky clouds rolling in or away. Before or after a storm. In the middle distance, a small red boat, eerily empty.

Hardly what I'd call bright, I observed.

The colours are pretty, she said, looking at it again.

She hung it firmly on the wall, adjusting it one way, then the other.

There, she said with finality, stepping from the footstool. *A woman's touch.*

She came down to meet me in the foyer. Her hair was pulled back from her face with a filmy scarf and she wore a peacock blue Chinese dressing gown belted tightly at the waist. She looked at me cautiously.

You're out early. I saw you go. I thought maybe you were on your way to work?

Ah, no. I work at home, actually.

Do you?

I thought I'd mentioned that.

I don't think so. I would have remembered. Anyway, I saw this, she said, brushing a hand against her own chin, *and knew you couldn't be going to work, anyway.*

This?

Your beard. It's growing quite thick.

I lifted a hand to my own chin, felt the stubble there. It was hardly what one would call a beard, and, of course, I was aware it was there, but with the lack of a mirror in the upstairs apartment, I hadn't noticed or cared.

It looks rather dashing, I think, Flossie said. *Some of my brother's friends had them, back in Indiana, even though they're not the fashion. But then nothing is, back there. I had crushes on them all. The friends, that is. How's your aunt?*

My aunt?

With the grippe.

Grippe?

Were you visiting her?

I collected myself. *Indeed. Yes. Improving. Thank you. For asking.*

Home soon?

Home? Yes. I hope so.

But then you'll leave, won't you.

She leaned against the wall in the light from the window. Her face scrubbed and shining, eyelashes so pale they looked golden. At times, I thought, in the right light, she gave the impression of being so ethereal, so translucent, one could see right through her. So different from Jane's solid, dark handsomeness.

Anyway, that makes two of us, I guess, Flossie went on. *Working at home. No auditions for me today. I suppose you guessed as much.*

Why's that?

I'm not exactly gussied up, am I.

The Midwestern turn of phrase was charming. She misread my slight smile, looked embarrassed.

Oh, you must find me awfully unsophisticated.

On the contrary.

Anyway, I'm hoping something will come up tomorrow, some hostessing work or something at least, maybe up in Boston, some stupid convention where they want girls to stand around with trays of business cards, smiling until their feet bleed or something.

Not exactly acting.

It's acting, all right. Believe you me. Oh, there I go again. Anyway, if there's anything going, I'll take the train up, but this miserable spring is putting a damper on things everywhere, no pun intended. Or so my agent tells me. But then one never knows with agents. Sometimes I think they just tell you what you want to hear.

You want to hear there are no auditions?

Well, not that, of course. She looked solemn then. *I'm glad you're not angry.*

Why would I be angry?

The other day. What the neighbour said. It was stupid of me.

You're hardly to blame for any nonsense some neighbourhood crank spouts.

I'm glad you feel that way. You seemed so angry. I've been just a wreck about it all. I couldn't bear to think you were upset with me. Say, do you have time for coffee? I just made a fresh pot. And there's a lemon cake I picked up at that little Italian bakery. I swear the box weighs ten pounds. I broke a darn sweat carrying it home and I'll just die if you make me eat it all myself. I'll have to starve for a week. Unless you're busy, working?

The best answer, of course, would have been that in fact I was working and could not spare the time. Flossie stood staring at me, waiting. The bright room behind her looked so inviting. The day was still young and the Aspirin was doing its work and with everything that had happened, and the conversation with my employer still heavily on my mind, a cup of coffee and a slice of cake with a pretty girl in a silk dressing gown seemed at that moment too pleasant to pass up. And then, too, I recalled, Helen was back. I was quite eager to meet her, as if she were a strange player come late to the stage.

Just a quick one, then, I said. *I do have a good deal to accomplish today.*

That sounds intriguing, she said, closing the door behind me. The locks rattled from their hooks.

You know, I could remove those for you, I offered. *They're quite unnecessary, I assure you.*

Yes, she said, turning the music down, *you said that already.*

Have I?

Anyway, I don't mind. It's kind of pleasant, in a way. A poor girl's door chime. And a good reminder, too.

Really. Of what?

Beats me, she said, *but something. Independence?* And she laughed again in that odd way she has, when a thing doesn't seem at all funny to me.

She disappeared into another room I supposed was the kitchenette and I stood looking around. The room was supremely untidy. On the coffee table, bottles of nail polish and wadded tissue like crumpled flowers amid several half-drunk cups of milky coffee; the floor and sofa littered with women's magazines and catalogues, torn-out pages on the carpet in some inexplicable feminine order. A saucer of hairpins. An opened jar of hand cream. A single, nibbled sugar biscuit. As if there had been quite a party.

But there was more. On the sofa were several violet silk cushions that had not been there before. The heavy green draperies had been replaced with sheer ones in a similar shade of violet, and a thick white rug rolled out beneath the coffee table. The potted ferns were gone and in their place were several vases of white chrysanthemums. A crystal candelabra dripping with light stood on the mantel where the horse had been.

Flossie returned with a silver urn of coffee and a cake on a tray.

I mean, she said, setting the tray on the table and licking frosting from her finger, *the lock could be done up. From the inside or from the outside, it doesn't matter. Either way, they'd be locked. I'd be locked. See what I mean?*

That sounds very New Thought.

And why not? I believe in the power of positive thinking. That you can create yourself, just by imagining yourself how you want to be. I suppose you think they're a bunch of kooks or something.

It's not my cup of tea, I said, clearing a spot on the sofa.

Well, I like to think I can change my destiny. Not just who I am, but who I will be. Who wants to be all locked up like that? I wasn't very independent, back in Indiana. My family doesn't encourage that sort of thing. And then I wasn't very independent here, you know, at first. But now.

Now, I said, thinking again about what she'd told me at the wharf, about Helen, and the implication. A gloominess passed across her face and I wondered if she was remembering it, too, and her tears afterward, and I said nothing.

She handed me a slice of cake and a cup of coffee, which I doused liberally with milk and sugar. I caught her watching me, amused.

Sweet tooth, is that right?

Not really, I said distractedly, then followed her gaze to my cup, where I'd deposited several teaspoons of sugar. It was scattered all around the saucer and I brushed it into my palm. Then, not knowing what to do with it, I dumped that into my cup as well. *Wasn't paying attention.*

I stirred and sipped, thinking I'd surely ruined the coffee, but in fact it tasted quite pleasant.

Flossie leaned back in her armchair, watching me with a curious amusement. Her white feet were bare, her toenails painted a bright Chinese red. I tapped my fingers on my coffee cup. Flossie smiled and wiggled her toes. I looked away.

I see you've made some changes, I ventured.

You noticed. The ferns were dying anyway. God only knows when they were watered last.

And what does your friend think of the changes? Helen?

Helen?

Isn't she back?

Flossie frowned. *Why would you think that?*

I paused and lowered my cup, looking at her carefully.

I haven't heard a word. She set her cup down with a clatter and bit at her thumbnail. *I don't know what to think. I tell you, I'm just about ready to write to her folks, in Indiana.*

Why don't you?

I don't want to worry them. I mean, if she isn't.

Perhaps she's on extended holiday, I offered.

I thought of that.

Or some other reasonable explanation. From what you told me, she seems just the sort of girl who would leave an unfinished meal and disappear for a few days. Unpredictable and all that.

It's true, Flossie said, considering. *She really is.*

Well, she does seem to be of a type. From what you've told me. Girls like her are not uncommon, I think. Seeking attention. Dramatic, I suppose.

Oh, terribly. You seem to understand her perfectly. It's as if you know her.

She does seem to be a certain type, I said again.

Difficult, yes. The stories I could tell. She did have, you know, problems.

Problems?

Oh, I don't know. It's just what my friend always said, her sister, Harriet. She looked at me carefully then. *Arthor, what I said, the other day, about Helen. I . . . really don't know for sure. It's just, there was always talk. I wouldn't want you to think badly of her.*

I understand.

She nodded. *And, anyway, would you really think it was so terrible?*

As you said, it's not for me to judge.

She seemed satisfied.

Maybe it's even best she's not here. It's been sort of good for me, to learn to be on my own. That independence, like I said. I think it's starting to suit me rather well.

Liar, I said.

She looked up, shocked.

You hate being alone.

She flushed then, looked away, forced a laugh.

It's true, she said. *I do hate it. You see right through me, Arthor.* She poured out more coffee though her cup was almost full. *Anyway. We'll see. I hope she won't mind, Helen, about the changes. When she's back. It was just so awfully green.*

Easily remedied if she doesn't. But if you decide to put in a new bathtub, you should probably wait till she returns. I laughed uneasily; it was a stupid, inappropriate thing to say, but she had not taken the remark so. It was pleasant, in Flossie's company again. The awkwardness between us dissipating. But, still, there was the question of the girl I'd seen in the garden. I'd been sure it was Helen. If it had not been . . .

Flossie, I began, leaning forward.

Mm?

I wonder if you wouldn't mind my asking a personal question.

Ooh, she said, *my favourite kind. Ask anything.*

I set my coffee cup down with a sharp clack I had not intended.

I thought I saw you out in the garden the other night.

She looked up in surprise.

Me? What was I doing there?

I'm not sure.

Well, you must be mistaken. I hate gardens, all dirt and earthworms and cat droppings. Reminds me only too well of my rural routes. Weeding—is there no worse hell.

It was late. Perhaps you were sleepwalking.

I sleep like the dead.

She held my gaze steadily. A beat, perhaps, too long. Then she lifted the coffee pot and eyed me, suddenly coy.

I do like that you thought you saw me there, she said. *It's kind of romantic. Was I wearing a flowing gown?*

In fact, I said, holding my cup out to her, *you were.*

Flossie laughed, delighted at the idea. She refilled my cup and set the pot down.

This is fun, she said, leaning back against the violet cushions and crossing her bare white ankles on the coffee table. *Like playing hooky. Well. You are. Not me, I guess. What I wouldn't do to have something to play hooky from. But all in good time, as they say. "They" being the ones currently working. Anyway. I'm keeping you from your work. And you haven't even told me yet what it is you do.*

I took a long sip of my coffee and put it down on the table.

I'm a writer.

What else was I to say? And anyway it was out, and I could not take it back.

Are you? she said, leaning forward. *How exciting. What do you write?*

Oh, fiction, mostly.

What kind?

The usual.

Romance?

I considered my employer's stories. *Hardly.*

Oh. She pouted prettily. *That's too bad. I love romance novels. It's the only kind I'll read, when I have the patience to read at all. It's not that I mind it so; it's just I'd rather . . .*

Yes?

Live. She looked at me brightly. *I hope I haven't offended you.*

Not at all.

Good. We were just getting to be friends again. So, what do you write?

I suppose it's called . . .

What?

Horror? Or, what was the term he'd used in his letters, in the magazines. *Weird fiction?*

She wrinkled her nose. *What on earth is that?*

Like horror, I suppose.

I see.

I'm not sure how to describe it.

That's all right.

We sat a few moments in silence, sipping our coffee.

I could tell you, I said finally, *about the story I'm working on now. If you like.*

Is it scary?

I'm not sure. Maybe you could tell me.

I don't like to be scared.

Then perhaps I shouldn't tell you.

Well, I suppose you have to tell me now, she said. She tucked her legs up beneath her on the armchair and cradled her cup in both hands. *Okay,* she said. *Go on. But if I get too frightened, you must promise to stop.*

It's about a hotel. Right here in Providence. Quite a popular one. On Benefit Street, beyond the university. I wonder if you know it?

Oh, don't tell me which, I might have to stay there sometime.

And it's about a girl.

Young?

Around your age, I would think.

And is she pretty?

Very.

Good, she said, settling into her chair. *Every scary story should have a pretty girl.*

2

WHEN I DESCENDED in the afternoon, I found Flossie's door standing open, as if she had been waiting for me. I hesitated a moment on the lowest step, my hand on the balustrade, uncertain. I had been surprisingly untroubled, after our coffee, at my own growing lies, even though Flossie must surely, sooner or later, learn the truth. My employer would not be ill forever. And what was I to do then?

But the fact was, I was enjoying my little charade. Surely as much as Flossie was enjoying hers. Oh, I was not a complete fool. That late-night return from across the way, from the boarding house. I knew very well what she was. And I did not mind. It made it easier for me to do my own pretending. A kind of independence, as Flossie had said. An opportunity to be, however briefly, someone other than who I was. The man I might, with better fortune or wiser decisions, have been.

It was then I heard the second voice, from within, lower than Flossie's, but unmistakably female. I couldn't help overhearing; it was hardly eavesdropping. And I thought, illogically, with something like panic: Jane has come.

Arthor? Flossie called out. *Is that you?*

Her yellow head peeped around the door. *You must come in.*

I'm just on my way out, I lied.

Oh, but you must, she insisted. *You've a visitor.*

I CONFESS MY HEART clenched. I could imagine only Jane seated there in Flossie's sunny apartment, her hair drawn back starkly from her beautiful, unhappy face. How she would have aged. I knew without having to set eyes upon her. A visitor. It had to be Jane. There was no one else.

But, of course, it was not Jane. Seated there on the green sofa amid the violet silk cushions, just as I had been mere hours ago, was a dark-haired woman quite unlike my wife. Her hair was pinned back rather untidily, her neck long and drooping into her shoulders. She wore a mannish cardigan and a grey skirt. I would not have called her ugly, but there was nothing of grace in her. And though she was not old, there was about her something distinctly crow-like. She rose when I entered. I almost expected wings.

This, Flossie announced, *is Mary.* Then added, *She's a writer.*

The woman, Mary, looked embarrassed.

I'd hardly say that, she said.

Oh no, Flossie said, *she's written ever so many stories, and had some published in magazines. Magazines I've heard of, even. Poems too, isn't that right, Mary?*

Mary agreed that it was.

She's a—what did you say again, Mary, what kind of writer?

Literary. Though lately I've taken an interest in weird fiction.

Hard to imagine, Flossie said. *Anyway, she's come all this way, all the way from Canada, can you believe it, just to meet you. She said she knows all your stories, isn't that right, Mary?*

Again, the woman looked embarrassed.

She didn't know the one about the hotel, though, Flossie mused. *Of course, that's because you've not even finished it yet, have you. I'd just been telling her about it.*

Pleased to meet you, Mary, I said, finally stepping forward. Her handshake was cold and damp, but in that moment I could have clasped her in an embrace, so relieved was I.

It's such an honour, she said.

From Canada, is it? I said.

Flossie fluttered around us. *Oh sit, everyone, sit. I'll make coffee. You will stay for coffee, won't you? Oh, I beg you, don't go upstairs. Do stay and visit here. It's sort of like a party, isn't it. You know, I knocked for you, Arthor, some time ago. Didn't you hear me? Poor Mary's been waiting. All the way from Canada. Just imagine. Where was it you said, again?*

It was not until I was seated next to Mary on the sofa, listening to Flossie chatter on instead of making coffee, that I realized, with no small degree of shock, that I was not—of course I was not, what could I have been thinking—I was not the man she was seeking. How easy, how easy it was, to slip. Had the woman not mentioned my employer's name to Flossie? Not made it clear the writer she sought?

Isn't that marvellous? Flossie was saying to me.

The backs of my hands prickled with a cold sweat.

I scarcely know—

Mary is, what did you say your last name was?

I didn't, Mary began. *But—*

And you, Flossie said, patting my knee, *you sly fox. All this time, letting me call you Arthor.*

I laughed nervously.

What have you got to say for yourself? Flossie demanded.

In fact—

A pen name, of all things. Mary says you've got hundreds.

Not hundreds, Mary corrected.

Are you really so famous? Do you know, Flossie said, turning to Mary, *I didn't even know he was a writer until this morning? I even thought he might be making it all up, you know, trying to impress me or something. Yes, that's right. You've been a very naughty boy, Arthor. Or should I call you, oh goodness, I've already forgotten. Mary, what did you say the name was?*

I EXCUSED MYSELF before we'd even had coffee, sick at my growing deceit, Flossie frowning after me as I ascended the stairs.

An hour later, I was in the kitchen, scraping food into a bowl for the cats, feeling rattled still over the encounter, when I heard someone at the door. I started, turned to see the latch twist, the door open. I scarcely knew whom to expect.

It was Flossie.

She stood there in the front hall, staring coldly in at me. I stepped forward, repressing the urge to usher her back out. I glanced quickly toward my employer's door. I hardly expected him to emerge, but even so.

Flossie stood waiting, it seemed, to be invited inside. Gone was her sparkle. I thought at first she was only angry at my premature departure, but it seemed more than that. She stood as if holding herself in restraint. I noticed there was a plate in her hands. She looked around the apartment with obvious interest before settling her eyes back upon me, her gaze hard.

I've brought cake, she said.

I set the pot I was holding on the counter.

Why don't we go down to your apartment, I suggested. *It's so much more pleasant.*

Flossie crossed the room, as if she hadn't heard, her heels sharp on the linoleum, and set the cake heavily upon the table. I cast my eyes again to the hall behind her, the closed study door. She followed my gaze.

Might I have a knife? she said, and seated herself firmly at the table.

I confess I deliberated, given her murderous tone. She appeared to be wound, as they say, rather tight.

What did you think of your admirer?

She seemed very pleasant.

She didn't seem . . . crazy, to you?

She seemed quite sensible. Why do you ask?

No reason. She stabbed the knife into the cake so forcefully the plate slid dangerously toward the edge of the table. She yanked it back.

We had an interesting conversation. After you left. Mary and I.

Did you?

Yes.

She flipped a slice of cake onto a plate and smacked it down on the table.

Aren't you going to offer me coffee?

I put the kettle on to boil, all the time glancing nervously out into the hall. Flossie watched me carefully.

You seem . . . , I began.

What?

I cleared my throat. *Angry?*

Just surprised, she said. She stabbed the knife into the cake again.

Oh?

Mary certainly seemed to know a good deal about you.

Is that right.

From some press club or something, some amateur something association. I can't remember the name.

Indeed?

Yes. She told me quite a bit. She said, for instance, you live here. With your aunt. That's how she found you here. From the amateur press whatever membership.

Yes, I told you that.

No, you said you were staying with her. Just for a while. Just to take care of things, until she is well.

And that is true.

Mary said you live here.

I forced out a small laugh. *Well, then, Mary must be right. Come now, Flossie, I don't even know the woman.*

But she knows you. It seems you're quite famous. In certain circles. Weird circles. Horror, I mean. Or, whatever you call it.

I wouldn't say that, I said, uneasily. I thought of my employer, possibly listening through the wall. I wished desperately that she would lower her voice.

Oh, yes. Quite a bit is known about you. You have quite a following.

Is that so.

And anyway, what should I even call you?

Call me Arthor, of course, as you always have.

The kettle screamed and I plucked it off the range.

And another thing, for instance, another thing Mary happened to mention, is that you are married. That's another thing.

I tipped the kettle, sloshing boiling water out over my shoes.

You needn't look so startled.

I set the steaming kettle back carefully on the range.

Is it true?

Flossie—

I thought you were different, she said, looking at me steadily.

I wanted to say, *We are, none of us, different.*

Coffee, she demanded, and swiped at her eyes, though they were dry.

I poured the water and brought the coffee. Flossie reached out and sloshed it into her cup before it had even brewed. She lifted it scalding to her lips.

So tell me about her, then.

About?

Your wife. This Sonia.

I stared. *Sonia?*

Oh, don't be stupid. Tell me about your wife. Is it true you are married?

I . . .

Mary said you are married but not living together. She didn't know why. Is that true?

I don't know what to say—

Say the truth.

What was the truth? I had no idea.

Keep your voice down, I said instead.

She looked astonished, then furious.

And why should I keep my voice down? Who should hear me, your aunt?

She's not here. I told you that.

Are you married?

Flossie, please.

Answer me.

Yes, I said, in a low voice, casting my eyes down the hall. *Yes. I'm married.*

It was out. I'd told her. And I might have told her all of it, everything, the truth and not a version of it, but all at once she was on her feet.

My god, she said, *she's here. Your wife. Isn't she. Has she been here the whole time? All this time?*

Before I could stop her, she was out in the hall, calling, *Hello, I'd love to meet you, Mrs. Crandle, Sonia. I've brought a lovely damned lemon cake.*

I had the eerie, awful vision of a door opening, and Jane stepping darkly through. Who on earth was Sonia?

I grabbed Flossie by the arm, feeling her skin pinch between my fingers, but she wrenched free and made for the door at the end of the hall.

Ah, she cried. *Is she here?*

She grasped the latch. With a cry, I stepped forward and pulled the door shut with a sharp smack.

What are you hiding from me?

I pulled her back down the hall toward the apartment door.

She isn't here, I said. *She isn't. I haven't seen her. It's been—*

Flossie lifted her hand, pressed her fingers to my mouth, fiercely. I flinched. I'd thought she was going to slap me.

Don't, she said angrily. *Don't. I know. All right? You don't owe me anything. I know that. I know. It's too old-fashioned, to think that way. And not free at all. Right?*

I'm sorry, I said. I was.

It's the lying, she said, *that really bothers me*. She turned from me then, angrily, her hand on the latch. *You needn't have lied, Arthor.*

I know that, I said.

3

I WOKE IN THE NIGHT from terrible dreams, shaking, as though I would retch. I rose and went to the window, feeling a chill the weather alone could not account for. It seemed all was crumbling. I had gone down twice to the foyer to rap at Flossie's door, but she was either not home or she did not answer. The house seemed darker again, sadder, without the certain knowledge of Flossie's brightness somewhere in it.

Outside, a storm was dying. The rain had ceased, though the wind was still up. Across the hedge, the boarding house glowed warmly. I imagined the boy there, James, seated near a flickering hearth, staring into the flames with that pale, otherworldly gaze, a cat curled purring in his lap. I had not seen any of them in days, and I wondered if perhaps the man Baxter had found a job, if they had moved on.

I was just about to turn away from the window when I saw her again, the girl.

There, in the garden, in the moving grasses, she stood. In all that wild motion, she was herself unmoving, utterly still, in a pale nightdress, the hem dragging heavily in the wet, her face upturned in the broken moonlight, staring with cold intensity at my attic window. But it was not Flossie; it was no woman.

It was a child.

I stepped unconsciously backwards in the force of its terrible, dead stare, my heart pounding. But just as soon as I'd glimpsed her, she was gone.

I shivered where I stood at the window, and raised a cold hand to the glass. The print from my sweating palm remained a moment, ghostly, then evaporated, was gone.

FOUR

I
===

WE DO NOT ALWAYS meet life directly. We turn aside, let it strike us on the cheek. I thought of my other life sometimes with a kind of horror, as of something unstoppable, something unnatural, to which I was still hurtling, or which was still hurtling toward me, sideways, just out of the line of my vision.

It was two years ago last December, in the week before Christmas. Molly was yet an infant, not quite three. All across Boston, candles glowed in small-paned windows, pine smoke cut the air, snow fell. There was a commitment I had at my workplace—all right, it was a party, as Jane insisted. A Christmas party. Molly was ill. Some minor ailment, congestion, fever, that sort of thing. Nothing serious, certainly. Jane had come down with the same. She had been ill with it a good while, I recall, and I had begun to wonder, I'm ashamed to admit it, if she was being willfully ill. Things were rocky, then. Jane was lonely. I worked long hours. Someone had to pay the bills, and even then it was already not easy, the economy in a downward slide. We argued, often. She infuriated me. I was weary.

Then, this commitment, this . . . party. I was in the bedroom, fussing with a black silk tie, smoothing pomade through my hair, adjusting the tie again, too short, too long. But I had to go. I really could not get out of it. It was scarcely a matter of choice.

Assuming what I judged a suitable air of reluctant obligation, I smoothed my jacket and stepped into the sitting room.

Jane was on the sofa in the shabby dressing gown she favoured. Chenille, she called it. I thought it a bedspread. She had not washed her hair in some time and wore it pinned up untidily at the back of her neck. She did not bathe as much as she might; when I kissed her she smelled of onion peel, soured milk. Molly rolled feverishly in her lap.

Jane looked up at me in shock. I was instantly annoyed.

I really cannot get out of it, I said, adjusting my tie again. *A work thing. You know how it is around there these days. Swinging axes. If you're not looking, you'll get it in the back of the neck.*

You're going, she said, *to that party?*

It's hardly a party.

Just then headlights pulled up in front. One of my co-workers—all right, it was the daughter of my boss—who'd offered to give me a ride, being aware Jane and I did not own an automobile.

Who is that? Jane asked, peering out between the curtains.

Well, don't stare, will you.

I said it rather sharply, I confess.

She let the curtain fall into place. Molly sat up, glassy-eyed, whimpering, and Jane jiggled her knee ruthlessly. Molly began to cry.

Jane stared at me, waiting, I realized, for an answer.

It's—to my credit I did not lie, certainly I might have, another man would have—*Constance.*

Jane rose with Molly against her shoulder, bending her knees deeply, as if warming up for a race, and looked back at me blankly. Something in me was perversely irritated that she did not know who Constance was. Everyone knew Constance. Everyone in our circle, certainly. Possibly everyone in Boston.

Morris's daughter, I said, pulling on my galoshes. *She helps out around the office sometimes. Helps out, you know what I'm saying. Morris's make-work project. Wants to keep her busy, I suppose. If she lifts a finger, it's only to check her nails. Been to one of those snooty girls' schools, Radcliffe or something, I don't really know. Home for the holidays. She offered a ride. I told her I could just hoof it, but she insisted, decent of her, after all, and I suppose it's just easier. I'll be home sooner this way, you see.*

I buttoned my overcoat in the alcove as I spoke. Jane stood in the sitting room. Molly cried.

Well, I said briskly. *Home soon. Try to get some rest.*

And I pulled the door shut behind me, hurrying, lest Constance, dressed as I knew she would be, scandalously, should, god forbid, come to the door.

When I stepped into the snowy street, smoothing my hair, I made a point of not looking back. I did not need to. I remembered the expression on Jane's face well.

I suspect I will remember it always.

THE EVENING WAS A GREAT success, as such parties in
poor times must need be. Constance was clearly having
a splendid time, into the gin punch and the men equally
enthusiastically, and some of the women as well. I stood
over by the window, sipping a ginger ale, watching her dance
the Charleston on a table in such a manner as to make it look
fashionable still, her bobbed hair damp against her cheeks,
her silvery dress throwing hard sparks in the candlelight,
like armour. I tried not to think of Jane and Molly, ill at
home; tried not to think of them, out of a kind of mis-
guided spite; but they were on my mind nonetheless and I
had begun to regret my decision.

On the table, Constance reached up and pulled down a
silver garland with a gesture at once obviously calculated
and yet so seemingly natural. The girl, I thought, was mas-
terful.

You know what I call a dame like that? said someone at my
shoulder.

No, I said, without turning. *What.*

A Chicago overcoat.

Chicago overcoat?

I turned, then, to look at him. I did not recognize him
from the office. He had a bright spot of cocktail sauce drib-
bled on his tie.

I thought that was a coffin, I said.

The man drained his highball before responding. The
ice clacked against his teeth.

Bingo.

The band, winding down, launched into the syrupy "Stardust" and Constance slowed too, swaying there on the table, one hand outstretched, swinging the silver garland like a tail, the fine straps of her dress looped down over the tops of her white arms.

Want my advice, the man said, chewing an ice cube, moving away into the crowd. *Take a cab.*

When I turned back to Constance, Morris, absurdly furious in a velvet Santa hat, was pulling her down from the table. He steered her into a corner. She was easily as tall as her father, and she stood with her head thrown back, half-reclined against a table, her long legs stretched out like a man's, while he spoke angrily into her ear.

She caught my gaze then, across the room. I held it a moment too long. Morris glanced over, following her look, and I turned quickly away, toward the window. I lifted my glass of ginger ale but it was empty. I set it on the window ledge.

The snow had begun to fall harder, spiralling in great flakes, drifting against the parked cars along the curb, the dead lawns, then swirling back up to stick against the steamed windowpane. The lights of the city were dying. One by one, guests drifted over to the window and rubbed the glass, peering out, frowning. The air stank of stale tobacco, soured wine. The band already packing away their instruments in great black cases with self-conscious ceremony, like magicians, the chatter of the crowd all at once shrill in the absence of music. A couple stood in the doorway, locked in intimate, groping conversation. An elderly man dozed in an armchair in the corner. Someone had removed his shoes and socks, and his feet against the dark carpet looked bloodless and sculpted. A fat woman wrapped a string of silver paper bells around his throat like a boa; another threw back her head and laughed. A pretty young woman I recognized from the office stood surrounded by a circle of girls, like horses, in the centre of the dance floor, shaking her head and weeping.

Constance, it seemed, had disappeared. I sat on the window ledge, folding and refolding a paper cocktail napkin, waiting. I imagined Jane and Molly would be asleep by then on the old sofa in a yellow pool of lamplight.

Slowly, the room emptied, the guests trickling away with the weather and the hour, leaving cocktail glasses, and trampled party favours, and plates of oysters half-eaten. Soon it was just me and an old Negro who emptied ashtrays into a tin bucket beneath the drooping garlands. I wanted to go home.

I made my way to the abandoned coat check and found the last two in the back row, hers and mine, ominous as hanged bodies. The feel of her coat on my arm, some sort of inky fur, was as of a live thing, at once sensual and alarming. I wondered what sort of state I might find her in, and where.

It did not take long. She leaned against the wall outside the ladies' room, her cheek pressed up against the gilded paper, hair damp against her forehead, scarlet lipstick bleeding beautifully.

She raised her head slowly at my approach.

Ready? she said.

2

THE IMAGE OF THE CHILD in the garden haunted me. There was something about the pale wispiness of her hair, a certain sturdy set of the shoulders. Something achingly, impossibly familiar.

But I could not think it. I pushed it from my mind. My head pounded. I worked sporadically, slept fitfully. During the night, I woke to the feel of a small hand against my cheek, cold, cold. I left the light in my room burning, and rose in the morning only to cross to the window and look at once down into the empty garden with a feeling of dread. I did not know what I feared to see, what sort of apparition— no, that was not right: I knew exactly what I feared to see. But there was nothing. Only glittering morning, only rain-drops hung from bare branches like purses of pure light.

I fumbled my feet into my shoes and went sockless down, through the foyer and around the outside of the house to the back garden, wanting proof. Something concrete, tangible, bare footprints in the turned soil, an unlatched door.

I found only last summer's weeds and long grasses, untrampled, beneath limbs so overgrown and diseased they'd been peeled smoothly of bark. I tried the latch of the garden door, which seemed to be, as I had thought, a sort of back entrance to Flossie's suite, but the latch was padlocked and looked to have been so for some time, cobwebbed, the metal dripping rusty stains down the white clapboard siding. Mossy clay pots stood stacked in front of it, still filled with soil and dead plants from summers previous, mouldering leaves packed against them in drifts. No one had come that way, clearly.

I circled the house slowly in the cold air, all the way back around to the garden. Nothing. As I stood pondering, the silver tabby appeared out of nowhere, curling himself round my ankles in a long, serpentine stretch. I bent to rub the top of his head, but he shot away into the long weeds, gone.

When I straightened, I saw on the cobblestones at my feet a little grey sparrow, its head twisted at a terrible angle. Squeamish, Jane had often called me, and I could not have honestly disagreed. I bent to look closely. The bird blinked its black eye, horribly, and the silver tabby reappeared at the edge of the grass. What could I do? I left the bird to its bloody fate, reminding myself it was, after all, too late.

ON MY WAY AROUND to the front of the house, another possibility occurred to me. A plausible one. I cut back through the yard again, pushing between the hedges to the yellow boarding house. I could smell bacon, coffee, on the wet air. I stepped up onto the whitewashed verandah and rapped at the door. It was opened shortly by a plump, red-faced woman in a stained apron. A blast of oven-warmed air and breakfast table chatter and clinking dishes wafted out behind her.

Morning, she said cheerfully, wiping her palms on her apron. *Afraid we're full up just now.*

Then, before I could set her straight, a funny look crossed her face. I saw her glance down at my bare ankles and I recalled I had hardly bothered to dress, much less wash or comb.

Forgive me, I said. *I'm just from over the way.* I gestured to the house behind me, and the woman's eyes glanced there but she said nothing.

This will sound strange, I began awkwardly, *but do you know, has there been anyone out in the garden at night, between the two houses? A guest of yours, I mean.*

The woman blinked at me.

A child, perhaps? I said. *A little—*

The woman turned abruptly and called over her shoulder. *Mister, can you come out a moment here.*

A man, about the same age as the woman, and with the same ruddy complexion, appeared at her shoulder. A husband or brother, he could have been either.

What is it, Missus, he began. Then, seeing me, he said, *Oh . . . hello, then.*

Good morning, I said. *I'm not sure; perhaps I could speak to the owners, or the caretakers, or what have you, or perhaps you are—*

You can speak to me, the man said, not rudely.

He's wondering, the woman said, *has there been a child . . . in the garden . . . at night.* She seemed to be weighing her words oddly.

A child?

I told him we've got no child here.

There's James, said the man.

That's right, too, said the woman. *I forgot about him.* She looked at me. *There's James. Quiet one, he is. Hardly know he's even here.*

Is it James you're looking for? asked the man.

No—

Well, that's all we've got. There's no other children. Isn't that right, Missus.

Yes, it is.

Just the boy, the man said.

James, the woman confirmed, nodding. *There's just James.*

I noticed the clattering of dishes, the hum of voices, had fallen silent in the room beyond. The man Baxter appeared at the door. I was pleased to see him and told him so.

I've got it, he said to the couple.

They exchanged a glance and, nodding at me solemnly, disappeared back inside the house.

I began to ask how the job search was progressing, then stopped myself. It would hardly have been tactful. At that moment, James appeared beneath his father's arm.

Quietly, Baxter said to the boy, *I told you—*

But, I wanted to ask, the boy said.

Ask what? I said.

James, the father cautioned, taking the boy by the arm. *Go back inside.*

Could she come here sometime? James said to me.

What? I said. *Who?*

She waves me over, but Papa won't let me.

James!

Who? I demanded, laying a restraining hand on Baxter's arm as he pulled the boy inside.

James stepped back a little, frightened by my tone.

The little girl, he said.

What little girl?

Up there, he said, pointing. *In your window.*

3

I WOULD NOT WISH to suggest she pursued me, the child.
But I found I could not cease to think of her all the rest of
that day and into the evening. I did not go out and, though
I rapped at Flossie's door many times, she did not answer.
Flossie's absence left a dark, cavernous void which seemed
to make room for the child. I struggled to focus on my work,
my employer's correspondence and the book of grammar,
trusting my efforts to weary me so that I could sleep the
terrible hours away.

But, too, some part of me longed to see her again in the
garden below me; and my gaze would drift down, through
the trees, and I would catch myself staring, waiting, waiting. She seemed to be there always, just out of sight. Not
only in the garden; everywhere. She was outside my window
in the hours after nightfall, walking the lane, lingering outside the kitchen door in a groan of weathered boards, in the
faintest scratching. I would yank the door open only to find
the silver tabby perched there, staring out into the garden,
moon-eyed, solemn as a sphinx. Waiting also.

She was everywhere, moving with me through the
house, in the stairwell, the front hall, on the landing. In

every dark room just before I turned on the light, and just after I turned it out. Up the blackened stairwell ahead of me, only the tender white soles of her little feet flashing in the darkness.

I FELT I MUST GET OUT of the house or go mad. I took my overcoat and made my slow way across town, down to the bay, retracing the route I'd walked with Flossie. She'd told me she went there often. I did not really expect I would find her there, but I did not know where else she might be.

I stood on the boardwalk where we'd stood. The water of the bay rippled with filaments of light. The sand was stained and damp; the tide, on its way out, seemed to push off from the shore, gently, like a girl striking out into calm water. Out in the bay, islands floated darkly. On the smallest of these, a house stood, cragging up from the rocks, itself angular, mineral, black against the bright water. Boats moved just above the line of the water, hovering, a trick of the light. The beach stretched out, glinting broadly, empty in both directions.

I descended the splintering boardwalk and onto the beach, the sand beneath my shoes still tight with the retreating weight of the sea. There was no sign of the strange group we'd encountered the other day. Perhaps they were not of the wharf, after all. And no sign of the tentacle either, though I paced the spot where I thought it had been, crunching blue mussel shells beneath my shoes.

Needing a destination, I turned in the direction of the pier where, there in the distance, I could see the silhouette of someone standing on the rocks. Flossie, perhaps, or even just a fisherman, with a rod and reel, staring patiently out at the water. I walked quickly, in spite of the drag of the sand, and soon I was out of breath and weary. I had been walking some time, yet, looking up, it seemed I'd grown no closer to the figure there on the rocks, and I increased my pace, huffing now, the sun on the water blinding, wondering why it was that the closer we came to a thing, always, the farther away it seemed. Gulls circled inland and cried, diving at pipers racing in the foamy wake. I stopped and squinted up my eyes, shading them from the white light fracturing up off the water. The figure was still there and I realized, looking behind, that I'd covered a good deal of distance. I walked on. The figure, at last, grew larger. I slowed, and slowed, and finally stopped, dismayed.

It was no figure at all, no fisherman, certainly not Flossie, but a broken piling, laced in creamy barnacles, casting out over the water. The green tide lapped against it.

I was winded; my legs trembled from the exertion, reminding me that I was not strong, still. I stopped at a big rock and, brushing the sand from it, sat a moment to rest, my palms against my knees. I looked up and down the shore. The day was bright.

I picked up a stick and scratched my name into the sand. I sat staring at it a long while.

Then I rose and made my slow way back up, toward home.

THAT NIGHT I OPENED the door of my room to find the child there, as I knew I finally must, standing unnaturally still in the window, her back to me, her long white night-dress hanging slack to her tiny feet, bare and terrible.

I paused, my hand still on the latch, the metal cold. The air stank of rotted cherries. The child did not move. She seemed to be staring at something out the window. It was that same dormered building she faced. I noticed the furniture I had rearranged in my room had been put back in place, all of it, oriented to that one view, that building, and in that upper dormer window, the light, on and off, on and off, filling the room with an eerie, staccato pulse. My throat was tight; my heart pounded. I could not move. Could not speak. I felt my eye sockets grow hot, dry. As I stood, snow began to fall, big, billowing flakes, there, in the black room.

Molly? I finally said.

The child stood unmoving a long, dreadful moment. Then, just a little, she lifted the fingers of one white hand. She turned her palm upward, watching as the snowflakes settled there. She seemed about to turn. A curdling scream rent the air as the door blew shut in my face.

I gasped into wakefulness, the scream still ringing in the darkness. I fumbled the room into light and waited, propped frozen on my elbows against the pillow, alert to any small sound, a movement, a shifting outside my door, beneath my bed.

The knock sounded so abruptly I started up, grabbing

my trousers from the floor. I pulled them on hastily, hesitated only a moment before unlocking my door and opening it.

The empty landing was dark.

I stepped across and opened the adjacent door.

Nothing there, either. Then, just as I was closing the door, I glimpsed a small light shining from behind the cornbroom against the wall. I crossed the room, my feet loud against the worn boards, and I set the broom aside. A small knothole was punched through the floor. I crouched and peered through it, unsure at first what I was seeing. Someone there, below, in the dark stairwell outside the apartment door. I got down on hands and knees on the dirty floor and put my eye closer. A flash of blue as something moved out of my range and then back again—a figure. A woman.

Flossie.

She knocked again, louder.

I rose and hastened down the groaning stairs to the apartment door and opened it.

Flossie stood looking pale and frightened in her Chinese dressing gown and I took her arm, guided her firmly out. I shut the door softly behind me.

What are you doing? she said in the darkness.

The skin of her arm was so silky, I at first thought I was touching the fabric of her gown. When I realized it was warm flesh beneath my palm, a thrill ran through me and I quickly snatched my hand away.

What is it? she said. *What's wrong?*

This way, I said, leading her back down the dark stairs.

On the landing, she stopped abruptly and turned back to look at me. I realized I had somehow taken hold of her arm again, was gripping it tightly. I tried to press her forward, but she would not move from the landing. It was so dark there, so oppressive, that just for an instant, I shrank back. Her arm felt waxen in my palm. I stepped quickly past her, stubbing my toe on the footstool she'd abandoned there, and took her by the sleeve, all but dragging her down the rest of the way to the foyer. A patch of streetlight shone through the window and I pulled her into it. Behind us, her apartment door stood open, the room blazing with light. I pulled her toward it.

What is it? I said finally. *Has something happened?*

Didn't you hear it?

What?

That scream, she said.

My blood chilled.

My god, she said, *it was terrible. I can't even describe . . . don't tell me you didn't hear it.*

I shook my head. Felt a slow sickening.

At first I thought it was someone outside, on the street, you know, but then it sounded as if it was . . .

What?

Coming from here. From inside the house.

She had heard it, too. It had been no dream.

Don't look at me like that, she said. *I heard it, I tell you. It sounded as if it were coming from right upstairs. I thought maybe you'd been, I don't know, attacked or something. I've never been so frightened. I almost called the police.*

I forced a laugh. *It must have been someone outside, as you said. Or you were dreaming.*

I wasn't dreaming, she said, pulling her arm away. It wasn't until then that I realized I'd been holding it again. How good it was to have her back.

I was standing in the middle of my bloody living room with the lights on. You can bet I wasn't sleeping then. I heard it. You think this is a joke? I thought you'd been . . .

What?

She shook her head in frustration. *I am calling the police.*

What on earth for?

Someone might be in trouble.

In Providence?

Oh, for god's sake! Not that again.

We've been standing here some time and haven't heard a thing.

But before.

What will you tell them? "I heard screaming? Before? It's gone now? Sorry to trouble you, constables?"

She looked over her shoulder, back at her apartment door, considering.

Whatever it was, I said, *or whomever, it's gone now. There's nothing we can do.* Then I remembered. *Wait. Where have you been?*

What do you mean?

All day today.

I've been here.

I knocked.

I didn't hear you. I thought you were angry with me. That you didn't want to see me. Because of that . . . scene, upstairs.

I thought you were angry with me.

She seemed to consider, and in that instant, something in her face changed. Then she said, in a different tone, and as if it had only now occurred to her, *Why did you bring me down here?*

What?

When I came upstairs. Why did you bring me down here? Why did you shoo me out like that?

I forced another laugh. *I didn't shoo you out.*

You did.

Well, I thought something was wrong. I thought something had happened. Down here.

She stared at me a long moment in the light from the street lamp.

Arthor?

What?

Is she here?

The image of the child flashed before me.

Who?

Your wife? Is she here?

No, I said, relieved. *No, I told you. We're married, yes, but not together. We're not together. In any way.*

She kept looking at me, steadily. *Were you working?*

When?

Just now.

Yes.

Writing?

That's correct.

But you didn't hear the scream.

I had been working, I clarified, *but I may have, what do you say, dozed off for a bit.*

While you were working?

Do consider the hour.

She studied me again, a long time, and I repressed the urge to explain further. I did not want to make it sound as if I was lying.

AFTER I'D SEEN HER into her apartment, I checked the lock on the front door again, for no particular reason. Then I mounted the stairs. I was just past the landing when the hair on the back of my neck all stood on end. I turned.

There, below me, just a glimpse as it slipped across the darkened foyer, gone, with the quick movements of a child.

I gripped the stair rail, my heart racing. This was no vision, no dream. I was wide awake.

I descended the stairs, still gripping the rail. The streetlight fell against the polished boards. The door between the potted palms stood slightly ajar. I hesitated, then pulled it open to find myself at the top of a narrow, dark stairwell. I felt around on the wall for a light switch, but there was nothing.

Sliding one of the heavy palms over, I propped the door open and stepped inside. I descended slowly, my hands against walls swollen with damp, the concrete steps cold and crumbling beneath my bare feet. The air smelled of root cellars and earth and wet stone. I almost expected to hear water dripping. I inched my feet forward along the rough stairs, feeling for the edges, careful of my footing. Streetlight fell in faintly from the foyer above me but did not reach very far down the passageway. Surely there could not have been anything—anyone—down there. And yet.

My foot dislodged a chunk of masonry and it tumbled down the stairs with an echoing clatter. When it stopped, I could hear my own breathing. I pressed my palms against the walls to steady myself.

And then I became aware of something else: *it* was there with me, too, in the stairwell. That old malevolence, that darkness. What I had felt on the landing that first day, and outside my employer's door. The thing, whatever it was, that was feeding on him. There, more powerful than I had ever felt it. As if I had come to the terrible, cold heart of something. And yet there was a dreadful sense, too, of nothingness. The sense that I could keep descending forever into an infinite darkness.

A scuttling across the floor at the bottom. I stopped. A quick, cold movement passed me up the stairs. My skin crawled. I turned to look behind me, but before I could do so I felt, very clearly, the press of two small hands—a child's hands—firm between my shoulders. I froze.

And then they gave a savage push, and I was falling, tumbling forward, down and down, into black emptiness.

I CAME TO IN A HEAP at the bottom, though whether I'd actually lost consciousness, I could not say. All was blackness. I was blinded. I blinked and blinked but no sight came. The door to the foyer above me was shut fast. I felt stunned, battered, my palms and knees tender and stinging. I touched a hand to my temple and it came away wet. I wiped my hand on my trousers and slid my back up against the wall. I sat a moment. All was silent. My head throbbed.

I was alone.

And yet I could recall precisely the feel of those small hands on my back, touching me, there, between the shoulder blades. I could feel the place on my back still where I'd been shoved, as though the prints of those palms had been burned there.

I scrabbled my feet on the rough concrete floor, trying to rise, feeling the wall for something to hold onto, dizzy still.

But it was not the damp wall I felt upon reaching up. It was a wooden door, cracked and splintering. My hand found the latch and, pulling myself upright, I leaned there a moment in blackness, breathing. Then, thinking to find a light within, I opened it.

A smell of rust and mothballs and rot. I felt around inside for a switch, my skin crawling. When I found it, the room fizzled with a weak, tea-coloured light, the bulb over my head glowing by a single corroded filament.

A storage room. Or, not even a storage room, a crawl space. Not big enough to stand up in. I leaned inside and poked around. Nothing, it seemed, of any importance. Boxes of curios, china figurines, books, old furniture, silvery Christmas bulbs packed in tissue like eggs in a nest. A cord was strung from beam to beam of the low, cobwebbed ceiling, and hung with metal clothes hangers. A dress dummy leaned against the far wall, white as a corpse, its shoulders disappearing eerily into the shadows.

The electric light fizzled. I bent to pry the lid off a sealed box, the cardboard dusty and damp. Children's toys, a red engine upturned over strips of jumbled railway, as if there had been some disaster. I opened another. It appeared to be filled with crusted rags. I plucked one off the top, exposing a nest of baby rats, groping blindly. An awfulness in their vulnerability. I straightened abruptly, dropping the rag, disgusted, and in doing so, jostled the hangers with a terrible metallic clatter and the light fizzled again and went out.

I reached up to touch the bulb, scorching my fingers as the light flickered on weakly, then went out again. I felt around for the rag and, using it to protect my fingertips, reached for the bulb again. Touched it. The light flickered on.

She was there: crouched among the boxes.

I recoiled, plunging the room again into a terrible darkness. I grabbed the bulb, heedless of burns, and the light came on and stayed on as I screwed it in tightly.

Of course, there was no one. Could not have been room for anyone besides myself. It was my mind which had seen the child, not my eyes. I could picture, still, its face there, peering out, horrible, from among the boxes. Not Molly's face at all. It could not have been. I swallowed a terrible tightness in my throat as I stood there in the doorway, aching.

Then I backed out of the room and punched off the light, groping my way back up the stairs, blind.

4

Constance careened us through the twisted streets of Boston's South End, the gas lamps ghostly in the falling snow. The drifts were all across the road. Constance plowed through them, her father's Lincoln halting and swerving and chugging on again.

She sang, at first, full tilt in a flat contralto, *Di-ner, is there no one fi-ner, in the state of Caroli-ner,* but forgot the rest of the words and finally just hunched silently, maniacally, over the steering wheel, propelling us through the dismal Victorian streets, reeking of sweat and gin punch and Tabu gone stale with the hour. Her coat was open over her lap and her dress hiked up to the top of indigo stockings, her thigh lean and finely muscled. I would not have called her beautiful. Handsome, perhaps. But more than this, there was a certain careless strength to her. A certain recklessness. A certain darkness.

The Lincoln slammed into a drift and stopped. The engine died. Constance cranked the starter brutally, again and again. Nothing. She put her forehead against the steering wheel and laughed. All around us the snow fell and fell in the dead city.

When she finally stopped laughing, the silence was profound, enormous. She turned her face toward me, her mascara all looped blackly under her eyes like a soldier.

She was, I admit, irresistible.

WE ARE NONE OF US free from the terrible humiliation of our humanness. Our bodies betray us. Our emotions likewise. Our minds, perhaps, most treacherous of all. Everything subject not to what our heart but to what our psychology conceives.

Lack of love, they say, is not what makes an unhappy marriage, but lack of friendship. In Jane, then, there was neither friendship nor love. But neither was there in Constance.

Inconstance, an unhappy accident of language.

AFTERWARD I WALKED the Boston streets alone, the wet, heavy snow to my shins. It seemed to take hours. I imagined the scene which would greet me at home: Jane sitting on the sofa in the same old sour dressing gown, Molly asleep on her lap. I would enter, shaking snow in the alcove. *Finally out, eh*, I would say. *Must be a relief. Snowing like the dickens out there.* I would hang my overcoat carefully, fiddle a long while with my galoshes. *Arthor*, Jane would say, evenly. *I called my mother.* She had threatened as much in the past. I would step into the room, peer at her in the lamplight, as if I could not conceive what she was saying.

She would look as if she had been crying, but she might not have been; she'd looked that way for weeks. *Do you know, she would say, what time it is? I cannot believe you went out tonight, to a party.* I would tell her again it wasn't a party. She would wipe her nose on a wadded hanky, tell me she was going back to Rochester, back to her parents. I would act honestly astonished, honestly confused. Oh, we'd had these scenes before. *I cannot believe, she would say, you went out this evening.* I would tell her I had no choice. She would say that was what I always said. I would be unable to deny it. In fact, it was how I often felt in those days. As if I had no choice. I would say, *I don't understand why you're so upset.*

If you want your secrets kept, they say, cloak them in candour.

My god, I would say, then, gaping. *You think I've been unfaithful. Is that it?* She would rise, struggling with Molly's weight, tell me she was going to bed. *Nothing happened between me and the girl,* I would say, angrily. *Between me and anyone. Not even between me and you in quite some time.*

She would turn and cast me a long glance, then shut the bedroom door firmly behind her. She would be frosty in the morning, unresponsive. I would act as if I did not care. And maybe I did not. Maybe I was tired of caring. Maybe I, too, was tired of such scenes. Tired of feeling old. Just tired.

I steeled myself for it as I turned onto our street. We were the last on the block, the lower floor of a slumped brownstone in a row of slumped brownstones, cloaked now in patches of snow, as if diseased things. Light fell through the drapes onto the unshovelled front steps and I tripped on my way up, ready for the confrontation but hoping too, maybe, just a little, that this time it would unfold differently. I pictured them again, as I had earlier in the evening, but tenderly now, curled together in a pool of lamplight on our old sofa and I softened.

I slid my key into the lock, but it was already open. Strange, I thought, and pushed the door ajar, stepping quietly inside. I paused a moment in the alcove. The sofa stood empty and orange in the light of the lamp still burning there. It was not like Jane, frugal always, to leave a light burning unnecessarily. I stamped my snowy galoshes lightly, then crossed the wood floor to where our bedroom door stood gaping weirdly. Streetlight fell coldly in through the window. The bed was as I had left it. Unmade, empty. I punched on the light.

Jane? I said.

I crossed the room, wrenched open the closet door, looking for her travelling case. I rummaged about in the heaps of soiled laundry.

A faint knocking at the front door and I turned and stepped back into the living room, my wet galoshes slipping against the wooden boards.

Mrs. Hill, who lived upstairs, teetered in the alcove in her husband's greatcoat, wringing her tiny red hands.

I stood staring at her dumbly, something, a certain numbness, already settling over me.

What is it? I finally managed.

Oh, Mr. Crandle, was all she said.

MR. HILL DROVE ME in his old Chevrolet and we made slow progress. I saw nothing: snow, the black river—did we cross it? I think we did; we must have—the ghost lights of a predawn December.

When, at last, we pulled up in front of the emergency room at Weymouth, all blazing with light, I stepped out and then asked, for some inexplicable reason, *Aren't you coming in?*

What things we do in times of crisis.

Mr. Hill just bit his lip and shook his head, his face green with the dashboard lights, there in the Chevrolet wafting plumes of exhaust over me. I shut the door, a groaning, clipped sound in the winter air. I can hear it still. But he did not leave. And I did not leave. I stood and stood. And finally he turned off the engine and got out and I followed him, this man I scarcely knew, who rapped the floor of his apartment above us sometimes, but timidly, a gentle reminder, when our shouting grew too loud. He led and I followed, stupidly, the snow banked up to our knees, and through the front doors, not bothering to stamp our galoshes, and inside to a desk, where Mr. Hill spoke quietly to a nurse who stood looking at me over his shoulder—oh, good Mr. Hill, where are you now?—before leading us away, down that polished hall, shedding snow as we went in great, heavy clumps and no one seeming to mind about that, no one seeming to care. And then Jane was there, hunched over in an armchair, as if someone had delivered a great blow to her stomach, as if she could not catch her breath, and I stood looking at Mr. Hill, as if he should do something, as if this were his story. And then he was gone. And we were alone, then, in that white room. Just Jane and me.

WHO CAN SAY HOW THE DAYS thereafter unfolded. There were vague impressions, and memories, sometimes so sharp I could taste them, feel them. The smell of flowers. A soft blue sweater with pearly buttons. A certain waxed wood beneath my palm. Or had I imagined that, the last bit? I no longer knew.

There are things I would not remember. Things I told myself I did not. And when you shut a thing up, when you shut it—

No. There was everything; and then there was nothing. That is the way with loss. It does not come in gradations.

AT SOME POINT it was day again, brutally. The light seared my eyes. All down our street the snow had browned from passing automobiles. There was nothing anymore of beauty in it. There was nothing. Only Jane climbing into the front seat there with her mother while her father slammed the black trunk shut, and no one looking at me, no one. As if I had never been there at all.

WHAT IS IT ABOUT the darkness which draws us? At once inward and outward. I had always been too easily drawn, too easily, Jane would have said, had said, too easily enveloped. I, who feared once, as a child, not the witching autumn, but spring, that clear-lighted season of ghosts when Jesus rose from the tomb, bloodless and terrible, rolling away the stone in the sunlight with his own deathless hands. I imagined Jane's shock at hearing such a confession.

Oh, yes, the darkness drew me. Had drawn me always.

There was something in me, I knew, something perhaps in us all which, no matter our rational selves, was haunted.

FIVE

I

SOMETHING HAD CHANGED in me. Was changing. There was something sinister in Sixty-Six. Something sinister in the face of that child, something ugly, angry. It was not Molly. I knew that. But, then, who was it? And what did it want with me, attached as it seemed to be to my employer? It meant to tell me something; I was sure of it. But what?

That night of my fall down the stairs, the child did not return. I slept badly, dreaming terrible dreams of being propelled up and up to where darkness thinned and into the grey aether toward some terrible knowledge which lay just out of my grasp, and then I was falling, hurtling into something cold and black and soulless, something that chilled me to my very core, that roused in me a feeling of despair which made me want to weep as I had not done in a long while.

And then I was awake, and alone. Two letters lay on my bedside table, weighted down with the chunk of gravestone. They had surely not been there the night before. My door, of course, remained shut and locked. I picked up the letters. The first was another from my employer to his mother. A fresh wave of guilt washed over me. I still had not delivered the first. The hours and days seemed to slip away from me always, in fragments, as if they were not in my control, as if broken things that crumbled in my hands. I lifted the second envelope, addressed to me. I saw with no small degree of shock it was from Jane.

I rose hastily and opened it at once, hands shaking so terribly I tore the pages. I could scarcely believe what I read. I sat down on the edge of my bed, reviewing the letter several times over before dropping it onto the table in dismay.

Jane had booked train passage: she would arrive in three days' time. What I had hoped for so long had come to pass now that I no longer desired or even welcomed it. The way of all things.

It could not be. But how was I to stop it? What could I tell her?

She could not come, and yet come she must.

I VENTURED FORTH early into the misty streets with single-minded determination, my collar buttoned against the cold and a woollen muffler wrapped snugly round my throat. I clenched the letters addressed to my employer's mother tightly in my fist in the chance that some ill wind would snatch them away and send them drowning into the Seekonk. Certainly, there had been enough of such diversions over the past week to set me off my course.

And, then, I marvelled: a week. Only that. It felt like years.

Jane was to come. God only knew what I was to do when she did. I would lose Flossie. I would lose my position, to be sure. And so I must, at least, finish what I had been asked to do. I felt compelled to, now, having seen him so broken. I knew, only too well, that kind of loss.

Hope Street wound down toward the river, empty still at that hour but for a lone man in a trenchcoat waiting on the corner with a briefcase, checking his wristwatch. I cut sharply up Lloyd, past the winter-dead rose bushes of St. Sebastian church, its grey stone tower medieval in the fog, and on into wide, tree-lined Blackstone Boulevard with its storeyed mansions set well back from the street. Shining automobiles rattled by with regularity. In one of the curving drives, a child in a cowboy hat and fringed vest crouched slapping at the gravel with a toy shovel. A housekeeper raised an upper window with a sharp smack and leaned out. I thought she would call to the child, but she only watched a moment, then shook a white dust cloth briskly, as though in surrender, and slammed the window shut again. An elderly gentleman rode a bicycle up the sidewalk, bells jingling. I stepped into the street, out of his way.

Morning, Sheriff, the man said to the boy, and the child pulled a toy pistol from his holster and fired after him.

I was nervous, unsure what I would find in my employer's mother. A monster, he'd said.

But, no, that was not right: it was she who had called him a monster, not the other way around.

I followed Blackstone for what seemed a long time. The yards began to broaden out into farms and the mansions thinned and the trees grew more densely and I wondered if I'd come too far. It seemed I had left the city behind and entered the countryside. All was brown and grey and tattered gold. The air smelled of wet feathers, of ice just come off the mud at the river's edge. A flock of crows or starlings or some raucous dark birds blasted out of the shrubbery like devils in a rattle of leafless branches. I had almost resolved to turn back when I noticed the landscape ahead seemed to become less wild again, more orderly. Rounding an obviously groomed bank of junipers, I came to an expanse of lawn. And paused.

I looked behind me. I checked for street signs. There were none. I walked closer, looked with a kind of wonder over the clipped brown lawns rolling out vastly and the curving drive and the circular flower beds still dormant with cold, the clipped hedges of box elder and rhododendron and, there in the near distance, the red-brick edifice I knew so well from my window. I stood marvelling. What a strange coincidence. There it stood, at the crest of the property. I was quite pleased with such fortuitousness. I could inquire inside about the address I sought and get a look around the place at the same time. Killing two birds with one stone. I walked nearer. The building was even more handsome than it had appeared from my attic window, luxurious even, and yet there was about the whole place a taint of something else, something marshy and decayed. There was about it the sort of restrained stillness one finds in only the unhappiest of houses. I walked to the foot of the lawn where a discreet sign rose up from the grass next to a gravel drive. I stared.

Butler Hospital for the Insane.

And, beneath, an address. I felt a coldness settle over me. I lifted the envelopes. The address was the same. It was this very building I sought.

I looked over the grounds again. The whole place had darkened, it seemed. A flatness to it in the early light. The dark windowpanes reflected nothing. The ivied brick had a wet, heavy, salty look, as of some fortress on the edge of the sea.

I roused myself and followed the curving drive to the main building, my shoes crunching in the cold silence. The place might have been abandoned, the kind of place one reads of in ghost stories. I followed the drive as far as the sweeping front entrance, then hesitated at the foot of the wide white-painted stairs, looking up at the blackened windows for a sign of life.

A movement to my right startled me and I turned to see a young woman stepping through the shrubbery, picking at the twigs in her hair with one hand. She looked up at me in surprise. A white face, plump in a pleasant, full-featured way. Her eyebrows so fine and highly arched that I realized what I'd taken for surprise was merely her natural expression. She wore a nurse's cap, slightly askew. A white collar poked out from beneath an old black woollen winter coat covered in cat hair which she clutched about her shoulders. Her skirt and stockings and shoes were white also, though on the tip of one shoe, the right one, there was a large brownish stain. I averted my eyes, noticing then that she held a cigarette behind her back.

I've startled you, she said.

Not at all.

I can't imagine the look I must have had on my face.

I'm afraid I didn't notice.

Polite, she said.

You work here, I take it?

She raised those eyebrows even higher and sighed. *I think I was just deciding.*

Difficult morning?

Difficult night. One of those shifts. The ones you hear about in nursing training but believe will never happen to you. Not used to it yet, I guess.

To what, may I ask?

The nights, she said. She lifted the cigarette then, with an embarrassed pursing of the lips. *Do you mind?*

Not at all.

I don't think there's any rule against it, per se. But I don't really know. There might be. I've been wrong about so many things. She puffed on the cigarette, exhaled. *And one doesn't like to take chances. You know, right off.*

You're new, then?

Day three. She tapped ash onto the lawn and ground it down with the toe of her stained shoe. *They tell me it gets better.*

Do you believe them?

No. She laughed humourlessly. *I mean, this is what I signed up for. It's just, things are so different in theory. On paper. If you know what I mean.*

Yes, I said. *I think so.*

I'm what my mother calls thin-skinned, I'm afraid.

It makes for a good many bruises.

Let me guess, she said. *You're the new doctor.*

Hardly. I laughed. *What makes you think so?*

Hmm, she said, tilting her head. *You just have that look about you. Of analyzing things. You know? A good observer, I would say.*

I've certainly been called worse things.

Me too. Only a few moments ago.

She laughed ruefully and flicked the ash from her cigarette, looking at me curiously.

I'm visiting someone, I said, anticipating her question.

Oh. That's too bad. Visiting hours aren't until after lunch, I'm afraid. Mornings are for treatments and therapy. Routine is crucial. Any minor change . . . She finished with a shake of her head.

I see.

You must be new then, too.

You could say that.

I'm sorry.

For what?

She shrugged and looked up at the building.

I mean, it can't be easy, either, she said. *Having someone in here. That's all.*

In there, out here. None of it is easy, it seems.

She looked at me doubtfully, sympathetically.

I suppose I shall have to come back, then, I said. Then, on second thought, I pulled the letters from my overcoat pocket and added, *Say, would you mind delivering these? I'd be awfully grateful. Just until I can make it back.*

She took the envelopes. *Two letters, my. Who's the lucky lady?* Her face blanched. *I'm sorry. That was stupid of me. I'm still getting used to the things you should say, the things you shouldn't say. Every day brings a new list of mistakes.*

It must be difficult.

It is. But I shouldn't be complaining to you. Mistake number 201.

Not at all, I said. *Well. Good day, then.*

Wait, she said behind me, *the name. I don't even know it's a woman you're here to see. I just assumed. It usually is, you know. The ones who get visitors, I mean. The men, hardly anyone comes to see them.*

Seems a shame. I wonder why.

I think they're more frightening, the men. The women—it sounds silly—but one almost expects it, madness. I don't know why. That sounds terrible, doesn't it? And it isn't fair. Some are worse than others, of course. The stories I could tell. But insanity in men? It's quite a different thing. It's—I don't know—bigger, somehow. So much more violent. The women, they mostly only hurt themselves.

That stands to reason, I suppose.

Does it? I wonder. The only thing is, she added, *the thing I really can't bear, if there are children involved—the things I've heard, I can't, I honestly can't—*

She stopped abruptly and turned away from me. Her hair had pulled loose from the bun in back and hung in lopsided strands down her neck. It was an uncomfortable moment. I wondered if I should speak, but then she turned back to me, eyes shining.

You told me you aren't a doctor, she said, *and here I'm talking to you like you're mine. You were about to tell me the name.*

Of course, I said. Yes. *It's Mrs. . . . Phillips. Or, no, Lovecraft.* She stared back at me with that perpetual look of surprise. *You're not sure?*

I—

Oh, I'm sorry. She waved a hand. *There I go again. I shouldn't pry. These things can be complicated.*

Yes.

I understand. Well. Phillips-Lovecraft. I'm not sure I know her. I'm still getting acquainted with all the wards. But I'll be sure she gets the letters. I'll give them to Sister Clem. She knows everyone. Whether they like it or not.

Clem?

Clementine. An old sourpuss, so goes the saying. I'm a little afraid of her myself, actually, but she's been here forever. She makes it her business to know them all. She put a hand up over her mouth. *Oh,* she said. *I didn't mean "them," not the way it sounded.*

Not at all. In fact, I had been thinking much the same.

I'll make sure she gets the letters.

Much obliged.

I was about to tip my hat in what I hoped was a gallant manner, when the nurse suddenly straightened, dropping the cigarette in the grass and stomping it out with her shoe. I heard footfalls coming toward us on the gravel and I turned.

An older gentleman in a grey woollen overcoat and spectacles stood behind me. He carried a large black leather satchel.

Forgive me, he said. *I have interrupted your pleasant conversation.*

He smiled in a friendly, easy, open way. He was a man whom people trusted, you could see that immediately. You could see he knew it, too. His silvery hair was combed back in a neat wave from his forehead, hiding, as it were, nothing.

Excuse me, the nurse said abruptly. *I'll be sure to deliver . . .*

She flapped the envelopes at me without looking up and was off, stumbling up the first stair and struggling a moment at the door, pushing instead of pulling, and finally gone.

The gentleman adjusted his gleaming spectacles.

How are you this fine morning? he asked.

I am quite well, I said. Pleasant fellow.

You seem lost, the man said, tentatively, inquiringly.

Not at all.

Or, perhaps, at a loss.

No indeed.

The man looked up at the hospital and then back at me.

Friend of our Ivy's, are you?

Ivy? I looked back at him blankly.

The young lady you were speaking with.

Ah. No. I just happened upon her, here. I gestured at the shrubbery awkwardly, then withdrew my hand.

Mm, yes. Out lingering in the rhododendrons again, our Creeping Ivy. His smile faded. *Out for a stroll, then, were you?*

Quite, I said. I tried out my own smile, felt it quiver.

Sweat prickled beneath my armpits. I had never been fond of doctors. It was not an uncommon reaction.

Are you—were you—on your way inside? He gestured at the asylum.

Not just at the moment.

I was aware I must look quite suspicious. I groped for something to say. What I really wanted to ask about was the lighted window I had seen every night, and the slow telegraphing that came to me sometimes across the darkened city. But how to phrase it?

This building . . . , I began. But I could not ask.

Yes?

Do you know, perchance, when it was built? I said instead.

Built? He pursed his lips, tilting his head up to look at the building. A trick of the light blacked out his spectacles. He shook his head. *I confess I haven't the foggiest.* He looked back at me, the faintest trace of a smile, I thought, flickering around the corners of his mouth.

Was it built as such? I stumbled on. *As an asylum?*

I believe it was. He looked at me carefully, seeming to consider. Then he said, *If you'd like to come in with me, I'm sure we can find out the particulars. Someone is bound to know. One of the sisters, perhaps. I sometimes think they came with the building, just between you and me. And I've been here a good while myself.*

I wouldn't want to trouble.

No trouble at all.

You know I have of it the most remarkable view, from my study window. Over by the university.

Indeed?

Yes, most remarkable. It looks, I said, *almost as of a castle at night. Lit up, you know.*

Does it?

Quite, I said, nodding. Then, for lack of anything else, *Quite.*

We stood a moment in uncomfortable silence.

Well, he said, and hesitated. He appeared on the brink of saying something further, then seemed to think better of it. *Good day to you, then.*

I watched him mount the wide stairs and cross the verandah, his clipped footfalls resonating across the empty lawns like the shots of hunters in autumn. At the door, he paused beneath the wide white portico and glanced back at me. I repressed the urge to lift a hand. He nodded, once, his spectacles darkening over again, before stepping inside, and I turned away, relieved and trying hard to make it look as if I were not.

I HAD TO RETURN, of course. I had to bring my employer some word of his mother before Jane arrived and everything, the entire sham, collapsed around me. I felt, however irrationally, that I owed it him.

The young nurse was not there smoking in the shrubbery, though I had somehow expected she would be, as if she came with the landscape, the angel at the gate. I lingered a moment at the foot of the stairs, feeling overwhelmed, sick, at the thought of entering that building, an asylum. Finally, mustering my resolve, I swung the heavy door open and stepped inside.

I was hit with an overwhelming odour of bleach and paste wax and distant, starchy cooking. The day had grown bright and the sunlight filtered in coldly through the many windows into the main foyer, luxurious with blue velvet arm-chairs and draperies of a light, airy fabric, though the hall-ways leading away in either direction were dark in spite of large windows at their ends, lit by dim orange lights which reflected on the gleaming floors like pumpkin lanterns. Down the passage nearest me, a man in baggy clothing moved with a bucket and mop, making wide, graceful sweeps. He looked up abruptly and stopped his motion, waiting for me to move on. I turned away, back to the bright foyer. The bitter taste of paste wax hung in the back of my throat and I swallowed hard. My palms sweated inside my overcoat pockets and I pulled them out, wiping them against my trousers. No one seemed to take any note of me. There was an air of bustle and purpose. Nurses moved, clacking across the polished floors, calling to one another. It was not what I'd expected from the outside. Still, in spite of the many windows and polished floors, there was an air of oppressiveness, of heaviness.

If you gaze into the abyss, I thought, the abyss also gazes into you. I wondered where I'd come across such a phrase, for it was surely not of my own invention.

I gripped the chunk of gravestone in my overcoat pocket and walked directly to the admittance desk. The nurse there frowned deeply over her typewriter and, when she looked up at my approach, frowned more deeply still. I wondered if I had the visiting hours wrong after all.

She was older than the nurse I'd met on the steps, and thin, with dark hair pinned in tight coils around her sharp face. Her lips were rouged heavily in a cracked, unbecoming colour that reminded me of old geraniums.

Good afternoon, she said, and far from the voice I had been expecting, hers was melodious, silvery.

Good afternoon, I said. *The nurse I spoke with earlier said visiting hours—*

You were here this morning?

Yes, only to drop some letters.

Whom did you speak with?

A nurse, I didn't get her name. She's new, I said. *Three days, I believe. About so tall.*

Fat?

Plump.

That would be Ivy. Did she say her name was Ivy?

She didn't say her name at all. No, wait—I recalled the doctor—*it is Ivy. Was Ivy.*

But she told you to come back later?

She said visiting hours were this afternoon. Am I mistaken?

And you gave her letters?

Yes, I—

Please wait a moment, she said, and rose from her chair, walking briskly to a windowed room just behind the reception area. Inside, two nurses and a hunched, aged sister stood flipping through a chart, and when the nurse spoke, they all three looked out at me. They seemed to be in mild disagreement over some matter, and finally the sister, a shrivelled crone of a woman, handed her clipboard to the reception nurse and came out, tapping along on an ivory cane, her black habit buckling with starch. She fixed me with a gaze so rheumy it was impossible to tell what colour her eyes might once have been.

Can I help you, she said.

I hope so, I said mildly. *As I explained to the nurse, I left some letters this morning—*

The sister plunged a hand behind the reception desk, rummaging there blindly until she came up with the envelopes.

Are these your letters? she asked, looking hard at me. I wondered just how poor her eyesight was, how much she could see.

Why, yes. May I ask—

Who are these letters for?

I noticed then that the seals on both letters had been broken. Someone had opened them, perhaps read them. I suspected it had not been my employer's mother.

For . . . Mrs. Lovecraft . . . , I began cautiously.

Mrs. Lovecraft, she said. *I see.*

The reception nurse had followed her back out and waited poised at her chair, watching. In the room beyond, the other two nurses stood at the window. When I looked at them, they turned quickly away.

Is there some problem? I asked.

Problem? You have brought letters. For Mrs. Lovecraft, you say. The sister looked sidelong at the nurse. *But, as you must know, we have many patients here, don't we, Nurse?*

Yes, we do.

We want to be sure, of course, that anything left for the patients, flowers, or small gifts, or personal items, or letters, say— she flapped them and I had the distinct image of a white bird in her clutches, trying to escape—*we would want to make quite certain they are received by the correct patient, would we not, Nurse?*

Yes, we would. Ivy said—

That's quite enough, the sister said to the nurse, snapping her cane against the desk. I looked down to see that the bottom corner of the desk was pocked with dents. The pink-lipped nurse retreated instantly into her former subordination. It was an impressive power this sister wielded.

Ah, I said, remembering something Ivy had said that morning. *You must be Sister Clementine?*

She looked at first surprised, and then sly, narrowing her eyes and stepping closer.

So, she said. *You do know me.*

Only by reputation.

I tempered myself. I would, after all, not want to say anything to put the pleasant nurse from that morning, Ivy, in any jeopardy.

And what, Sister Clementine said, *do you know of my reputation?*

See here now, I said, refusing to be bullied by the woman. *If there's some confusion, some trouble, I'd appreciate if you'd out with it.*

Sister Clementine smiled slowly, revealing remarkably lovely teeth. The contrast, the impossible perfection of those teeth, somehow made her face all the more terrible.

Is it, she said mildly, *is it, this Mrs. Lovecraft . . .*

Yes?

. . . is she a relative?

I almost lied. I almost said yes. But at the last moment I caught myself.

Certainly not, I said. *I am no relation to Mrs. Lovecraft. I am merely delivering letters on behalf of her son.*

And yet you've come back, Sister Clementine said.

Yes.

During visiting hours. Clearly you wish to see her, do you not?

On behalf of her son. He is my employer, and . . . look here, I hardly think this bears explaining to you.

Sister Clementine turned then on the nurse, who stood looking rather terrified.

Make yourself useful, she commanded, and the nurse was gone.

You see, she said, watching me closely. *I have some unfortunate news. For your employer.*

Has something happened?

You might say that.

I waited, impatiently.

Your employer's mother, have I got that right?

Yes, I snapped.

Is dead.

She said it flatly. It was a moment before the meaning, in fact, registered. Sister Clementine seemed to be waiting for me to say something, a very particular thing.

My god. When?

She paused, satisfied, and showed her teeth before responding.

Fifteen years ago.

I COULD NOT SLEEP for thinking of it.

I rose and paced the room, sat at the desk in lamplight, flipping pages without seeing them. Stretched out on my bed again and, taking up the magazine that had arrived only that morning by post, I tried to read one of the stories, "The Albino Deaths." I read the same paragraph three times before tossing the magazine to the floor. It lay face up, its cover—a shackled woman in lingerie, crouching in fear before a red-cloaked figure with a whip (the latter, though hooded, looking also distinctively female)—seemed more absurd, more objectionable, than ever. I rose and kicked it under the bed. Then, not liking the thought of it there, got down on my hands and knees and rummaged it out again, throwing it in the trash.

I turned out the light and undressed and stood a long time at the window looking out over the night city. Scarcely a light shone anywhere. Even the asylum, for once, was dark. The thought of it brought the taste of paste wax to my mouth, and the image of Sister Clementine's milky eyes.

Fifteen years ago. Fifteen years.

I rubbed my own eyes to rid myself of the image of Sister Clementine, then pulled from the bedside table my bottle of Aspirin and shook out the last two tablets—had I emptied it so soon?—into my palm. I ground them to powder between my teeth, chucked the bottle into the trash can with the magazine. I lay down on the bed. Thought of Jane. Wondered what, in fact, we would say to one another.

The horror magazine stuck up over the lip of the trash can. "The Albino Deaths." What rot. Life, in my experience, provides all we need of horror.

I MUST HAVE SLEPT. The sound of church bells roused me, ringing against the cold windowglass, and I wondered if it was Sunday. I'd lost my grasp on the passing of days, on the most elementary order, as if I had entered some void in which the laws of time and space were meaningless. There was a kind of comfort in such drift, I was aware. The chiming of the church bells ceased.

I lay brooding still over the events of the previous day. I wanted answers, a reasonable explanation to it all, to this mistake. I felt almost certain Sister Clementine was in error. It was too macabre. Too inexplicable. The woman was clearly senile and should have been relieved long ago of her responsibilities there. I felt I must get to the bottom of it all; I did not relish the thought, but I resolved to return to Butler and settle the matter clearly, to demand an audience with my employer's mother.

As I lay in bed I could hear voices, silvery in the street. A child's trill and the slamming of automobile doors. How remote it all seemed. How ethereal. The circumnavigatory light of the attic room.

I closed my eyes again, just for a few moments. I was not ready to face it. For if Sister Clementine was not mistaken—but this I did not wish to consider.

2

I RAPPED FOR SOME TIME at Flossie's door. But she appeared to have gone out again. The cellar door stood closed, the potted palms in their places, ordinary, as if none of the events from two nights previous had happened. I felt the wound crusted over on my temple. That, at least, was real.

I rapped once more at her door, just to be certain, but there was no answer.

The house was silent around me as I stood with one hand on the opened padlock. The steel felt cool to the touch. I pressed my ear to the door, then got down on my hands and knees and tried to look beneath it, but it was impossible. I could see nothing.

If she did not wish to see me, very well. But surely she did not need to hide herself. I wrote a hasty note inquiring after her health and slipped it under the door, then made my way hurriedly out into the sunlight.

SISTER CLEMENTINE BLINKED her eyes in the antique light.

Back again?

She nodded to one of her underlings, dispatching the girl post-haste. I leaned with both hands on the polished desk, firmly.

I'd like to speak with someone in charge, please.

I am in charge.

Then I would like to speak with a doctor.

About Mrs. Lovecraft. Your employer's mother.

I'm afraid I must insist upon speaking with a doctor.

In fact I've already sent for one. Phillips, of course, was her maiden name. When she first came here. Sarah Susan Phillips. She was a maiden once, too, Sister Clementine said, displaying again those impressive teeth. *They all were.*

Sister Clementine, a voice said sharply behind us.

Ah, Sister Clementine said. *Here is your doctor.* And disappeared in a slow, stiff flapping of black down the hall.

I turned to see with some relief the friendly older gentleman I had encountered on the grounds upon my first visit.

The doctor extended his hand. *I'm glad to see you again. I am Dr. Tinseley. I was hoping we could have a word.*

Were you?

Indeed.

May I ask about what?

Why, the doctor said, smiling easily, as if we were old friends, *about the building, of course. The architecture. You had some questions for me. Don't you remember?*

WE WALKED DOWN one of the dark halls, our shoes echoing on the polished floors. The doctor moved briskly, swinging his arms, as if we were out for a bit of bracing exercise. The orange lights shone on his spectacles when he turned to smile at me over his shoulder. I tried to keep pace, to breathe shallowly of that bleach-wax stench, to not look from side to side, into the glass windows of the closed doors which lined both sides of the corridor, afraid of what I would see there.

At the end of the hallway, an abandoned wheelchair stood in the cold light from the window. We were almost alongside it before I noticed there was someone sitting in it. A girl, a child, perhaps. Her swollen head, listing over to one side, against her tiny shoulder. She wore an absurdly ruffled gown of some velvety fabric, and someone had taken a good deal of care in combing her sparse blond hair into two grotesque pigtails, as if to draw more attention still to the awful, ballooned head. On her curled hands, terrible, garish rings. I could not honestly tell if she was woman or child.

Polly, I thought the doctor said, greeting the girl. But he seized the wheelchair and spun it round to an open doorway, calling, *Louise, Louise!*

Yes, Doctor, came a voice from inside the room, and a young nurse poked her head round the corner.

Eh, the doctor said. *I thought this was Louise's ward.*

Louise is off sick.

Nothing catching, I hope.

I, the nurse began, glancing at me, *don't know.*

What's this doing out here?

Doctor?

He rolled the chair—and the girl, Polly—toward the nurse.

I was just changing—

Well, mind you don't, he said crisply. *Policies.*

Yes, Doctor, the nurse said, pulling the chair back inside the room and shutting the door.

The doctor set off again. *Policies,* he said, *policies.*

I followed.

Your office is a long way, I said, to make conversation.

But the doctor only looked over his shoulder at me again.

Two orderlies passed with an enormous metal cart piled with towels and linens that stank of bleach and, worse, a repellent humanness. Not blood or urine or fecal matter, not sweat, but something both less and more bodily; it was something like foul breath which permeated the air. I felt my lip curl in disgust.

Behind the orderlies was the pleasant, plump nurse I'd met on my first morning, Ivy. She was holding the arm of an elderly woman, overdressed for the outdoors, as if she were a child, a thick knitted hat plugged on her head.

Ivy, I said, slowing as we passed. *Hello.*

Though I was certain she recognized me, the nurse looked quickly away.

But the woman in the knitted hat grinned back at me.

I'm getting out, she said.

IN HIS OFFICE, crammed with books and stacks of file folders and dirty coffee cups, the doctor held out a sheet of paper upon which someone had written some hasty notes.

What is this? I did not take it from him, averse as I was to touching anything in that place, to breathing, even, that tainted air. But the doctor kept holding it and so I reached out and took it with the tips of my fingers.

Please, he said, gesturing to a chair across from his desk, *sit. I've done a bit of research, as you can see. You piqued my curiosity. I found out a few things, architecturally. The building is not a "true colonial," for instance.* He smiled.

I sat in the chair, pretending to glance over the notes, nodding with false interest. *Very interesting. Very interesting, indeed. Thank you, Doctor.* I handed the paper back to him, unread.

Of course you may keep that.

I hesitated, then folded it into my overcoat pocket. *Sorry to have put you to any trouble.*

Not at all.

It was only a passing interest.

He waited, studying me across the desk. He seemed to struggle with something, or expect something from me.

Many thanks, I repeated, and patted my overcoat pocket awkwardly.

He smiled.

Bit of an accident? he asked.

I'm sorry?

He tapped a finger against his own temple, and remembering, I raised my hand to the scab there. It had become unhinged at one corner, where I'd been worrying it, and it stung afresh at the touch of my fingertips.

Yes, I said. *A slip on the stairs, I'm afraid. Careless of me.*

These things happen.

We sat a moment, nodding at each other.

In fact, I began, *I was hoping to speak with you about another matter.*

Is that so, Mr. . . .

Crandle.

Crandle. You may speak to me about anything. Anything at all. You will find we are quite accommodating here at Butler.

It is concerning one of your patients.

That would be your employer's mother, I take it.

You've been speaking with Sister Clementine.

She insists upon it. He laughed easily.

I must ask, I said. *Sister Clementine led me to believe—*

He held up a palm. *May I ask you something first?*

Certainly.

He leaned forward across his desk. *How well do you know the . . . family?*

He is my employer, as I say. Not well at all. I've only just started there, just a little more than a week now.

I see. So you never actually met the woman yourself, then. You never met Mrs. Lovecraft?

I can't say I ever have, nor for that matter could I say as much of her son. Not really. Not what you'd say met.

The doctor stared back at me, waiting.

It's been a confusing time, you see, I said. *I'm just with him temporarily, from the agency. And my employer is not exactly what one would call, shall we say, forthcoming. And then he has this funny tic, of writing under false names, dozens of them, that for some days, I wasn't sure exactly who he was. And then he's been quite ill, so I've scarcely seen him. Haven't seen him at all, come to think of it. It's rather an unusual situation,* I added. *Writers, you know.*

Of course, the doctor said, *of course. It only stands to reason. Things can at times become very confusing. No one knows that better than I.*

Something in me, some alarm, went off. The doctor was, I thought, not being merely odd, but disingenuous—worse, carefully disingenuous. As if he were trying to glean some information about my employer from me.

He rose from his desk then and came around the other side and leaned there, crossing his ankles, in a pose of false ease.

Well, Mr. . . .

Crandle, I finished, with some annoyance.

Crandle. He leaned forward and narrowed his eyes at me. *May I ask, how much do you know of Mrs. Lovecraft's condition?*

Nothing at all, really.

Perhaps I could enlighten you.

I would be only too grateful.

Well, it's quite an interesting family, you see, he said, going back around his desk and sitting. He lifted a glass decanter. *Water?*

I shook my head.

He poured some out into a glass anyway and pushed it toward me across the desk. *Quite an aristocratic family, able to trace their lineage all the way back to the Massachusetts Bay Colony, or so they claim. This kind of thing is important here in Providence, you no doubt are aware, so they were quite a prominent family. Wealthy, too, her father, Whipple Van Buren Phillips, having made a fortune as an industrialist, I believe. They lived on one of the large estates on Angell Street, quite a mansion in its day, I am told, in that modest New England way. Orchards and fountains and carriage houses. A library housing some twenty thousand books, apparently, belonging to old Whipple. Unfortunately, it was all lost, as many fortunes were in those days. Everything.*

He poured himself a glass of water and drank. He seemed to be waiting for some response from me.

Shame, I said.

He set down the glass.

Yes. The mother, Robie, was dead by then, and Whipple and his daughters, as well as your . . .

Employer?

Yes, your employer, were forced to give it up, the old estate, and move to rather diminished quarters. Old Whipple died not long after; the strain was too much for the old man. He left his three daughters what little he had. And so it went, the Phillips women had fallen hard, and your employer, then but a child, would have felt the loss keenly. No doubt.

He pushed his chair back from his desk, crossed his legs the other way, and I repressed the urge to do the same.

But, I said, *what of his father? Surely the mother was not entirely on her own.*

Ah. In fact, she was, then. Apart from her sisters. Terrible busi-

ness. It sometimes goes this way. You see, your employer's mother was not the first of her immediate family to be a patient here.

No?

Her husband, that would be—he consulted a folder spread open on his desk and I tried not to reveal my own interest in the papers—*Winfield, was his name. Funny fellow, as I recall. What one would call a poseur. I remember him well. An Englishman, you'd put money on it, though he was born and raised in upstate New York. English parentage, I believe, but he was one to put on airs, as they say. At any rate, Winfield preceded his wife by some fifteen years. He was brought in under complete restraint, I'm afraid. You see he'd been away on business, staying in some hotel somewhere or other, I forget just where, when someone in a neighbouring room reported hearing terrible screaming.*

Something in me chilled.

When they found him, he was completely out of control, claiming his wife was being assaulted by someone in an upstairs room. There was no reasoning with him. He had gone, as they say, completely insane.

Good lord, I said. *What happened?*

He was in and out of this hospital for some five years—mostly in—sometimes better, sometimes worse, as it seems to go, often, in the early stages.

Worse, how?

Hallucinations.

I lifted my glass, drank carefully.

When he was finally admitted for the last time, he hung on only some three months or so.

He died here?

I'm afraid so. General paresis is listed as the cause of death. I've checked the files. Of course, this was all some time ago. Almost forty years.

So long.

Indeed. His wife visited him here, but there is no evidence among our visitor files that his son—that would be your friend—

My employer, I corrected.

*Forgive me, your employer. No record that he ever did, though his father was, as I've said, here quite some time. His wife, Sarah Susan did not arrive as a long-term patient until—*he checked his folder again—*1919. She had, how shall I say it, episodes, before that, of course.*

What sort of episodes?

Hallucinations. Much as her husband had. Susie was always what one might call a weak sister, of spirit, mind, and body. Dramatic, you know. The least toothache was a tragedy. She was a born sufferer. And a woman of narrow intelligence, limited interests. I first met her as a young woman. She was brought in by Whipple and Robie. She'd been having difficulties, trouble sleeping, terrible headaches, she had become reclusive and, her parents thought, strange. Behaving strangely, is what I mean, he said, as if that needed clarification. *She was here only a short time, then. I was not her doctor. I had, in fact, only just arrived myself, fresh out of medical school. It seems a lifetime ago now, and I guess it was. But Susie was only very young, perhaps seventeen or eighteen. Pretty, in a way. But silly, also, if you will forgive me, in a rather needful way. Seeking attention, always. She had an inordinately pale complexion, quite the whitest I'd ever seen. Achieved, I am told, by drinking arsenic. At any rate, it soon became clear there was nothing wrong with her, or nothing we could detect at the time. She seemed healthy enough, mentally.*

He put inordinate stress upon the final word, and I took that he meant her problems were of a physical nature. I was tempted to inquire, but he pressed on.

After we released her, she spent several months in reclusion, I understand. When she finally emerged, she was deeply changed. Less silly and frivolous. She was, of course, always a bit odd. But after Winfield died, she became a recluse again, this time permanently. People saw her sometimes lurking around her yard, hiding. The hallucinations grew worse. This is how it often goes. She began to see, it seemed, creatures rushing out from behind buildings, from the corners of rooms at dusk. Shadow people, she called them.

Good god.

Mmm. He folded his fingers beneath his chin and stared at me, waiting. *She grew worse after her admittance; it was quite rapid. It was these creatures, you understand, these shadow people. Monsters.*

How terrible, I said. *It must have been difficult—*

On your friend.

My employer, yes.

In fact, it was. Susie had what one might call an unhealthy fixation on her son. She babied him terribly, as an infant. She dressed him in pretty nightgowns, let his hair grow long as a girl's. He was often mistaken for such, a little girl. It was quite a battle when he got older and was teased by the other children. Finally, when he was already six, she relented and sat next his barber chair, weeping, I am told, while his hair was cut. Even then she wouldn't let him out of her sight lest something should befall him, the least bump or bruise. Then, all at once, she was repelled by him. She told people in passing he was monstrous, deformed, too terrible to look upon. She could not bear to be touched by him. She wanted him hidden away.

Because he was a monster, I said.

The doctor eyed me curiously. *He has spoken to you about this?*

No. I looked up at him. *No, we don't discuss such things. It is just something he said once.*

After a moment he nodded. *Well. She believed, yes, that he was deformed. Hideously so.*

And? I said. *Is he?*

He eyed me narrowly and leaned back again in his chair. *Might I ask about your . . . personal interest in the matter.*

I wouldn't say personal, I said, affronted.

I don't mean to pry, the doctor offered.

Of course I'm concerned.

For your employer.

Yes.

He's had a bad time. More than anyone should have to bear, when you think of it.

But how terrible, I said. *How terrible for him. His own mother. And his father already insane.*

This family history now shed an awful light upon him. I considered speaking to the doctor about it, but something in his mannerisms, in his watchfulness, made me hesitate.

Well, I said, setting my water glass back on the desk. *Thank you for your time, Doctor.*

You're not in any hurry?

I do have a number of errands to get through before the close of the business day.

Your employer keeps you busy.

Indeed he does, Doctor. I considered. *One thing more . . .*

Yes?

I mentioned I have a view of Butler, from my room.

The doctor waited.

There is a dormer window, on the upper east corner . . .

Yes?

I see a light there sometimes—it sounds strange, I know—a light going on and off. As if someone were pressing the button.

Indeed?

Yes.

The doctor stared back at me. I felt he was waiting for more. I knew not what to say.

The light, I said again, *just flickers on and off. Sometimes for several minutes.*

Strange. The doctor smiled. *Perhaps the cleaners, wiping down the buttons. We have stringent codes of cleanliness here at Butler, you know.*

I nodded. *Yes. No doubt you do.* I tapped my fingertips against my knees. *Well,* I said. There was no putting it off any longer. I rose, felt the letters in my pocket. *I appreciate your taking the time,* I said, and pulled out the letters. *If you'll kindly direct me to the correct room.*

He looked up at me a long moment, frowning deeply.

What is it?

He paused, studying me. *Surely Sister Clementine told you?*

I felt a sinking at the pit of my stomach, and I sat slowly again in the chair.

I'm sorry, he said. *I thought you understood. It was a gall bladder operation. She claimed the day before the procedure she had no wish any longer to live.*

She is . . . dead, then?

Buried in the Swan Point Cemetery, out back, along with her husband, Winfield. You can easily find her gravestone there in the Phillips plot.

But, I said, *so long?*

Fifteen years, yes. He tapped his fingers lightly on the desk, then leaned forward. *These things*, he said, *they are often genetic, you understand. They pass from one generation to the next, as easily as blue eyes or curly hair. You understand?*

I understood. I tucked the letters back into my pocket, felt them burn there.

At the door, I turned back. *And did the son*, I asked, *ever visit the mother here?*

He looked at me a long time. Finally he said, *He did. They would stroll by the river and sit at length on a little bench there. They were very close, at the end. Yes, he was here often. But . . .*

Yes?

As far as I know, he never once, in all those years, ever came inside. He seemed to consider. Then he said, *You know—forgive me, I've forgotten your name.*

Crandle.

Crandle, yes. Forgive me, Mr. Crandle, but may I make an obser-
vation?

Certainly.

You seem to have become rather deeply involved, yourself, in the
matter.

No, I said. *I wouldn't say that. Concerned, yes. But, someone in*
such close proximity, suffering so, really, how can one not be aware?

Yes, the doctor said, nodding slowly. *That is often the question.*

I STOOD ON THE STEPS of Butler, glad of the cold, the
fresh air, and felt I could begin to breathe again, though the
weight of the asylum loomed enormous at my back, throwing its shadow over me. I felt a chill and stepped out into
the sunlight.

The grounds spread out before me, dull with the last
of winter, the sky big and blue above, a full-blown sky. A
breeze rustled the browned vines along the wall at my back,
sent a clatter of leaves to the ground, and I crushed one
with my shoe until it was dust. The doctor's words weighed
heavily. He had managed to shed both light and darkness.
No place worth knowing, I thought, yields itself at sight;
no person; no thing. And I wondered where the phrase had
come from, if it had been something the doctor had said. I
could not recall.

Down at the far end of the building, past a pared bed
of bloomless rose bushes, I could see the young nurse, Ivy,

leading the woman in the knitted hat by the arm in the clear light, as one would a tentative child. As I watched, Ivy stopped and knelt with her white stockings in the damp brown grass to tie the woman's shoe. I had to turn away at such an intimate, such a humble, motherly gesture.

I descended the steps onto the gravel drive, feeling in my overcoat pocket for the chunk of gravestone. And stopped. All at once I knew exactly where it had—where it must have—come from.

I turned and followed a swept cobbled path briskly along the front of the asylum. The vines up the bricks rattled drily. At the edge of the building, a man in dirty overalls stabbed the dirt with a spade and I was forced to step off the path into the wet grass.

Rounding the corner, I saw the manicured grounds spread out in a long sweep down to a wooded bluff and the river beyond. I walked across the wet lawns and, picking up a path there again at the edge of the woods, followed it through stands of leafless shrubbery and bare, mossy hardwoods to a little fieldstone shelter with a graceful shingled roof. I was astonished to see there, all along the base of the southernmost wall, daffodils, just budding. They were dwarfed, reluctant things, and I marvelled, rubbing my chilled hands together, at the thought of such tender buds braving that frosted air. Above them hung the sign I had been looking for. I opened the low iron gate, which creaked into the still air, and stepped inside, let it swing shut again with a clang.

From that prospect, it appeared to be a park. I followed a groomed path curving between long, glossy walls of holly and came out in a little clearing, with a view of a pond upon which mergansers sailed serenely, cutting the water in long, black Vs. An elderly couple sat on a bench there, muffled, holding gloved hands, their breath pluming out beautifully in the hard sunlight. There was a smell of new grass and a sweet, pleasant scent which must have come from a big, willowy tree, blooming with stars, which hung over a stone wall near the pond. Life, it seemed, as if conscious of the near proximity of death, burst forth sooner there.

I ascended a series of stone steps, slippery with dew, and then I was in the cemetery proper.

The place was larger than I'd expected. I spent a long hour winding among headstones—some so mossed and weathered as to be illegible—and winged angels and Russian crosses and stone obelisks. There were cracked slabs dating to the late 1700s, crumbling and browned, the earth all around sunken and soft beneath my shoes. Trees dangled their branches protectively round fenced family plots typical of a certain misanthropic New England mentality. The grasses where I'd strayed from the path to examine carvings and inscriptions—*As You Are Now, So Once Was I*—were long and wet, and my shoes were soon soaked through and I was chilled and weary. I sat to rest on a mossy stone wall. Then, as if fate had led me there, I saw it. *Phillips*. I rose again and crossed the grass, circling the family plot: *Robie, Whipple, Winfield, Sarah Susan*.

I felt a thrill: there, round the back of his mother's grave-stone, a piece was missing near the base. I felt of the chunk of stone in my pocket. Of course, it made perfect sense.

But I could not help being saddened, then, at the thought of such a memento, and I wondered if perhaps my employer thought he'd lost it. I made a mental note to return it to him at the earliest possibility. Crouching down, I pulled the chunk from my pocket and held it up to the gravestone.

It did not fit.

No matter which way I turned the piece, I could not make it do so. I turned then upon Winfield's stone. But his was perfectly intact.

I stood a good while in the cold sunshine, turning the piece of gravestone in my fingers, baffled. A flock of birds lifted from the treetops in absolute silence. I watched them disappear.

Then I propped the letters in their envelopes very care-fully against the mother's grave. The sky was enormous, filled with light, and all around me the gilded branches burst out over the bluffs; beneath, the slow, coldly muscled coursing of the river. A wind had come up off the bay; the sky felt unbear-ably, icily blue, and though it was the middle of April, it felt for all the world like winter was only just setting in.

3

FLOSSIE SEEMED TO HAVE GONE for good. I felt anxious
but also angry, somehow, as if she had simply abandoned
me to the darkness of Sixty-Six. In truth, I suppose, I had
come to hope—hope, yes—that something might grow up
between us. Some good thing, some light thing.

And, then, when I was honest with myself, I knew there
was a part of me that was glad also. Or, perhaps not glad but
relieved. Jane was to come. Jane must come. And it made
things much simpler if Flossie was not there.

I saw no one when I returned to Sixty-Six. Even the
child, the presence, seemed to have gone. Only the silver
tabby appeared at the kitchen window at dinnertime, or just
past, when the streets were already bathed in dusklight.
He sat on the shed roof waiting, like a ghost, until I raised
the glass and put out a bowl of something good that I had,
again, failed to eat. I had no appetite still and my trousers
hung from my hip bones. I'd had to use a kitchen knife to
work another hole into the leather of my belt.

As for the tabby, he was, in spite of his ghostly colour-
ing, muscular and real. I had come to regard him with a kind
of wonder and horror. There was about him nothing of the

ephemeral; he was what he was, no less and no more. When
he pushed against my palm, I pushed back, feeling the agil-
ity in him, the strength. The heat of all that blood.

THAT NIGHT I KNOCKED, softly, at the study door. I could
not put it off any longer. I felt none of the dread, or fear, I
had used to feel, only a kind of embarrassed pity. There was
nothing, it seemed, that life from some people would not
wrench away.

When no answer came, I tried the latch. It was unlocked.
I inched the door open and called, quietly, *It's me, sir. Crandle.*

A rustling as of blankets and a sigh and then, *What is it?
May I come in?*

I waited outside the cracked door. More rustling and
what sounded like a shifting of furniture across the floor, a
dragging, and then he said, *Come.*

The heavy draperies were drawn against the dusklight.
A lamp shone dimly on the table by the door, and I realized
this was the constant light I must have seen from beneath
the door. Beside it was a dusty jar containing a dead snake,
mottled, dessicated, blind. Someone had taken pains to pose
the creature in a manner the effect of which was hardly life-
like. I looked away in disgust.

The matches I'd dropped days ago still lay scattered
across the carpet. I stooped to brush them quickly into my
palm before looking about the room.

By dim lamplight, the space was much larger than I

would have thought, and crammed with furnishings and papers and books, a maze of bookshelves, really; an antique rifle hung on one wall and clustered photographs and illustrations and shelves of curios; an elegant classical bust of a woman veiled in cobwebs; armchairs and occasional tables and two large desks, at opposite ends of the room, as if it were arranged for two people instead of one. The larger of these was situated under the window facing the street. The room was, in fact, so crammed with things that at first I could not make him out; it was like those children's puzzles in which one must find the hidden figure.

Finally I saw him, hunched in the big Morris chair in the shadows at the far side of the room, just outside of the pool of lamplight. He appeared so heavily covered in blankets that I could see only shoulders—rather broader than I'd imagined—his face indistinguishable in the dim light.

Tell me, Candle—he smacked his lips drily, as of someone waking from sleep—*when is spring to come.*

I was puzzled at first, wondering if he was speaking metaphorically. I struggled to shape an adequate reply, but then he said, *I don't recall a springtime ever so miserable as this one.*

It strikes me as a bit milder today, sir, I said.

Not in here.

I stood uncertainly in the doorway, wondering would he invite me in.

I have beheld all the universe has to hold of horror, he said, sounding as if he was quoting someone, *and even the skies of spring and the flowers of summer must ever after be poison to me.*

I'm afraid I don't know who that is, sir.

No, he said, heavily.

I felt of the gravestone in my pocket.

I believe I have something of yours. It only occurred to me today you might be wanting it.

Yes?

It's . . . I pulled the stone from my pocket. *May I come in?*

I am not well, Candle.

I apologize, sir. I just . . . perhaps this is of some importance to you?

Well?

I took this as an invitation and stepped tentatively toward him across the room. I almost thought he might warn me back, but he did not, and the closer I came, the more I could make out his face dimly there in the shadows. It seemed, much to my astonishment, from what I could see, quite normal.

I'm sure I stood staring, gaping perhaps. It was a face quite long and narrow, lantern-jawed. Withered by illness, the face of a sick man, clearly, gaunt and strained, drained of all colour, but hardly monstrous.

Will you speak, he said then, *or is this to be some parlour game?*

I beg your pardon, I said. *I wanted only to give you this.*

I handed him the chunk of gravestone and he took it with hands long and fine-fingered. As he leaned forward, his face spasmed and twisted, as if with great pain. He raised a hand self-consciously, to hide himself.

Forgive me, he said, from behind his hand. *It is a condition I've had since childhood. Saint Vitus' Dance. Enchanting name for an ugly syndrome. Worse when I am ill or tired, I'm afraid. I know it is unpleasant to look upon.*

I made motions of denial, but I had to admit it had been grotesque and frightening. He leaned back in his chair again, turning the stone over in his hands.

Where did you find it?

Upstairs, I said, *in my room. If I'd known . . .*

Known?

If I thought it had any significance to you, I would have returned it sooner. I've been carrying it around. I'm not quite sure why. An embarrassing admission. I half-expected to be upbraided by him.

Do you know what it is? he asked instead.

I didn't, at first. But then, after a while, I thought it must be a piece broken from a gravestone.

Yes, he said. *And no.*

He was quiet a long while, and when he finally looked up at me, it was as if he was surprised to find me still there.

Please, he said, *sit. A proper meeting has been a long time coming. I hope you will forgive such rudeness.*

I sat on the edge of a rocker a few feet away. It groaned beneath me and I stiffened to stop the noise.

In fact, Candle, he said, lifting the piece of stone, *I have not seen this in quite some time. A childhood memento. I had wondered where it had gotten to, and then time passes, and we forget, as we do with all things that once meant a great deal. It is necessary, I suppose, such forgetting. A blessing, really.* He lowered the stone to his lap, where it lay cupped in his palm.

You know, Candle, I was handsomely indulged as a boy, by my mother in particular. We had an idyllic estate, the most beautiful in Providence, I dare say, in what was practically the country, back then. My grandfather, with whom I was close, fell on hard times. When he lost his fortune, everything else hit an inevitable downslide. When he died, it seemed all was lost.

The rocker creaked beneath me and I stopped it.

So it is from his grave.

He closed a weak fist over the stone.

It is not. You see, I spent a good deal of time as a boy with my grandfather. My mother needed often to be alone. She suffered terrible migraines, was so sick from them she had bouts of vomiting so violent it left her gaunt-eyed and shaking. And, of course, she was always what she called "nervous." My father was not much in my life. A salesman, away a good deal, with a demanding position. And so he fell ill from the pressures, was paralyzed, died not long after. My grandfather the only other male in a house filled with women, and so it was only natural we should have a certain affinity. He was a great reader himself and loved especially a good ghost story. Perhaps this is where my own interest began. No doubt it is. He used to love telling me scary stories when I was a boy, and in truth I did not often feel afraid. Only once, when I'd expressed some discomfort at bedtime over some nonsense tale or other which he'd spun, he took me and led me, long after everyone else had gone to bed, through the darkened house, room by room, pointing out ordinary objects, touching them with me, exploring the familiar places that seemed so transformed by lack of light but were in fact still ordinary, still the same. After that night, I don't recall ever feeling afraid again. It was as if he'd taken the mystery out of the darkness and replaced it with himself, the comfort of his presence, and of his voice.

At any rate, he had a story for everything, every phenomenon, every landmark, every person we'd meet all up and down Angell Street. Even the servants who lived up on the third floor, he had stories for them, dark stories that made them more than human to me, mythical, as if every ordinary face hid secrets, and magic. Every place on the estate, the carriage house, the orchard, the woods, he had stories for them all. I spent a good deal of my boyhood exploring all of those places, and creating my own imaginary populations and cities among the grass and the dirt.

It was while occupied thus one afternoon that I came across a spot behind the carriage house, back near the woods in the tall grasses near the empty neighbouring lot, where someone had placed a small concrete marker. I thought at first it was only a rock, all overgrown and covered in moss, but then noted its unusually square shape and I pulled away the long grass and brambles and rubbed at the moss only to discover, engraved there—can you imagine?

I shook my head dumbly.

The name of my own mother, Sarah Susan Phillips.

I watched my employer uneasily, but said nothing.

Of course, I had no idea what it might be, or why the name of my mother, alive and well, might be written there, but I played for some time around the place, using the stone as a fortress wall for a village of Arabs I'd imagined there, until one afternoon my grandfather happened upon me in that place and asked what I was doing. I told him. He seemed odd about it and advised that I find another place for my games, and being myself a rather precocious child, I sensed his demeanour had something to do with the stone, and so I asked him about it. I believe I may even have said something about it looking like a grave and remarking how strange it was that I should find it here with my mother up and around and quite well indeed. I believe I pressed the matter, no doubt I did, irrepressible as I was. I threw a bit of a tantrum, as I was wont to do in those days, and finally the old man said he would tell me but that it must be a secret just between the two of us and that I must never let on to my mother or anyone else what he was about to tell me. Of course, we had many good secrets, he and I, so this was hardly unusual, and so I agreed, knowing quite well this was the way he prefaced all of his best stories.

He told me then that it was a special place, that my mother had buried something there, a silver pier glass of some remarkable value, years ago, in darker times. Naturally I asked why she would do such a thing. He leaned in, then—I can picture his face still, with its big white walrus moustache—he leaned in and said, "Howard, if you can explain to me the confounding ways of women, I will be much obliged." And we had a good laugh, then. In fact, he often made such jokes, about the women; it was a sort of them-and-us situation. It was a fine joke. And I moved my little Arab village and thought no more about it.

But then we lost it all, my grandfather died, and everything changed. He changed. He was no longer the man I had known. Sometimes, I caught him looking at me blankly, as if he could not remember who I was. One afternoon I was passing by his study window and I caught sight of him. I stopped there, peeking out, despicably, from behind the shrubbery. He was standing on the old moth-eaten scarlet carpet my grandmother had always hated, and which I'd always loved, woven as it was into a sort of tapestry of the gods. He was standing there, adrift in the centre of this great room, staring into the palms of his upturned hands. He stared and stared. Then, as if he sensed my presence, he looked out the window, at me, and I did not move. I thought I would catch hell from him. Privacy was sacrosanct among all us Phillipses. But he only stared at me the same way he had, a moment previous, been staring at his own hands. With nothing of recognition there. Not that he did not know me, but that he did not even know what I was. You understand?

I think so.

I was still a child, really, not even quite a young man. I wanted to weep. Instead, I grew angry. I went to him. I barged into his study, where he still stood on the scarlet carpet and I railed at him. A tantrum, as I hadn't thrown in quite some time. And something in my vitriol reminded me of that treasure my mother had buried out behind the carriage house. The priceless pier glass. I stopped short, myself silenced by the revelation. I marvelled, felt I had saved the day. I came forward, eagerly, reminding my grandfather of it—how could he have forgotten? How could we all have? Surely it was worth quite a lot. He had told me as much himself. Oh, I was very pleased with myself.

But the old man, he just put his head in his big hands and he wept and wept. I had never seen him cry. It was terrible for me. It was that moment, I think, when I knew things would never again be the way they once had.

When, after the old man's death, only a few weeks later, my mother told me we were to move, that we would be leaving the house on Angell Street forever, I went out behind the carriage house and, *taking a shovel, went back to the woods. I intended to dig that pier glass up—it was valuable—but once I was there, I could only stand dumbly, staring. I don't know why, even now. And my mother calling, her voice ringing out across the evening lawns, until I could stand there no more. I raised the shovel up over my head and brought it down with all my childish, adolescent rage and grief upon that stone, so hard my palms rang with pain. I dropped the shovel. A chunk of stone fell away into the grass. I could hear my mother coming then and, wiping my nose on my sleeve, I grabbed the chunk of stone and ran back to her.*

"What are you doing?" she said when I'd come round the side of the building.

"Nothing," I told her. And she looked at me oddly but said nothing more. That's how it was with us, you know. It's the aristocratic way. The New England way. It is how I, too, have lived my life. I often think how it must build and build and I wonder how any of us stand it.

Mother became quite ill, sometimes I think from that very thing. From all that pretending. Then I grew ill myself. Again. Sometimes I think I have never been truly well. Time passed. I grew to understand it was just another of my grandfather's stories, and I wondered even if there had been a name on that stone at all, my mother's name. It seemed always that he and I walked such a fine line together between reality and fancy. There has been so much that feels real in my memory but which I know cannot possibly be.

He turned the stone again in his fingers and then passed it back to me. I was taken aback.

Forgive me, sir. Don't you want it?

He waved his hand at me, the stone still held loosely there, but did not reply.

What could I have done? I took the stone and in so doing my fingertips brushed his; they were cold, so cold he might have been one of the dead. I repressed the urge to wipe my fingers on my trousers.

Change is the only enemy of anything really worth cherishing, he said. *I have been homesick my entire life. I imagine I will die so.*

We sat awhile, then, without speaking. The rocker creaked again beneath me, offensively, and I stilled it. My knees ached with the effort.

He leaned his head back against his chair and closed his eyes.

I fear I've tired you, I said.

I am tired, Candle. Yes. You will have to excuse me. One cannot spend one's youth gazing at the stars and not feel hopeless, as I'm sure you understand only too well. If there's something else you need, I must ask that you put it in a letter.

Of course, I said.

It was a moment before I realized he had dismissed me and that he would say nothing further. I thought of his mother, dead there beneath the still-brown grass of Swan Point. I thought of his letters. But I could not tell him. I could not.

Taking the chunk of gravestone and yet another sin of omission, I left the room, closing the door behind me.

SIX

I

THAT NIGHT I WENT TO THE AUNT'S ROOM. I thought I'd heard a noise there when I was fixing a cup of tea in the kitchenette. And perhaps I had. But my employer's story—and the sad truth I'd discovered at Butler—had made me curious, too. It was the one room in the house I had not entered. And, then, I wondered: Was there even an aunt at all? Was she mad, too? Or dead?

Still, it was more than uncertainty, more than curiosity, which drew me there. I was drawn, as we always are, by something outside myself also.

I tried the latch; to my surprise, the door was unlocked.

I stood, listening, for a long moment in the darkness. I was thinking still on the story my employer had told me, turning it over and over in my head, wondering at the strangeness of it and of the details I had learned at Butler. That Sixty-Six was a disturbed house, I had no doubt any longer; and that this disturbance, this haunting, this child I had seen, was connected to the darkness at Butler Hospital, the darkness of my employer, I had come to believe a certainty.

I opened the door and stepped softly inside, pulling it shut behind me.

I was hit by that scent of overripe cherries, and I realized it must be some sort of perfume or talcum. I pushed the button of the electric light and the bed chamber swilled yellow.

A bed, a matching set of dressers, all of a dark, carved wood, mahogany or walnut perhaps, expensive. The coverlet the deep yellow of daffodils not quite fresh. A round braided rug, just a shade darker, lay upon the wood floor. A framed photograph had fallen to the rug and I picked it up, placed it carefully back among the little bright glass jars of cream, the pots of powder. I reached for the nearest jar and opened it. I stuck my finger inside, then rubbed my hands together and smelled: lemon verbena, not the scent of cherries I was seeking. I closed the jar, wiped my hands on my trousers.

Several framed photographs sat among the jars and bottles. I picked one up: a young man of about fifteen, serious and rather handsome in a prim, aristocratic way. I realized it must be my employer as a much younger man. I set it back down.

On the nightstand was a vase of dried lavender gone dusty with age. I touched a stain of lipstick on the rim of a glass of nearly evaporated water. The peachy colour flaked away on my fingertips. Again, I wiped my hands on my trousers, then opened several of the cupboard doors, for what I could not say, merely exploring, I suppose. Women's things—shoes, cardigans, hats, chiffon scarves, unidentifiables laced and crocheted and embroidered, an entire shelf of washed jelly jars containing buttons and safety pins. Among them, a smaller jar holding what I at first took to be tiny ivory pebbles until I poked my finger inside. It was a collection of child's teeth, small and sharp as splinters of bone. In my disgust, I dropped the entire jar onto the carpet and it rolled away beneath the yellow bedskirt, scattering its contents.

I could feel my heart loud in my chest. I got down on my hands and knees to collect the teeth, depositing them in the palm of my hand, then stretching my arm beneath the bed for the jar. I felt around, trying not to be repelled by the dust and other debris I discovered there, and by that other feeling that spaces beneath beds have always roused in me, making my skin crawl. I found the jar lodged against a stack of papers and I pulled them out.

It was not a sheaf of papers, as I had thought, but rather a packet of photographs. The first was of a young man in spectacles, obviously my employer, that lantern jaw; the second of a young boy who bore a vague resemblance to the other, and I assumed this, too, was my employer at a younger age. Across the face of the third was clipped a handwritten note which read, *When I am gone, darling, keep these and know you were never terrible to look upon. It was only her sickness which caused her to speak so.*

It was then I heard, distinctly, a voice.

I froze there, my blood racing. It had not been the voice of a man, not my employer. I held my breath. Nothing. I knelt down to hastily stuff the photographs back under the bedskirt, and just as I did, something clattered behind me. I swung about to see the photograph I had found on the rug earlier toppled again from the dressing table. I bent and picked it up and this time turned it over. My skin crawled.

It was the child. The one I had mistaken for, imagined was, Molly. Slowly, I peeled back the note from the third photograph in my hand. It was the same child. And it was no little girl. I recalled what Dr. Tinseley had told me of Susie, how she'd dressed my employer as a little girl.

Arthor.

The voice came from outside the closed bedroom door. Seizing the latch, I flung it open in a panic, scarcely knowing whom, or what, to expect.

There, in the shadows, stood Flossie.

SHE WORE HER BLUE velvet cloak and clutched her white leather travelling case in both hands, looking remarkably as she had when I'd first seen her. But now there was in her face something sunken and weary that I regretted to see at once. She had only just returned, she said, and could not find the key she had left under the potted palm in the foyer.

Then she added, with what seemed to me a strained cheerfulness, *I thought maybe you could put me up for the night.*

I must have given her an odd look, for she said sharply, *You needn't look so shocked, Arthor. Did you think I was gone for good?*

I took the case gently enough from her fingers and pulled the door of the aunt's room shut behind me, and led her wordlessly out to the stairs.

Where have you been? I asked in a low voice.

Did you miss me?

I led her down to the foyer and set her case on the bottom-most stair and rolled up my sleeves.

The key wasn't under the palm? I said.

Without waiting for an answer, I tipped the heavy pot to one side and felt underneath. There was the key.

Oh, how did I miss it under there? Flossie said flatly.

I straightened, wiping my hands on my trousers.

I passed by the other day, I said. *And the lock was undone.*

Impossible, she said, taking the key. I watched her struggle with the lock an unreasonably long time. The clock chimed out the quarter hour and seemed to rattle her further. She shook the lock in frustration.

I could remove that for you.

Yes, you keep saying that, she said sharply.

She seemed to note this sharpness herself, for when she spoke again her voice was softer, though still strained.

I've been up in Boston, if you can believe it. That convention I told you about. My feet are killing me. Standing around eight hours a day in heels. They can have it. I told my agent so. I don't need to work that bad. But how have you been? Come in and have a nightcap, do. I want to hear all about what you've been up to. How's your aunt?

My aunt?

Silly, she teased flatly, batting my arm. *You always say that.*

But she was only going through the motions. Even I could see that.

Finally the lock clicked and she opened the door. I thought she seemed rather odd about it, pausing there a moment on the threshold, as if she did not want to enter. I handed her the travelling case.

Aren't you coming in? she said, and I detected, I thought, a note of panic there.

I hadn't better.

Oh, please.

I've a good deal of work.

Oh, you terrible great baby, she cried. *You're sulking.*

Nonsense.

You were worried about me, weren't you.

I scarcely knew how to reply. Flossie had struck me as the sort of girl who always landed on her feet, but I judged it best to allow her to believe I had been anxious indeed. Relations between women and men are often fraught with such little deceptions. What a laugh, as Flossie would say.

Then I noticed she held something in her hand. A rolled magazine.

What is that?

What?

In your hand?

She genuinely seemed to have forgotten about it.

Oh, she said, handing it to me, *I picked it up upstairs, in your apartment.*

It unfurled slowly in my palm. The *Weird Tales* magazine I'd thrown into the trash can of my attic room.

Where did you get this?

I told you.

You were in my room?

What? Don't be ridiculous. It was sitting right there on the kitchen table. I went in there first, looking for you. The light was on.

But I certainly did not remember taking it there.

Anyway, she said, smoothing the magazine flat in my palm, *I saw it sitting there and picked it up, awful thing. I mean, really, Arthor, she's hardly wearing anything at all; they needn't have bothered. But, look*, she said. *She looks a bit like me.*

Now that she'd mentioned it, there was a faint resemblance. I rolled the picture of the woman, essentially nude, up again, embarrassed.

You know, you might have left word, I allowed. *A note, at the least.*

So you were worried. Well, good. I'm glad. I hope you were sick over it. A girl likes to be worried about now and then, you know. Now throw off your pouting and come in and keep me company while I put up my poor, bruised feet. You never know what sort of creatures might have found their way in here. Maybe one of yours.

One of my what?

She seized my arm, then, and to my surprise pulled me violently inside and shut the door behind us. I stood, rubbing my wrist, in that bright living room.

Honestly, Flossie. Don't be a child.

She tucked in her chin, looking hurt. *I just meant those things you make up, those monsters and things, like in that magazine you've got. I don't like them, you know.*

Well, I don't like them either.

You write them.

It doesn't mean I like them.

Who sounds like a child now?

How had things devolved so quickly between us? I was glad to see her, I really was. But Jane . . .

I'm sorry, I said. *I've just had this terrible headache.*

She uncrossed her arms and stepped toward me then, laying a hand on my arm. *Poor you,* she said, sincerely. So different from Jane, who could nurse a grudge into the wee hours of the morning.

Sit here, Flossie said, *and put your feet up and I'll make you a hot drink, to help you sleep. There now.* I saw then a bottle of Aspirin stood on the coffee table. She cranked the top off the bottle and shook two into my palm. *Take your precious Aspirin and just relax.*

She disappeared into the next room with her travelling case. When she was gone, I shook out two more Aspirin into my mouth, leaning back into the sofa.

I confess a part of me was pleased. I'd felt starved for the kind of light Flossie emanated; she was all clear sunlight where everything else was murky, dark. I put my head against the violet cushions. The electric light shone against the draperies, making the room dreamy, ethereal, and I closed my eyes, just for a moment.

I must have dozed off. When I opened my eyes, the light had changed; the apartment was still and cold. The bottle of Aspirin lay in my lap with the magazine. I listened for the sounds of Flossie puttering about in the kitchen but all was quiet. The air had, somehow, greyed. Something—I cannot explain it—felt so awful just then, so, I don't know, frightening, so empty, that I was afraid to rise from the sofa. I pressed my eyes shut again.

And then all at once Flossie was there, with two steaming mugs on a tray, smelling of cinnamon and green apple.

Silly, she said. *I saw you open your eyes. You can't fool me. You're going to have to sit up here and drink this like a good boy and keep me company.* She stared at me hard, then. *My goodness*, she said, gently touching her fingertips to my temple. *What's happened?*

I scarcely know.

Poor you, she said again.

She sat down on the coffee table, facing me, and gave me a wobbly smile. Then, all at once, she started to cry.

I stared at her, dumbfounded.

What is it? I said. *What's happened?*

She shook her head, fumbled for a tissue in a box on the table, smiling as if she were surprised by it herself, as if it were not her but someone else weeping there.

Something, obviously, I said.

She was crying heavily now, great wracking sobs, and trying to catch her breath as she wept. *I didn't want to tell you, before.*

Tell me what?

She shook her head again.

For heaven's sake.

Helen, she choked out.

What about Helen?

Oh, it's too awful. I can't.

I stifled my growing irritation and poured her out a tumbler of water from the pitcher on the coffee table and had her sit in my place on the sofa and take a few sips and blow her nose.

After a few moments, she said, *I wasn't truthful before. I wasn't truthful at all. I don't like to lie to my friends, but I just couldn't tell you; I just didn't even want to say it.*

Say what, for heaven's sake?

I wasn't in Boston for any silly old convention. I was in Miami.

Indiana.

Yes, Indiana.

All right—

For a funeral. There. I've said it. And I hope you're glad, because I certainly don't feel any better. She began to sob again.

Flossie . . . , I began, after a moment.

It's too terrible, she said through her tears. *I didn't even like her, really. But still, I wouldn't wish it upon anyone, and then me just sitting here like a fool and I didn't even call her parents or, or the police, or anything, just sat here wondering where she'd gone like the idiot that I am. And you were no help, really, telling me not to worry. She's on holiday, you said. She'll be back soon. And all the time I knew, I just knew. Why are you all so stupid that way?*

She's . . . , I began. *But . . . is she dead, then?*

Yes, she's dead, Flossie cried. *For god's sake. That's just what I've been saying. It was . . . oh, Arthor . . . it was . . .*

What?

Suicide.

And she put her head in her lap and sobbed again.

I sat down on the coffee table, astonished.

My god, I said. *She shot herself?*

Flossie raised her reddened eyes and wiped a wrist across her nose. *What? Shot herself? No. Why would you think such a thing?*

I don't know. I just assumed—

I don't see why you'd think that.

Of course not. I don't know why I said it.

I poured her some more water and she pushed it away, and I handed her a dry tissue and pulled a throw blanket from one of the armchairs and covered her and coaxed her to lie down a bit on the sofa. But she began to cry again and I hardly knew what to do with myself. I turned on her radio, softly: that song that seemed to be always on—*Is it true what they say about Dixie? Does the sun really shine all the time?*—brought a renewed bout of sobs, so I turned it off again.

When she had cried herself out and lay silently on the sofa, I said, *But Flossie, why didn't you tell me? In the first place?*

I don't know, she said, staring glassy-eyed at the ceiling. After a while, she said, *I know you think I'm silly, Arthor, and scatterbrained, but I'm not, you know. I feel things, too. I may not be a writer, I may not be so bohemian, like you, I may just be a silly old actress, and not even a very good one, but I have feelings, you know.*

Of course you do.

You seem to think I don't.

Why would you say such a thing?

You seem to have this wrong idea, of who I am, the kind of person, as if you'd already decided . . .

She stared at me a long while, and finally turned her head away. *You treat everyone,* she said quietly, *like a character in one of your stories.*

If only she knew how mistaken she was.

Oh, I don't know, she said then, turning back to me. *Don't pay any attention. I'm just upset about it all. I guess I just didn't want to say it. Didn't want to hear myself saying it.*

Understandable.

And I wasn't very kind about her, was I? I said terrible things. Do you know what I remember about her most? I mean from when I was a girl?

Yes?

Well—she sniffed and dabbed at her nose with a tissue—*I was friends with her sister, Harriet, like I told you. She and Harriet didn't get on very well, and I thought her kind of strange even then, but in a mysterious sort of way, like you do when you're a child. And there was something appealing about that. Do you know what I mean?*

Only too well.

I can't say I liked her, and certainly she wasn't very kind to Harriet. I remember they had some argument once, something silly, about toast, and Helen went after her with a knife, chasing her around the kitchen. It was just a little butter knife and probably harmless, but it was terrifying at the time, and Harriet locked herself in the bathroom, screaming bloody murder, and me just standing there not knowing what on earth I should do. I thought Helen might go after me next, but she didn't. She came back into the kitchen holding that knife and just asked would I like some toast, nice as you please. Of course I said no thank you.

Good thinking.

I know it sounds crazy, but I'd felt, well, almost drawn to her, because of her strangeness. Even though I was afraid of her. Does that make any sense?

In fact, I said, *it makes perfect sense. To me it does.*

Oh, I don't know that I understand it myself. Not then, certainly not now. Back when we were children, Harriet and me, I remember Helen had this bottle, a plain old green glass bottle, a wine bottle or something, and she'd used it to hold candles, all different colours, I guess, so as the candles melted, the wax ran down the outsides of this bottle, making this pattern of all these colours, like . . . I don't know, just layer after layer. I wanted that bottle so badly. And one day while I was alone in their house—I don't know where Harriet had got to—but I was holding that bottle, just admiring it and prying a bit of the wax off with my thumbnail, when I dropped it. At first I thought it hadn't broken and I was so relieved. But then I picked it up and saw that it was only the wax that held it together and it was cracked apart in three big chunks. And do you know what I did?

What?

Nothing. I just left their house and went home. I thought Helen would blame Harriet, which Harriet told me later was just exactly what happened. Harriet said Helen was so angry with her, so upset, and that Helen had wept and wept about that bottle—that's what Harriet said—that Helen seemed herself so broken about it, and said terrible, hurtful things to Harriet, and Harriet said the ugly old thing had probably just toppled onto the floor on its own, but you could see Harriet was upset about it too, upset about whatever it was that Helen had said to her. She never did tell me just what, and I never did set Harriet straight about that. I never did set Helen straight. And then at the funeral, I'd been thinking about that silly old bottle, and do you know I still couldn't tell Harriet the truth. After all this time, and such a, such a terrible tragedy. I still couldn't even confess my own little deception, and I feel doubly horrible about it because now Helen never will know. It's too late.

I'm sure it feels important, I began, *but it could hardly matter, given the circumstances. It probably means more to you than it ever did to either of them. Guilt works that way, you know. It is you who are haunted by it, and not them.*

She seemed comforted by that, and more collected, and certainly more herself. I rose to go, but felt her eyes on me as I opened her door.

You'll feel better about it all in the morning, I said, in the way of things. I felt suddenly weary, and immensely sad. But as I made my way up the stairs, I heard her come out and follow me up to the landing. I turned again to her.

She was staring up at me, imploringly. The way the shadows fell across her face, I could not see her eyes, as if they were black holes there, empty. She rubbed her arms and I had an inkling, a premonition, of exactly what she was about to say next.

Arthor, she began, *I just, please. I don't want to be alone down there. It's just, it's too . . .*

I did not know what to say.

Oh, she said unhappily. She turned away. *I've been a terrible bother.*

Of course not, I said, coming back down the stairs. *I'm just tired. I need to go back upstairs and get some sleep. And work. I'm falling far behind. You must understand.*

Oh, please, she said suddenly, and grasped my sleeve. *Please don't leave me in that horrible apartment . . . with all of her . . . things, just sitting there. I've nowhere to go. You could bring your work down, or whatever you have to do, and sit in the armchair, and I'll just lie there quietly. I won't bother you, I promise. Please.*

The streetlight from the window fell in a soft outline along her cheek.

It could not possibly be prudent. I looked again at Flossie, so broken and so alone, the two of us, there on that grim landing while the darkness moved and moved around us.

God help me, what else was I to do?

I HADN'T INTENDED to fall asleep there. When next I opened my eyes, my back ached and my neck was in knots, and the windows were all dark, though whether it was late evening or the middle of the night or just before dawn, I had no idea. All the lights in Flossie's apartment blazed. But she was not there. I rose hastily and looked about the apartment, but all the rooms were empty and I felt a terrible, cold sinking, a memory creeping upon me.

I went out to the foyer, dark, though a light shone out from the top of the staircase, where my apartment door stood open. I took the stairs two at a time.

The door at the end of the hall—the door into my employer's study—stood open also and I moved toward it as in a dream. Flossie was there, standing in the middle of the room, her arms at her sides, looking vaguely disappointed.

She turned to me as I came in behind her. I looked around, but there was no one else. My employer was gone.

Forgive me, Flossie said, looking genuinely sorry. *I thought you'd been hiding something.*

I LEFT HER in her apartment. She did not try to stop me, try to make me stay. She thought I was angry; I could see that. I wasn't.

All I could think: Where had he gone?

On the landing I was met again by that oppressive cloud, as if it had been waiting for me. And I wondered if it had been there all along, that presence, what I had come to think of as the child, that it had never left at all. I felt it move with me up the stairs. It is amazing what we can allow ourselves to become used to, if necessary. It makes me think we must be able to withstand anything, if we only set our minds to it.

No, I do not mean that. I do not mean anything.

2

WE WENT OUT TOGETHER, heavily, late the next after-noon, Flossie and I. I could not be angry with her, was not. She did not want to be alone. Neither did I. I had spent the night awake, wondering. Twice, I had begun wording a telegram to Jane, warning her not to come, and twice I had thrown it away. There was something inevitable in her arrival, as there was something inevitable in my employer's absence. I could not make sense of it, and yet there was something fitting. Something right.

And then, if I were to rein my imagination in, it was not impossible he was simply feeling better, had gone out. Not impossible at all.

I caught Flossie looking at me sadly. She noticed and slipped an arm through mine as we walked. I was at once defensive against the gesture and grateful. It is ever thus in matters of intimacy.

We stopped in a little café on Prospect, where Flossie puzzled over the menu a long while, then picked at an egg salad, claiming she wasn't all that hungry after all. I looked out the café window. It was the magic hour, when shadows began to lengthen and the light took on a gilded, antique quality. The edges of buildings, trees, pedestrians sharpened, colours saturated, as if the ordinary and real had intensified into the extraordinary through a simple angle of light.

We stepped out into it, back on the street, where, coming toward us from the direction of Sixty-Six, was the man Baxter. He had his boy with him, James.

Good evening, I said.

The man looked up. He seemed surprised to see us there.

Evening, he agreed.

Good evening, James, I said.

The boy looked pleased that I'd remembered him. He wore no scarf but shouldered the heavy old overcoat nevertheless, unbuttoned a little at the neck. An odd look crossed the man Baxter's face and I recalled our last meeting. What the boy had said.

Bit of a hurry, Baxter said. *Good evening to you.*

And he propelled the boy along down the street. But the child looked back at me over his shoulder, with that pale, disconcerting gaze.

Well, that was rude, Flossie said.

He isn't the friendliest sort.

Still, a little common courtesy.

Country people, I said, by way of explanation.

I am country people, Flossie said, rather heatedly, *and I can tell you we aren't like that.*

Hard times, then. It tends to take the shine out of people.

I suppose. Still.

You pretty women are all the same, I said. *You don't like to be ignored. You needn't take it so personally.*

You think I'm pretty?

You know you are.

Is that so wrong? To know you're pretty?

But I was no longer listening. We had stopped in the shadow of the Van Wickle Gates, closed and locked, and I pulled away from Flossie and stepped up to the gleaming brass plate there, astonished at my reflection, warped and gilded. I would not have known myself. I was aware, of course, that I'd lost a good deal of weight, but I had not imagined my face so drawn and gaunt. My beard had grown in and there was a strained look about the mouth I did not recognize. I rubbed a sleeve against the brass to sharpen my reflection, but it merely wavered there, liquid, shimmering.

Well, Arthor? Flossie said softly, coming up behind me. She laid a hand on my shoulder. *Where are we going?*

The elms in the evening light had taken on a fuzzy, ghostly look.

Angell Street, I said abruptly. I said it without thinking. I did not turn around, and only after I had said it did I realize that was exactly where I did not want to go, and where I had been meaning to go all along.

WE WALKED THE LONG, wearying length of Angell Street as if in a dream, without speaking, without touching, the narrow street leading us farther out, until the city began to creep into farmland. I clenched the chunk of gravestone in my overcoat pocket, turning and turning it in my hand. At last we came in sight of the house. I knew it at once, without having to check the address. It could have been none other, looming up over the street, mythical and grand. Something in me lurched painfully and turned over.

Goodness, Flossie breathed.

It was a grey, impassive clapboard, set just back from the street on a high green terrace, handsomely shuttered, three storeys, with dormers and cupolas just beginning to sag with the weight of its history. I did not like the look of it, though I could not say why. Something about it was unsettling, though it was not extraordinary in any other way. The gabled front veranda was flanked by witch hazel, bare and spidering upward, where a handful of last autumn's leaves still clung, withered and rattling drily. From the low rise where we stood, I could see, behind the house, a sprawling carriage house or horse barn, and sheds and a garden, a marble fountain dead at the yard's heart. There was a lonely quality to the place, surrounded by willows and lawns and, away off to the edge, thick woods darkened already by the coming evening. It seemed the sort of place stumbled upon in a dream; there was a stillness about it, as if long abandoned. It occurred to me, then, I could hear no birds. Angell Street itself was silent. No automobile passed. Dogs did not bark.

It's so quiet, Flossie said.

I turned back to the house. The windows were all dark, as if they held already the coming night. The curtains were pulled open to the evening, and I thought I saw, just for an instant, someone stir there at an upper window.

Flossie said, *There's something kind of . . . lost about it, isn't there.* Her voice sounded strange, too, in the empty street, as if she were speaking from far away.

I imagine these lots used to be much bigger. You can see those newer houses now between the old mansions. I bet they were all parcelled off some time ago.

A breeze stirred in the witch hazel; a rasping sound, as of a voice long out of use.

Finally Flossie said, *Aren't we going inside?*

Just then, we heard the slow creak of a screen door opening, and a teenage boy in a neat collared shirt stepped out onto the verandah. He paused there, back under the eaves, watching us.

Wait here, I said. And before Flossie could object, I approached the wrought iron gate and laid my hands upon the cold metal. It creaked under my hands and I steadied it.

We've got no work, the boy called.

Forgive me, I called back, and looked down the empty street. *I wonder if I might have a word?*

The boy looked uncomfortable. He came forward a bit, out of the shadows.

I take it you live here, I said, *that your family does.*

The boy looked back at the house over his shoulder, then came reluctantly down off the verandah. He hesitated on the cracked sidewalk, as if he would go back.

I'm awfully sorry to trouble you. It's a matter of some importance.

He came forward, down the walk, and met me at the gate. His Adam's apple bobbed above his shirt collar.

Honestly, I wish you folks wouldn't keep coming around here. My father's about fed up, I don't mind telling you, and it makes Mother awfully nervous.

I'm not begging for work, I said. *I'm here—*

Oh, I know what you're here for, then. Same as all the rest. It's only ever one of two reasons. Like I said, my folks are about fed up with all of you.

There've been others?

Gosh, all the time.

But what do they want?

Same as you, I guess. One gal even took pictures.

Of what?

Why, the house, I suppose. I don't understand it. I've never even heard of the fellow.

The fellow?

The one who used to live here, or his mother did, or his family, or I don't even know. Some writer. I don't go in for any of that stuff.

What stuff?

He shrugged. *Ghost stories, or whatever. My sister's crazy for it. She gets this magazine, with these terrible stories. She's read some of them to me. I don't much care for them myself. Covers are all right. But if Mother catches her with them, I tell you.*

He stopped, then, straightened and lifted his chin.

Anyhow, you're lucky they aren't home right now, my folks, or you'd get an earful. I'm supposed to tell you to move on and not come around here anymore. You'd best do it.

Forgive me, I said. *But you misunderstand. I'm not a fan.*

No?

In fact, I'm a relative. A distant relation.

The boy stuck his hands in his pockets.

And I'm sorry to trouble you, but my aunt is quite ill. She grew up here, you know, and she was hoping I'd come have a look around for her, give her word of the old place.

Your aunt?

That's right.

What's her name?

Phillips. Annie Phillips.

The boy shrugged.

She's very unwell. Dying, actually. I'd like to bring her some word.

You can't come in the house, the boy said, frowning.

No, no, of course not.

I'd get a hiding, sure enough.

No doubt, I agreed, *no doubt. But I wonder, would you mind if I just have a quick walk about the place?*

The boy looked doubtful. *I don't think you ought, I'm just on my way out.*

My aunt would be ever so grateful, I said. *I don't know how long she has and, well, she may never have the chance to come back and see the place.*

The boy bit his lip. *I don't think so. My folks are up in Philadelphia.*

I wouldn't dream of asking to come inside the house. Just wanted a stroll about the grounds.

I don't know.

You say you're alone here?

The boy looked at me sharply, suspiciously. *I didn't say that.*

Your folks are in Philadelphia, you mentioned. I'm from near Philadelphia myself.

If you say so.

I shook my head sadly. *Well,* I said, *thanks. I'll, well, I'll tell my aunt the old place is still here, anyway. I guess that'll have to be enough.*

The boy chewed his lip. Then, in a quick movement, he unlatched the gate and, for a moment, I thought he'd changed his mind. But then he just stepped through and latched it behind him.

I'm awfully sorry, he said. *Maybe you could come back next week, when my folks are home.*

But—

I've got to go.

One thing more, I said and the boy turned. *There wasn't an older man here today? Sickly, gaunt?*

The boy just frowned at me. It occurred to me, then, that Flossie might hold more sway with him.

Might I just introduce my friend, and I turned to indicate Flossie waiting on the street behind me.

The boy looked over my shoulder at the empty street.

What friend? he said.

I FOUND FLOSSIE on the other side of a glossy hedge, seated on a low rock wall covered in moss. The shadows fell all around her. She'd slipped off her shoes and was massaging her stockinged feet.

What on earth, I said.

Well, you left me standing there so long, she accused.

It was not five minutes.

Well, I'm very tired, she said petulantly. *And these shoes are brand new and pinch my feet something terrible.*

Well, why did you wear them?

She shot me an irritated glance. *Honestly, Arthor, do you know nothing?*

I gave her my hand. *Come on, then.*

She slipped back into her shoes, making terrible grimaces. *Are we going back now?*

Not yet, I said. I peered out into the street to make sure the boy had gone. Then I opened the wrought iron gate with a slow, rusted creak that seemed to float out into the silent street.

Arthor P. Crandle, Flossie said in mock surprise. *Breaking the rules?*

I sighed.

How fun, she said.

I held the gate open for her, then latched it again behind us.

The sun was setting just beyond the woods which lay in a long line blackly at the edge of the lawn. I recalled my employer's story, his grandfather's story, the grave there. The shadow of the house was long and dark and we stepped into it. Flossie shivered and rubbed her arms as we passed in front of the verandah.

It is something, she said. *Imagine living in a house like that. It makes me just want to put on a long gown, you know, with a scandalously low back, like Ginger Rogers, and stand on the verandah sipping a pink gin. Oh, look, a fountain. Honestly, Arthor, won't you slow down?*

She had stopped beside the stone fountain just off the verandah. It was cracked and covered in bird droppings, its basin filled with black leaves. I thought I saw something scurry there.

Flossie laid a hand on the cold stone.

What a shame, she said. *Imagine this in its day. Has your aunt ever spoken about it? I bet it was something. That's where I would have been as a girl, anyway, sitting in the sun here on a summer's day, imagining all the possibilities.*

Which is exactly, I said, *what you should do.*

What?

Sit here and rest. Look, here's a lovely spot.

But it's dirty, she said. *And cold.*

I stripped off my overcoat and draped it over the fountain's edge.

There you are, I said. *It's a shabby old thing anyway. Rest your feet and daydream all you like, and I won't be a moment.*

Where are you going?

Just to poke around a bit, out back.

What for?

I shrugged. *Just curious.*

She bit her lip.

What is it? I said, growing impatient.

Is it true what you said?

What did I say?

About your aunt? That she is dying?

I laughed irritably. *Of course not.*

She looked at me reproachfully.

What else was I to do, for heaven's sake?

She lifted her shoulders.

Listen, I said, *just wait here a minute. I won't be long.*

I began to cross the lawn. The shadows had spread out fully across the ground, almost touching.

It'll be dark soon, she called after me.

I'm quite aware, I called back without turning.

Arthor? she called.

I stopped, exasperated, and half turned. The lawn was vast between us. She looked small, pale there in the shadow of the big house.

What time does the streetcar stop running? I don't want to walk all that way back.

I'll be just a moment. I turned away from her.

It's an awfully long way. Arthor?

But I was hardly listening. My blood had turned cold. That presence, that feeling from Sixty-Six, was there with me. My skin crawled. I lifted my eyes toward the dark line of woods beyond the horse barn. A glimpse of something, maybe, there between the branches, a quick shifting, and then it was gone.

I CAME AROUND THE SIDE of the carriage house in dread, past rusting rakes and shovels and burlap sacking and old buckets, toward the woods. I almost expected to see the child there, waiting.

But there was only the overgrown grass and the darkening woods beyond, the black tangle of branches. I could feel the cold damp air spreading out toward me, could smell the marshy, black rot stench of it. The sun was down now, the sky tinged barely pink above the black trees knifing upward. The grasses hushed and parted before me as I passed through. The marshy earth, sucking beneath my feet, seeped up water like cold steeped tea into my shoes.

Another quick movement: it could have been the black wings of a crow, so faint was the stirring in the gathered darkness there, or a conjuring of my own imagination. But I knew it was the child, leading me. I ran, stumbling through the tangled grasses.

And then it happened. I recalled the feel of those small hands on my back, and all at once, again, I was falling. I hit the earth, the wind knocked out of me, the sky gilded pink above and already fading, too beautiful to last.

THERE IT WAS.

Not two feet from my upturned hand. Overgrown with moss, long grasses, brambles. I would not have found it had it not, yes, found me. Had the child not led me. I pulled myself to my knees. I could feel the pulse in my head, throbbing. There was a gash in my ankle, the blood welling up sticky and bright, and I pressed a muddy palm against it as I clawed the weeds away. I rubbed the top of the stone with my shirt sleeve. The moss was slippery, wet, and came away easily, like a skin on milk. *Sarah Susan Phillips.* Etched rudely into the stone.

There, where I knew it would be, was the chip in the corner. I pulled the chunk of stone from my pocket. It fit. Exactly where it was supposed to. I almost wept.

Arthor?

I turned to see Flossie standing a few feet away at the edge of the grass. She held my overcoat before her, as if to hand it to me or fend me off. She had an odd look on her face.

What are you doing? she said.

Go back, I said, waving at her, lightly I hoped. *Go back; I won't be a moment.*

You've blood on your sleeve.

Blood?

She glanced behind her at the great house there on the rise, looking, darkened, down upon us.

Arthor, she said, hugging herself, *you're scaring me.*

Don't be silly. I've only cut myself on this stone.

I saw you go down.

That's right. I've just scraped my ankle a little. It's nothing. Go on. I'll be right there.

But she did not budge. As I knew she would not.

I don't want to go back there.

Don't be silly.

I have a bad feeling.

Flossie—

I'm not stupid, Arthor, in spite of what you may think. I can see quite clearly you're up to something, and if you don't tell me right now what it is, I'm going back to the street and calling for that boy. I'm scared.

He's not home, I said. I may even have laughed.

You're acting crazy, she said.

I shook my head. The darkness fell all around us. It fell and fell.

Flossie, I said. *Listen. All right? I'll tell you. It's probably nonsense, but there's this, this family lore, you know, in his—my aunt's family, about this silver mirror, or a pier glass, he said—*

Pier glass? Who said?

Buried here on the property. It's probably nothing. I thought myself it was nonsense. But I've only just now found the spot.

She stepped a few paces into the long grasses, then stopped.

Arthor, she said, *it looks like . . . a grave. Sarah Susan Phillips?*

It isn't, I said. *It isn't. She isn't buried here.*

How do you know that?

Because she's in Swan Point Cemetery, in the Phillips family plot, with the rest of them.

Them?

Us, I mean. The Phillipses. Lovecrafts.

Great god.

Flossie bit her lip, shivered.

She's the one who buried it. She's been dead fifteen years. But this, I said, running a hand across the stone, *is much older. It looks to be some fifty years at least. Doesn't it? Which would be right. That's when she was supposed to have done it.*

Flossie came closer, the long grasses shushing as she passed through. She knelt down beside me in the marshy earth.

Do you really think something's buried here?

There's a whole story about it. I can't tell you now. I leaned toward her. *Flossie, I know it seems crazy.*

She frowned but was curious too, I could tell.

Finding a flat, sharp stone, I dug a little hollow beneath one corner.

If I can get my fingers under, I said, digging my fingers into the soil, *and pry it up, and then if you can get your hands in, we'll just turn it over. There*, I said, lifting the corner up.

It wasn't as deep, or as heavy, as I'd thought. Flossie hoisted the stone over and we flipped it onto the grass. It broke into three pieces.

I ran my fingers over a black mulched hollow where the stone had been. It was latticed with the white roots of weeds, ghostly and beautiful in the dusklight.

It's getting dark, Flossie said.

I know.

All at once she was on her feet, her dress clinging muddily to her knees.

I know where there's a spade, she said. And she was off across the field toward the horse barn before I could stop her.

THE WOODEN HANDLE of the spade was worn and smooth in my palms. Flossie's face hovered next to mine, her hot breath on my neck.

Are you sure about this? I said. For now that we'd come this far, I had doubts. Looking under a stone was one thing. Digging into someone else's property—a grave, even a fake grave—was quite another.

There was a smear of dirt across Flossie's mouth. Her intensity, her excitement, was intoxicating. Her eyes glistened blackly in the half light. There was a pause, as if everything in that instant stopped, and then her lips were on mine, and they were cool and soft. I thought I'd never felt anything softer. She pulled her head away and looked straight into my eyes. I became aware all at once of the sweet spring smell of the night and the grass, the crickets, the stars wheeling over us, the sharp bite of her lipstick.

Arthor, she said, *hurry.*

I stabbed at the muck. The soil was soft and rich and wet as I sloughed it out into the grass. Not a foot down, the spade struck something solid. Flossie and I looked at each other. She grabbed my arm.

It may just be a rock, I warned.

It won't, she said. *It won't be. Hurry, we're losing the light.*

I dug all around the hard place, then got down on my hands and knees and scrabbled the loose earth away.

It's a box, I said. *My god. Flossie. There's really something here.*

Get it out, she said.

I pried the box up out of the earth with a sucking, wet

sound and sat back on my haunches, breathless. I put the box down on the grass between us and smeared the mud and dirt away with my palms. It was wooden and looked as if, at one time, it had been expensive. There was something engraved on the lid, but it was so clogged with dirt we could not make it out in the dim light.

It's a silverware box, Flossie said. *Like people keep their good silver in, so the air won't tarnish it.*

It's forks and knives?

I don't know. It would be, it could be, worth a good deal. Maybe. I don't know. But it could be anything in there. Anything.

I sat looking at it.

I can't, I said.

Her face was lost to me now in the dusk.

What do you mean?

I don't know. It feels . . . something's wrong.

She looked over her shoulder at the great house.

Oh my god, she said, grabbing my sleeve, *someone's coming.*

The distant swing of a torch moved across the grasses at the edge of the house, back and forth, someone walking this way.

Arthor, she said.

I can't, I said. *Something's wrong.*

Hello? came the voice, calling out across the field. *Who's out there?*

Flossie hissed, *For god's sake, Arthor*, and reaching out, she grasped the tarnished clasp and flipped the lid open.

We sat there, at first, not able to take it in, to understand quite what it was we were looking at in the falling darkness.

There, impossibly small and nestled in a bed of what must once have been a deep blue velvet, curled the white bones of an infant, badly deformed.

3

ALL ALONG THE STREETCAR ride back down Butler Avenue, Flossie sat turned from me with her head in her hands, weeping. We were the only ones on the car at that hour and I was glad of it.

The conductor looked at me strangely from beneath his cap as we were disembarking. *All right?* he said to me.

She will be, I said.

He frowned at me deeply before pulling away.

I took her arm and guided her back up College Street in the darkness, the streetlight pooling out beside us on the cobblestones, past the John Hay Library, and in through the front door of Sixty-Six. I saw her inside her apartment.

You'll want to wash up, I said, and when she looked at me mournfully, questioningly, I said, *I'll wait*.

The water ran a long time in the next room, and I sat with every light I could find burning to help dispel that overwhelming feeling of darkness, of heaviness, that had weighed upon me since Angell Street. I did not want to think about that old mahogany box. Did not want to think about what we had disturbed. I recalled us there in the darkness, putting the box back hastily and pressing the soil over it again with our palms and shoving the broken stone back in its place, with my own chunk of gravestone there where it belonged, before ducking off into the woods as the torchlight neared, someone calling out at us even as we fled. Then how we waited, huddling there in the woods, shivering, until all was, again, darkness. Sitting there in Flossie's apartment, looking at my soiled hands, I almost wept myself.

Flossie emerged finally with her wet hair combed back from a face pink and raw with scrubbing. She wore that peacock blue dressing gown, but all the charm had gone out of it.

Do you want coffee? she said flatly.

I shook my head.

She took the violet throw and curled up into herself in the armchair by the window, looking out at the streetlights and the night.

Finally, she said, *Why, Arthor?*

After a long time, I said, *I don't know.*

Will you stay?

I nodded. I did not want to be alone upstairs any more than she wanted to be alone downstairs. And I didn't see why either of us should be.

I just need some air, I said.

I stepped outside and stood in the spring darkness. The air was fresh, clean. The stars blinked through the bare limbs like fireflies, coldly. The sky looked closer than I'd ever seen it. The night was full. I stepped out into the lane and looked up at Sixty-Six. The second and third floors were, as always, dark. Light shone out from Flossie's apartment, and I could see in through the living room window, to the armchair. Flossie was not there. I felt a terrible loneliness, an emptiness. How saddened I would be when we could no longer be friends.

I went back inside and entered her apartment, closing the door behind me.

To my surprise, Flossie was there in the chair, with her forehead against the window, just as I had left her.

Where did you go? I said.

Nowhere, she said, sadly. *I've been here the whole time.*

MUCH LATER, WHEN I OPENED my eyes, I was stretched out on the sofa next to Flossie. All the lights blazed and she lay there dead to the world, covered in the violet blanket that she clutched bunched up under her chin like a child. Her back was to me and her yellow hair had fallen across her face, so that I could not see it.

I eased myself from the sofa and paused there a moment. I cannot explain it, but I had in that moment such a feeling of dread and horror. There was something so terrible in her stillness and in that ordinary detail, that Flossie in that moment did not have a face.

4

I PULLED MYSELF from the bath and let the filthy water drain away. My ankle throbbed and I doused it with antiseptic and taped it over with a bandage. It probably needed stitching, but it was, at any rate, too late for that now. I went upstairs and dressed and sat a long while thinking. Then I descended to the front hall. I paused outside his study. I considered knocking but did not. I was afraid to find him still not returned.

The light, of course, still shone from beneath the door. I hardly need mention it.

AT BUTLER, I SAT on the bench where my employer had used to sit with his mother. I had a kind of half idea I might find him there. But, of course, there was no one. I sat in the chill wind, watching the ducks on the river, moving between the brown reeds at the water's edge. So peaceful, they seemed.

I thought it was you, came a voice behind me.

I turned to see the plump, pleasant nurse from my first visit.

Iris, I said.

Ivy, she corrected.

She indicated the bench and I slid over to make room for her.

Her cheeks were pink from the wind and she blinked water from her eyes, seemed to wait for me to say something, though it was she who had sought me out and not the other way around.

I thought the other day, I said, *perhaps you didn't recognize me. In the hallway.*

She seemed embarrassed. *I recognized you*, she said. *It's just Dr. Tinseley. He's funny about things.*

Funny how?

A psychiatrist. They have a certain interest invested in . . .

Invested in what?

She shook her head, dismissing the matter.

Then she said, *I saw you afterward, you know. I walk this way to work and back, every day.*

Saw me where?

In the cemetery. In Swan Point. I walk there myself sometimes. It's so beautiful. I think it's my favourite place in Providence.

It is indeed beautiful.

After a long moment, she said, *I'm sorry, I don't mean to be personal, but . . .*

Yes?

Did you find it, then, she said, nodding in the direction of the cemetery, *in there? Did you find what you were looking for?*

What makes you think I was looking for something?

She stared out over the river. *You had that air about you, you know, that people have. Everyone does. No matter how many times they've been there, it's like each time is the first. They don't know where to go, just wander around awhile, searching.* She turned to me again. *Did you find it?*

I think so, I said. *But you misunderstand. What I sought, I mean.*

She looked around a bit, the wind blowing her hair across her broad face. She nodded, slowly. *You know, I don't agree,* she said, finally, *with the way they do some things. At Butler. I know I'm new, and maybe I'll get used to it. I don't know. I hope I won't. It isn't right,* she said. And her eyes teared up again and she wiped them. *This rotten wind,* she said.

I pulled a tissue from my overcoat and handed it to her. *It must be difficult,* I said.

She nodded, blew her nose. Then she said, *Do you know there's children buried here, in the woods?*

I felt a shock of alarm. It could not be mere coincidence. But she couldn't possibly, I told myself. I looked toward the cemetery.

Not there, she said. *I mean here. Right beneath our feet probably.*

I beg your pardon?

Not children, she said. *Babies. Stillborns, they call them, but they weren't, not all of them, not always. We dug a garden last week in back, for the patients, you know, as a kind of therapy, so they can plant it when the weather warms.* She shook her head, looked away, then back at me. *There were bones. The tiniest little bones. They push through sometimes in the springtime, between the trees, I'm told, after the frost is gone. Like violets.*

How awful, I said.

The women, sometimes they're pregnant when they get here. But sometimes, she said, *they aren't. The nurses, they used to help them. With the babies. You understand?*

I'm not sure I do.

One of the nurses said Sister Clementine . . . But then she buttoned her lip and it seemed she would say no more.

Sister Clementine?

She looked up quickly at the asylum, then said, all in a rush, *I really have to go. I just wanted you to know . . .*

Know what?

That I don't think it's right. Dr. Tinseley. I've seen him. He's like a cat with a bird.

I WAITED AT THE TRAIN station for an hour and Jane was not there. I wondered if perhaps there had been an error on her end; perhaps she had miswritten the information, or missed her train in Rochester. I waited until past dinnertime, the ticket seller casting me suspicious glances over his soup.

Finally, I rose and approached him.

Yes? he said, wiping his chin.

Is there another train from Rochester today?

He pointed at the schedule with a dripping spoon.

Last train from Rochester came in at 6:10.

Yes, I see that. But I'm wondering if maybe there isn't some other train, perhaps not up there, a late train.

Yeah, he said, *sure, like, say, a ghost train, maybe?*

I was thinking more along the lines of an unscheduled—

No such thing as an unscheduled train.

So there is no other—

Last train from Rochester came in at 6:10. On schedule. Like *the sign says.*

At a loss, I walked back to the post office and sent Jane a wire asking her to please send word immediately. I waited for a reply and, when none came, I sent a second. But there was nothing. When the clerk indicated he was about to close for the day, I had no choice but to leave.

I stepped out into the darkening street. There, not half a block away, disappearing into a narrow alley between the hedges, was a man I could have sworn was my employer, emaciated, stooped, slowly wheeling, of all things, a red bicycle. I called out as I ran across the grass and into the alley, hollering, yes, like a madman.

The man heard me and looked up, looked to his left and right, and then finally behind him. His whiskers were long and turned up at the corners, like a Civil War general. A bright bow tie sat tight beneath his chin.

I'm sorry, I said, stopping abruptly. *I thought you were* *someone else.*

Be off with you, he said. *I'm not in the custom of giving* *handouts.* He turned, muttered something about vagrants, and was gone.

I RETURNED, SLOWLY, to Sixty-Six. I felt like a man twice my age. And felt, too, there was still some final thing, one last discovery. I stopped, stood in the lane, staring up. Something looked different.

Then it struck me: a light shone clearly from the kitchen window, where I had left no light burning.

SHE WAS SEATED at the kitchen table with her back to me, though she rose slowly, carefully, when I came in, and turned to face me in the doorway. She wore a loose, old-fashioned floral blouse pinned at the collar with a pearl brooch and tucked into the waistband of her skirt. Her hair, an iron grey, was pulled back from a face that had likely never been beautiful and was now further ravaged by age and illness. Her dark eyes, nevertheless, were sharp, took me in at a glance. It could be no one else. My employer's aunt. Annie Phillips.

Allow me to introduce myself, I said, stepping forward.

No need, she said, waving weakly, *no need*. She sat again and gestured to the other chair, and I took it.

Across the table she seemed, upon second glance, younger than I had thought; her illness had taken its toll. She held herself with the bearing of one who has been long ill. When she moved, she winced visibly. Her eyes, though, were remarkable: bright, intelligent.

Can I get you anything? I offered. *Tea?*

She shook her head.

I was not expecting you so soon, I said. *Not until the end of next week, at the earliest.*

I came home early, she said. *I thought it necessary.*

I hope not on my account.

She looked at me sharply again, seemed about to say something, then changed her mind.

You've been feeding the cats, she said.

I hope that's all right. I've been rather short on instructions here. Your nephew himself has been quite unwell, I'm afraid. I'm sure he'll be only too glad of your return. I was surprised, yesterday, to find him gone out. I would have thought he was hardly up to it. I confess I've been quite worried . . .

She looked pained again and, lifting a hand to her ribs, looked away.

Are you all right? I said. *Is there nothing I can get for you?*

But she just waved me away and rose slowly, painfully.

I'm very tired, she said.

In the doorway, she turned and looked at me again with a curious intensity. *Good night, then*, she said.

I TOSSED AND TURNED and could not get comfortable. It felt strange, knowing the aunt was there in the house too, now, though I don't know why it should have.

In the morning, I rose bleary and clogged from another night of bad dreams, my body sore and sluggish from the abuse I'd suffered while being propelled by winged creatures out into the soulless atmosphere above the city. I was scarcely awake, and aching, and in need of a drink of water, when I fumbled my way down to the bathroom and pushed open the door.

She was naked from the waist up, a wet cloth in one hand, the other arm raised above her head as if in a balletic pose. Her old woman skin hung loose there, like a slack purse of flesh. And on her withered chest, where her left breast should have been, a long, ugly slash, curved like a sickle, raw and crusted over with dried blood.

She cried out—I may have done so as well—and dropped her arm in pain, and I yanked the door shut, so hard it rattled on its hinges, echoing through the quiet house, ricocheting around in the stairwell. I fled to my room, horrified, horrified at what I should never have seen.

I SOMETIMES WONDER where the flesh goes.

Ash does not answer, nor the dust.

We grow old, and the flesh, too, begins to reach earthward, searching or giving up. The soul, for me, is not the question. It is the flesh. All that blood. Our hearts. All the pains and aches and bruises. The feel of one's own skin. All the tactile memories held fast in the palms.

Where do they go?

SHE WAS IN THE KITCHEN, wiping the counters slowly. Her pained movements made sense to me now.

Good morning, she said when I entered. It seemed more of a question. She did not look at me. I felt grateful.

Forgive me, I began, but she raised a hand.

Please.

I nodded.

After a moment, she said, formally, *I have spoken with Dr. Tinseley.*

Tinseley?

From Butler. I understand you've been to see him.

I thought I detected a note of anger in her tone.

Yes.

She waited for me to say more. How could I?

Finally she said, tightly, *I'm so glad you've spoken with him. He's very good that way. Very good to speak with.*

I agreed that he was. Yet I was puzzled by the odd tone of her voice.

He says you're welcome anytime. He said you had a very good conversation.

I nodded, considering the matter. It seemed as appropriate a time as any.

As to your sister, I began.

The aunt looked at me sharply. She waited.

When I said nothing further, she said, *She is dead, yes. Is that what you mean to say?*

I nodded. But there was something yet more.

I realize, I said, *this is none of my concern. That this is terribly personal, but I wondered . . .* I hesitated. *Did she . . . had she ever had . . . other children?*

Did Dr. Tinseley tell you this?

Again I hesitated. *Yes*, I finally said.

The aunt turned away again. The cloth moved back and forth across the counters, steadily. I thought she had finished with me. That, surely, I had offended her.

Some things are best left in the past, she said, without turning around. *She was only a girl herself.*

So it's true.

Then he surely told you it was terribly deformed. She was never the same, afterward. Even after she married. She was never right again.

What happened to it?

It died, she said shortly. She resumed her slow wiping. *But you don't understand. It could never have lived.*

I sat there, uncertain how to take her words.

The important thing, she said fiercely, turning to me again, *the thing to remember, is that she was never the same. One cannot take to heart things said by*—she hesitated—*those who are not right in their own heads. In their own hearts.*

I understood. I thought I did. We stayed that way a long while. Finally she pulled the kettle from the drawer beneath the range and filled it at the spitting sink and put it on the stove. The blue flame gasped into life.

Outside the window, the cats sunned themselves on the shed roof. The silver tabby was there. The trees had begun to bud. A forsythia burst yellow against the stone wall. And beyond, the boy James, in his shirt sleeves, snaked a branch through the grass for one of the cats. Laughing, laughing, as if all was—as if all could be—set right again. As if he were, just then, outside his house in the country with a red barn open to the sunlight and his father in the fields and his mother cooking their breakfast at the little white range in their kitchen, ordinary, perfect.

When, I wondered, had spring come?

Will you have tea? the aunt asked.

Thank you, no.

It seemed as good a time as any to mention the matter of payment.

She moved slowly out to the hall and came back with a black patent purse, which she set on the table, pulling from it a generous handful of bills, which, to my astonishment, she did not bother to count, but handed to me in its entirety.

I hope this will cover things, she said, *for the time being. You will let me know, of course, when you require more.*

I scarcely knew what to say. I thanked her and pocketed the bills.

Will you eat something before you go? she asked over her shoulder.

I'm not terribly hungry, thank you.

She nodded, as if she'd expected as much, then went back to her slow wiping. She did not look at me again.

ON MY WAY OUT, I stopped in astonishment at Flossie's door: the locks hung loose and undone, the door standing slightly ajar. I knocked anyway, and when no answer came, opened the door a little and called inside, reminded of my arrival at the house only a little more than a week ago. My god, how fast it had gone. No answer came and so I stepped inside.

I stood a moment, perplexed. Gone were the violet cushions and sheer draperies and thick white rug. Gone were the bottles of nail polish scattered about the coffee table, and the magazines with their broken spines, and the blue china cups of tea half finished. Gone were the bouquets of white chrysanthemums. The ferns stood again in their stead, but were dried and crumbling at the touch. On the mantel sat the marble horse.

I bent and brushed a hand across the coffee table, leaving a broad, clear streak in the heavy dust, the dust of months. I wiped my hand on my trousers.

At a loss, I sat down on the sofa, as I had used to, and waited. I waited until the light faded and the room was dark all around me and the street lights came on, shining but dim through the heavy draperies.

I might have slept. I wasn't certain. When I opened my eyes, it was with the sense of a great deal of time having passed, and someone leaning over me in the half-light.

Howard, she said. *I thought I might find you here.*

She moved slowly, painfully, out of the apartment and up the creaking stairs and I followed.

I've made us tea, she said.

I stood in the front hall, watching her. The emerald lamp was lit at my elbow.

Then I remembered. *I must check the post*, I said.

What for?

I'm expecting a wire, or a letter at least, from my wife. But it sounded wrong.

From Sonia? Why on earth?

From Jane, I said.

She turned away.

I've made tea, she said again, flatly, and gestured toward the kitchen. She looked very tired. *Come,* she said. *You'll feel better.*

I almost did. I almost followed her to the kitchen and sat and drank tea and ate. It would have been so easy. Instead I turned and walked to the study door. I had an overwhelming sense of déjà vu. I heard the aunt come to the kitchen doorway and stand watching me. I reached out and grasped the latch. I turned to look at her. She seemed a bit funny around the mouth and eyes, a bit pinched.

Imagination, she said, *is a double-edged sword.*

As before, the latch clicked, and then the door was open and I looked in again upon the lighted room, the mystery, the heart of all my days.

And I went in.

═══

I DREAMED I WENT to Angell Street again.

All the lights blazed out from the windows there, as if for a party, falling yellow on the walk and on the grass and on the fountain trickling musically into the night. There were fireflies in the woods and they glittered faintly, floated up and up, cold stars against the blackened aether. Then the woods darkened, and the lights in the great house went out, one by one, in every window, and I was being led by the hand through its rooms, slowly, until my fear was gone. How easy to hide oneself there. And, hidden, to lose oneself.

But within all darkness is the possibility of light.

Providence, tonight, is lightless. All down College Street the old houses turn inward. Beyond the observatory, Butler Hospital lies like a dead star, consuming its own darkness. The moon is not yet risen, the stars still dark, though the river is there, winding its black way through the sleeping city.

Time is short. The night falls and falls.

I ask you: How much loss can we be made to bear?

ACKNOWLEDGEMENTS

IN THE SPRING OF 1936, Howard Phillips Lovecraft was chronically ill with the cancer that would kill him less than a year later. The aunt he lived with was in hospital recovering from a mastectomy, leaving him alone, a situation which, in spite of his reclusiveness, he'd never borne easily. Over the course of those few weeks, during which he believed he suffered only from the flu, he despaired over his lack of literary and, therefore, financial success, and he mourned the loss of his idyllic childhood, claiming he was on the edge of a nervous breakdown, not the first in his life.

For "facts" of this sort, I looked to Lovecraft's excellent biographers and to his own letters. But facts, like ghosts too, are perhaps best viewed from the corner of the eye. Lovecraft himself wrote: *Men of broader intellect know that there is no sharp distinction betwixt the real and the unreal; that all things appear as they do only by virtue of the delicate individual physical and mental media through which we are made conscious of them.* Although this work of fiction is based on the known "reality" of Lovecraft's life, I have taken liberties with certain details while, I believe, remaining true to the spirit of the man I found in his stories and letters.

Memories and possibilities, Lovecraft also wrote, *are ever more hideous than realities.*

~

MY THANKS to Lovecraft's biographers of the real. To Jane Warren, Martha Magor Webb, and Timothy Birch. To John, Gabrielle, and Julian. To my mother, Lorraine, as always. And, especially, to Steven Price; what a debt of gratitude lies herein.